The Diocese Dilemma

By

Timothy Imholt & Michael Garst

Also by Timothy Imholt

1) *The Forest of Assassins*
2) *Toddler Art*
3) *The Layman's United States Constitution*
4) *China Bones Book 1 – China Side*
5) *China Bones Book 2 – The Bamboo Caress*
6) *China Bones Book 3 – The Red Pagoda*
7) *China Bones – The Complete Series*
8) *The Layman's Articles of Confederation*
9) *A Collection of Mother Goose Tongue Twisters*
10) *A Study in Scarlet with Annotations*
11) *The Sign of the Four with Annotations*
12) *Laughing at a Military Enlistment*
13) *The Hound of the Baskervilles (Annotated)*
14) *The Last World War Volume 1: Trial by Fission*
15) *The Valley of Fear (Annotated)*
16) *Degrees Book 1: Saving the Earth*
17) *The Adventures of Sherlock Holmes (Annotated)*
18) *The Memoirs of Sherlock Holmes (Annotated)*
19) *Boston, Sort of Legal Part 1 – Win Some, Lose Some*
20) *The Return of Sherlock Holmes (Annotated)*
21) *Concusstitution: Welcome to Football*
22) *A Princess of Mars (Annotated)*
23) *Fighting Spirit*
24) *The Last World War Volume 2: Attempted Liquidation*
25) *The Diocese Dilemma*

Forward by Timothy Imholt

1) *Warbots*
2) *Warbots: #2 Operation Steel Band*
3) *Warbots: #3 The Bastaard Rebellion*

Also by Michael Garst

1) *The Layman's United States Constitution*
2) *The Laymen's Articles of Confederation*
3) *Laughing at a Military Enlistment*
4) *The Last World War Volume 1: Trial by Fission*
5) *The Last World War Volume 2: Attempted Liquidation*

Chapter One
A Bizarre Confession

Father Franklin Santini stood at the back of the ornately decorated Catholic Church admiring the view. His mood shifted quickly as a police siren came to life nearby, piercing the silence and speeding off to deal with some emergency somewhere. In here, inside the Church, was a safe place. In here the view was still worthy of being called a House of the Lord. The exterior was covered in a great deal of graffiti, but inside was in pristine condition.

He made his way down the main aisle of the Sanctuary, silently passing those few parishioners who'd come to this place looking for a silent place to pray. Father Santini came here knowing he'd find a quiet place for that very same purpose.

He rubbed at his temples, attempting to get even the smallest bit of relief from his pounding headache.

The stabbing pain behind his eyes had just started to subside when he heard a gunshot in the distance, and it came roaring back, worse than before.

He let out a deep sigh, reverently performed the sign of the cross as he knelt down in the pew and began to pray.

Heavenly Father, I've spent the majority of my adult life

searching for a positive way to make a difference in the world that You have so graciously gifted to mankind. Despite my lack of understanding of how to accomplish that, I am certain that You have a plan, for me and for all of mankind.

Despite my struggle, I have realized at least one thing. The number of people worthy of being welcomed into Heaven is rapidly shrinking.

In this, it is mankind that is failing You. As one of Your servants, I can no longer sit on the sidelines and watch this travesty continue.

We must bring people in here to listen to Your word. I know the official policy of the Church leadership is that we're to wait for people to come to us before attempting to spread Your Word. But I feel differently, I feel that we should work as hard as we can to bring people in.

As a member of the clergy, it is supposed to be my duty, my life's mission, it is my mission in life to bring Your message of peace to all mankind. Not just to those few who enter this tiny building in the middle of New England.

Another police siren came to life just outside the Church and sped away. Father Frank rolled his eyes and rubbed his forehead, but the throbbing continued unabated.

This society is clearly going in the wrong direction. Things are getting worse each and every day. I must alter my behavior – change my strategies – to push members of this society to live lives worthy of being welcomed into the Silver City.

I, and the rest of the clergy, must take Your teachings to the people of the world. By changing our behavior, we just might be able to put an end to humanity's decay. We must face this challenge head-on.

We must do this because society no longer reflects Your glory.

You deserve better.

The Church is no longer a consideration, or even a minor influence on the lives of most people.

I must act, and quickly.

I must bring people in those doors so that they may experience Your glory.

By any means necessary.

I must admit that I don't know more than anyone else in the Diocese.

I recognize my arrogance in suggesting an action different that from the guidance given by the Cardinals.

History has shown over and over and over again what happens when we ignore our obligations and cower inside these walls. To make matters more difficult our available resources to bring people into Your glory are diminishing.

Even the missionaries.

Those few who do choose to serve the Church are merely vacationing in exotic lands courtesy of Church funds. They are only there for adventure, photo ops for social media, or are trying to satisfy some vain hope they have of becoming famous and adored by millions of others. They are not there to spread Your Glory.

We must expand Your influence. We must go beyond our

congregations, and we need to do so without delay. We must start spreading Your Word by any means necessary until far more people experience the positive results of following Your teachings.

Being called into Your service saved my life. Before all of this – I feel like I was a different person on a different planet.

Your plans brought me to where I am today. I know it. You gave me the desire and skills to help all of those created in Your image.

On top of that, there is the challenged faced in the confessional. I must find a way to change my approach in dealing with those who are truly unrepentant. The ones who seek out confession as a way to justify their repeated sins, or worse still, the ones who sin without even so much as a symbolic attempt and repentance.

They are the wolves among the faithful, perverting Scripture, perverting the confessional, trying to use it as some kind of "get out of Hell free" card.

I must protect Your loyal followers from the evils of this world. I, and the rest of the clergy, must do better in the future.

I hope to fully understand Your plan one day. Until then I'll continue as Your loyal servant to the best of my meager ability.

In Your name I pray.

Amen

He stood and performed the sign of the cross, the traditional bookend of Catholic prayers.

Father Santini was oblivious to the sweat covering his forehead despite the chill in the air.

He blinked his eyes, relieved that his headache was finally receding. Prayer always helped in that regard.

He looked at the artwork around the room depicting the suffering that Christ endured on the day of the crucifixion as he made his way to the confessional.

Father Santini always manned the confessional on Friday afternoons, giving the other priests a break. There was nothing like people seeking a clean slate before their weekend fun.

No sooner had he settled into the confessional than someone entered the confessor area. The priest slid aside the divider to find an older woman who had removed the optional privacy screen.

Father Santini appreciated confessors who confessed in this manner. He felt it showed no desire to hide their feelings, which was key in the process of receiving this Sacrament. According to Scripture, a confessor who was truly sorry would be forgiven and eventually welcomed into Heaven. In order to be honestly repentant, the confessor wouldn't hide anything, including the motivations for their actions.

Father Santini found that looking into the confessor's eyes to be extremely helpful in the process. Since joining the priesthood, he had come to believe the eyes acted as a window to the soul, and the eternal soul was what really mattered.

"Bless me Father for I have sinned. It's been one week since my last confession," said Sister Mary

Anne Margaret, one of a dwindling number of nuns faithfully serving the Catholic Church.

"Sister, before you begin, may I say something?" he made no effort to hide that he was rolling his eyes.

"Of course," the old woman said derisively.

"Outside of your religious duties you've worked as a volunteer nurse for, what, thirty years?" he asked rhetorically. "On top of healing the sick, you've worked tirelessly to help the homeless. You are without a doubt, or even close competition, the most dedicated nun I have ever met. While I know you'll continue to come here every week seeking absolution, and I will continue giving it, I believe you're being too hard on yourself. Much of what you have confessed over the years isn't a sin, most of it is barely a concern, spiritually speaking. Please stop being so hard on yourself. If you feel bad about the money you took off me at the poker game, you had the better hand."

"Father, you, more than most, know we're all born sinners. Now, can we stop wasting time?" Sister Mary Anne asked.

"If you must," he waved his hand dismissively, wishing more people had a few of this woman's spiritual traits.

"As I was saying," she said, raising an eyebrow, "Forgive me Father for I have sinned. It has been one week since my last confession. While I wouldn't consider taking a few dollars from an over-confident priest who goes all-in on a lousy pair of jacks a sin, I do consider physical assault a sin."

Father Santini was surprised. He couldn't imagine this small, peaceful woman physically attacking anyone.

"You see, lately we have had a lot of younger people in the ER. There are a lot of injuries that wouldn't have happened if there had been proper parental supervision, more extreme drug problems in teens than ever before, not to mention one beautiful little ten-year-old child who had been 'accidentally' shot somehow. It seems to just keep getting worse. It all came to a head this week," she explained.

"How bad has this gotten?" Father Santini asked.

"Just a few years ago, if an injured child came in, there would always be a worried parent, someone who knew exactly what happened, who always assumed the worst possible outcome. It is what virtually every parent has done in the ER since I became a nurse, and likely long before that."

"Seems logical," Father Santini said.

"But lately that has changed. Kids come in alone, even when the injuries are just playground stuff. Now we see a lot of obvious physical abuse, horrific car injuries in children who weren't in any kind of safety seat, parents who think we can just push some magic button and make everything ok. It seems like it gets worse every – single – day," she wiped a tear from her face.

"That sounds just horrible, but how does that result in you coming in here to see me with the sin of violence towards your fellow man?" he asked.

"Well, I suppose this has been building up for a long time. I was at the hospital. I spent *nine* hours on the same patient. A teenage boy. Someone just dumped him outside the ER and sped off. They didn't even bother to stop, just slowed down a little as they pushed him out of the car. They just left him there on the ground, like a pile of discarded trash. Who *does* that?" she asked.

"Did they boy make it?" Father Santini asked.

"No, he didn't. He overdosed on something; we never could figure out what. The way he died was so horrible. So painful. He coughed up so much blood. We tried, but we couldn't do anything to help him," she said, sadly.

"Sister, I am so sorry," Father Santini offered, unsure of how to comfort her.

She wiped tears from her face and took a deep breath, "I had the unfortunate duty of informing the boy's parents. Normally I'm pretty good at this sort of thing, but that *man*. The boy's father. No matter how hard I try, I still just can't understand him, his behavior…"

"What did he say?" Father Santini moved forward far enough on his seat that he almost fell off.

"He told me," she made air quotes with her fingers, "that 'I've been telling him to stop that crap for months. Serves his dumb ass right.'

"Father, such disregard for human life. For his own son! I snapped. I cursed at him. Had there not been a hospital Orderly holding me back, I would've gouged his eyes out. He wasn't the first person in the ER to have such disregard for the suffering of others, and I suppose it's a hot button of mine, but this is the first time I ever snapped and lost my cool. Nurses are supposed to stay unemotional," she said, speaking very quickly.

He could see the stress leaving her body and just saying the words out loud seemed to be helping her.

"I think I can understand why you acted the way you did," Father Santini offered.

"The man was devoid of emotion, devoid of compassion. He just *stood* there while I screamed at him. He just shrugged. He had this annoying *smug* look on his face! Like it was more important to be proven right than dealing with what happened to his son," she was growing angry.

Father Santini finally had a clear picture of the situation, and felt he understood what had driven her actions.

He tried to figure out what he would have done in the same situation? Probably shoved the Orderly aside and pummeled the man.

God would've understood and endorsed the act.

She had certainly not sinned in the eyes of the Lord.

Clearly it was her duty as a nun to protect the innocent from evil. Her reaction to this absolutely evil man was completely justifiable considering her duty to the Lord.

"When I was a kid, in South Boston, we would've

said the man needed a beatin'. I'm one hundred percent certain that if anyone else on the planet had been there besides you, it would've gone far worse for him" Father Frank said honestly.

He paused to gather his thoughts, "I know that the Lord will forgive your actions. But you should find a way to help that family. Reach out. Perhaps send a handwritten letter offering your condolences and your help with the end-of-life arrangements. Maybe one day this week we can have coffee and figure out what else is bothering you. Get to the bottom of what drove you to violence, and how we can work together to turn things around. You aren't the only one who sees people living lives that are less in line with Scripture than ever before."

He wasn't exactly sure what else he could tell her but given some time to think he was sure he could find a way to put her mind at ease.

Listening to this woman made his headache worse. He rubbed at his temples trying to get it to go away.

"Now, please, go and do what you normally do on a Friday night. Go to the hospital for the overloaded night in the ER. Just, please, don't attack anyone this time," he joked trying to lighten the mood.

"Thank you, Father, I'll try," she said, leaving the confessional.

No sooner had the nun left than someone else entered.

Father Santini removed the divider to find a confessor who had decided to leave the privacy screen in place.

"Bless me Father for I have sinned," said the voice of a younger male parishioner.

"Bless you, please tell me your Sins," Father Frank said.

"Father, I feel so bad," he said.

"I understand, please just tell me what brings you to see me," the priest said.

"It's like this, my entire life I have wanted to get into an Ivy League school, but my grades aren't good enough," he said.

"That's no Sin, and ambition can be a good thing," Father Santini said.

"Well, sure, but that's not the problem," the young man said timidly.

"Ok, tell me more," Father Santini said.

"You see, my grades were almost good enough, but if I could get a high enough score on the SAT I could get in anyway, but my SAT test scores weren't good enough, so I retook the test. My second time through, I cheated, a lot," the young man said, obviously ashamed.

Frank smiled, thinking this was an easy one, "How far off was your score on the first test?"

"I was off by fifteen points from my goal, and I studied so hard the night before," the confessor said, clearly upset.

"Look, you shouldn't ever cheat, but fifteen points on

that particular test isn't very much. First, you need to understand that these exams are standardized tests to measure your aptitude, and not something you can necessarily cram for. If you stress yourself out it will impact your performance. What I want you to do is to go from here, sign up for the test again, get a lot of rest the night before, don't stress out about it and I'm going to bet you get the score you need. Then come back and see me after mass someday and tell me what happened," Frank said. "On your way out say five Our Fathers, and don't cheat anymore."

"Thank you, Father, I will do as you say, and please pray that my test score comes out the way I have always wanted," he said.

"I will, and Bless you," Father Santini said, glad someone came in who was truly repentant he could help and put back on the proper path.

The young man left.

Father Santini sat listening to an argument happening just outside the Church. It was uncomfortable to sit in the confessional and listen to the voices. It was impossible to make out the words, but the anger was undeniable.

He sat lost in thought until someone entered the confessor area. Father Santini removed the divider to reveal a repeat confessor who always removed the privacy screen, and *always* confessed the same sin over and over and *over* again.

She was a long-time parishioner of sorts, in her late twenties or early thirties, and very physically fit. She was one of the worst repeat offenders on his list of regulars who didn't respect the true intent of the confessional in any way shape or form.

"Bless me Father, for I have sinned. It has been two weeks since my last confession," she said.

"Go on," he said, struggling to contain his anger, feeling he could recite her side of this with how often the two of them had done this song and dance routine.

"Father, I have been…"

"Unfaithful to your husband," he interrupted.

"My, my, my, Father Santini, how did you ever guess?" she giggled.

Her joke caused his blood to boil. Father Santini sat forward in his chair, "You can't continue to keep ignoring part of your penance – to remain faithful – and assume God will just forgive you. Why? Why do you keep doing this? Lisa, what is this, the eleventh time now?"

"Father Santini, I'm still young, hot, and never had a chance to sow any wild oats before I got married. I mean we were so young," she became defensive at being challenged.

"That's no excuse. One offense we can forgive for the truly repentant, but eleven times? Double digits? Where does it end?" he waved his arms as he spoke.

"I won't be done until I have had enough fun experiences to give me a lifetime of fantasy memories to re-run when I am bored with my husband," she smiled.

Father Santini took a deep breath and rolled his eyes, "I understand the thought of a lifetime with someone can seem like it is going to be boring, but you will have a lifetime of experiences and joy with this person. A person that you *proclaim* to love," he said, trying to contain his anger.

"I know, you said almost that very same thing the last time I was here. But we all have bucket lists we need to check off before we die. Mine just happens to be different than yours," she claimed.

"What kind of list?" he asked, fearing he already knew the answer.

"I don't want to say," she said with a mischievous smile.

"You know whatever you say here in the confessional is said in total confidence," he reminded her with a sigh.

"I know, ok, fine, if you must know, it's a list of sexual conquests I wanted to make before I settled down," she said.

"Why didn't you refuse to marry your husband when he asked you to, especially if this was the case?" Father Santini inquired not trying to hide his frustration.

"Well, because I love him," she said defensively.

"Do you see the dilemma here," he rolled his eyes.

"Not really, but I'm almost done," she traced the divider between them with a perfectly manicured finger. "One more and I'll have everything I need to move onto some other diversion, well ok maybe two. But who knows I might decide I have more to add to this list I can't seem to manage to get this one difficult one."

"There isn't someone else, one of the many other conquests you have that checks this box?" Father Santini thinking that he might have found a loophole.

"Nope, not this one. You know, you're cute when you try to problem solve like this," she said.

"Why not? What's so different about this one conquest that you feel compelled to continue the chase?" he asked.

"Because, I have never had a priest," she smiled sweetly, attempting to look innocent, as if trying to appeal to some inner instinct Father Santini might have.

"Lisa," he rubbed his temples as much in frustration as from his pounding headache. "You have got to be kidding me. Propositioning a man of the cloth, while married, in the confessional, while confessing to infidelity? Seriously?"

Father Santini thought he had heard them all, but this was a new one.

He could empathize with Sister Mary Anne more and more with each passing minute.

"Lisa, enough. Just go home, to your *husband*, and come back when you are serious," Father Santini said in frustration.

"Fine, but seriously Father, you could have all of *this*. You don't want to miss out on this once in a lifetime opportunity," she chewed on her lip and winked at him.

"Lisa, go home," he commanded.

"Ok, but if you change your mind tomorrow night I'll be down at the Black Rose in the Irish District after eight," she slipped her purse over her shoulder. "I'd love to see you there. And I'm certain you would love to see *all* of me," she wiggled her shoulders.

"Lisa! Go, come back when you are ready to take this seriously," he rubbed his head.

"Fine," she left in a huff.

He could not figure out how anyone could believe they would be forgiven the way this woman seemed to believe it was possible.

Father Santini sat and listened to the few confessions that came in for the next hour. He grew more angry with that woman the entire time. Then he got angry with himself for not being able to help her.

Perhaps she was just beyond any help other than what was in the Old Testament. She was clearly someone who could not be dealt with passively.

How could he, a man of peace, a man of God, protect the innocent from such evil if he just sat back and *talked* about problems? It was time for action.

Lucifer himself must have sent her to walk among mankind. God had guided her into the Church, but she could not possibly be His creation.

Innocent people such as this woman's husband must be protected from the evil within her.

There had to be a way to protect the world from such evil.

Chapter Two
The Emergency Room

Sister Mary Anne was dressed in dark blue medical scrubs and comfortable white sneakers. Her hospital identification, stethoscope, pens and a blood pressure cuff were hanging off her body, all arranged for quick and easy access. The only indication of any religious affiliation was a small crucifix hanging around her neck on a thin silver chain. When serving at the hospital she considered herself a nurse first and a nun second.

By all outward appearances she was just another upper middle-age, hard working woman who probably enjoyed spending her time off playing with the grandkids. Maybe she was even planning on retiring to lead a quiet life of reading novels and taking trips just for the pleasure of new experiences. But that was only the appearance.

In reality, she had never even considered slowing down. She was fully devoted to her life of service to others' spiritual *and* physical health, which she firmly believed to be intertwined.

Sister Mary Anne stood in a private treatment room at a patient's bedside taking vital signs from a middle-aged man on the younger side of forty-five. Periodically she would put down a piece of equipment and enter some numbers into the man's electronic medical record.

She glanced at his file to remind herself of his name, "Well, Mr. Littlefield, based on your numbers, things are looking up. But now that we are getting the fever and dehydration under control, you should start feeling better any time. Our plan is to keep you here for a few days. Despite how you feel right now, you should fully recover soon enough but are just not well enough to go home yet."

"What – do – I – have?" he asked between wheezing breaths, obviously in pain.

"Probably flu. Once the lab results are ready, we'll know for certain. But you're young, so you'll be fine once whatever this is passes," she explained.

"Thank you – Mrs. – I am sorry. I – can't remember – your name," he admitted weakly.

"It's ok, you were really out of it there for a while. I'm Sister Mary Anne Margaret, from Saint Michaels Church, at your service," she said warmly, proudly fingering the silver crucifix adorning her neck.

"Wait?!? You aren't – a nurse?" he asked, alarmed enough to make a feeble attempt at sitting up straight and failing.

"Oh, don't worry," she said waving off his concern, "I'm also a registered nurse. I just volunteer here in addition to my duties at the Church. I just like to do that to people, it always gives me a little laugh watching people momentarily panic when they hear I am a nun," she gave the smile she always used to calm patients.

"Sorry, I didn't – mean it – like that," he wheezed, trying to hide his embarrassment.

She gave a smile and a wink; they both knew better. Controlling gut reactions was difficult when ill, and it didn't bother her, she had done it on purpose to try to take his mind off his pain. It was a trick she had used on many other patients to distract them from their suffering.

"You just rest up. We'll get you moved upstairs as soon as some paperwork is done," she entered the last of his vitals into the computer. "If you need anything, push that little button on that control panel next to the picture of the nurse."

"Thanks," the man said as he closed his eyes and sank back into his pillow, the embarrassment quickly passing.

She patted his hand to offer some comfort and left the room, wondering if he had any close friends or family.

He had come into the ER alone and was doing his best to not be a bother to anyone. Most people who behaved like this lived lonely lives. She wanted to hug those patients the most. In her opinion it was vital to the physical recovery process to do everything possible to lift the spirits of the patient while treating the physical body. Having someone close helped with that. Lacking friends and family, hugs from a nun had never hurt anyone.

Sister Mary Anne scrubbed her hands and put on a fresh set of gloves before heading to the ambulance entrance. Word had come in about a traffic accident requiring two emergency response teams and one, if not both, would be arriving soon.

She was standing by the ambulance entrance when Doctor Nancy Rodriguez came up behind her. The doctor was dressed similarly to the nun, with the addition of a white lab coat and her hair pulled back in a braided ponytail ready for another hard night's work.

"Good evening, Sister," the doctor, twenty years her junior, said politely with an overtone of exhaustion all ER doctors seemed to have on a continuous basis.

"Hey Doc, any idea how bad the incomings are?" she asked.

"Not as much as I would like. Only that there are three injured people. A male in his early fifties, who is a suspected drunk driver. A woman in her late twenties and a pre-school aged child. The man 'allegedly,' blew through a red light and slammed into the vehicle with the woman and the child. EMTs said one patient is in bad shape, but I don't know which one," Doctor Rodriguez answered.

"Let's pray it isn't that bad," she crossed herself, folded her hands and lowered her head.

A siren became audible in the distance and the two women tensed up. The noise was growing louder so quickly it could only mean the driver was coming in as quickly as possible, traffic safety be damned. Whomever was in the back had to be in serious trouble.

The siren grew almost unbearably loud until,

abruptly, there was an eerie silence.

The door burst open and a child, no more than a toddler really, was rushed in on a gurney surrounded by emergency medical technicians, one of them riding with the child on his knees so he could continue to work during transport. The child looked shockingly small surrounded by all the equipment.

Sister Mary Anne's stomach twisted. He was so young, so badly injured.

She'd seen similar situations like this before, but this one was getting to her. There was just so much blood, it was everywhere, and he was so small.

Too much blood for such a little thing.

Shoving her feelings aside, her medical training took over as she got to work.

"VITALS!" Doctor Rodriguez demanded, as only an ER doctor can.

"Weak, blood pressure is still falling. We are on the first unit of plasma, but that's almost gone," said one of the EMTs.

The pressure bandages on the child's head and chest were reaching their saturation point and blood was starting to pool on the surfaces.

Sister Mary Anne took some small consolation in that the child was unconscious and couldn't feel anything. No one should have to experience that much pain, especially someone so young, so innocent.

"Where's his mother?!?" Sister Mary Anne demanded.

"She is being helped out of the ambulance with a fairly minor leg injury," answered Paul, one of the EMTs.

They rushed into the treatment room and quickly transferred the boy from the gurney to the treatment bed.

"Get a pressure monitor on! We need Doctor Bogdanowicz from pediatrics," Doctor Rodriguez instructed.

"Doc, the head wound is bad, really bad," Paul's expression and tone spoke more than his words ever could.

Doctor Rodriguez carefully removed the bandages. A metal rod was sticking out of the left side of the boy's head. Blood bubbled up from around the wound. The scalp looked like a piece of meat that had been left out in the sun too long and had started to rot.

The bubbles were the most gruesome part.

One crimson bubble would burst, sending small droplets splattering in every direction, only to be replaced by another, and another.

Shredded bits of tissue were mixed together with the blood and coated the surface of the bandage.

"How deep?" the Doctor's voice shook, but she remained focused.

"Looks like it may have penetrated the skull," Paul answered, barely breathing.

Doctor Rodriguez hesitated but didn't stop, "Get Doctor Roberts down here, *now!*"

Sister Mary Anne took two steps back. Calling for Doctor Roberts made sense. A brain trauma expert was the logical choice for a patient that had a chance, assuming that the patient had a chance of survival.

Was that really the best decision for this child?

Did he really have a chance at something resembling a normal life even if he did survive this terrible accident.

"Nancy, he isn't going to make it. Let him rest. Let him find peace," Sister Mary Anne said between sobs.

"No! We don't give up in my ER. Not before everything possible to save the patient," Doctor Rodriguez continued feverishly working.

"He's simply not going to make it. Let the boy rest," the nun's shoulders slumped. Sadness filled her eyes and tears ran down her cheeks as she looked at the tiny, shattered form on the bed.

The tortured body filled Sister Mary Anne's mind and twisted her heart into knots as the rest of the medical team quickly continued doing their jobs.

Sister Mary Anne put her back to the wall and slid down to sit on the floor. The cool tile floor, the rushing of the medical team going completely unnoticed. The only thing she could think about was that there should be a little boy crying for his mother and his voice was silent.

All she saw was red. Angry red. Red flashing ambulance lights. Red blood from a child spilling onto a formerly pristine white floor. Red footprints on the once white floor left by the furiously hard-working staff.

Tears continued to flow, but she managed to find the strength to stand. There was no possible way to save that poor child. All the medical team would achieve was prolonging his suffering.

Why put off the inevitable? Why prolong the pain?

Head held high, her shoulders back, Sister Mary Anne left the room. She had to find his mother. No matter how emotionally difficult, she would make sure his mother had a chance to say a final goodbye. The child's soul deserved no less as it departed this world to make the journey into Heaven.

Sister Mary Anne knew the woman would suffer severe emotional trauma, but she would offer help. Nothing could compare, no words could prepare her for losing such a small child. At least the mother could say goodbye, and that was something.

Turning the corner, she saw a large man being escorted by two police officers and an emergency medical team. He was confused but other than some bruises and a cut above his eye, he appeared largely unhurt.

"Did I hurt anyone thish time?" he slurred, obviously drunk.

"Yes, you did, and this isn't the first time you drank and tried to drive home, is it?" asked one of the officers, almost casually.

"Noooo, but I drive so mush bettah aftah I had a few high ballsh, it calmsh mah brain," slurred the fat sweaty man without consideration to the police officers and their body cameras recording him admitting to a crime.

Hearing the man speak, Sister Mary Anne saw red again. Her desire to vomit was turning to pure rage. She wanted to punch the man in the face. She fought the urge and continued her quest to find the child's mother.

Sister Mary Anne found what had to be the right woman fidgeting in a wheelchair. She was in tears and looked terrified.

"Nurse! Do you know where Benjamin is?!?" the desperation clear in her voice.

"I'm going to take you to him. The doctors should know something by now," Sister Mary Anne pushed the wheelchair quickly down the hall.

"This won't get in the way of him starting pre-school next week, right? He's so excited about it. He keeps carrying around his backpack asking if it's time to go to school," the woman rambled frantically, like if she spoke fast enough, she could alter the reality of the situation.

Listening to the woman talk about her son was making Sister Mary Anne's heart ache even more. She had a duty, to herself, to this woman, to that tiny child, and to the Lord. She had a duty to protect the innocent from evil.

But how? How could she console this woman? How could she protect the innocent, like Benjamin, from evil?

The boy was dying with no hope of survival. Even if they saved his body, the brain injury meant he was already lost. He would no longer be the child this woman knew.

What words could she possibly say that would both help this frightened mother envision the reality of the situation while simultaneously consoling her?

Pushing open the door to the treatment room, Sister Mary Anne rolled the woman inside. Seeing the tiny little boy, the woman gasped in shock.

Three doctors and five nurses now circled the table.

"That's actually the inner layer of skin, not splintered pieces of skull, but it is amazing how often those two can be confused because they do look so much alike when on a bandage. Especially in trauma cases like this one as everything gets all mixed together. If we limit inflammation, we should be able to prevent any brain damage. Focus on getting the bleeding under control so we can get a better idea of the situation," Doctor Roberts said calmly.

"Sister, you're contaminating the room, please leave," Doctor Rodriguez snarled without looking up.

"Ok, someone please keep his mother informed as things progress," she said with her heart in her throat.

"We will, now get out," snapped Doctor Rodriguez.

Pale and shaking, the nun pushed the mother from the room, swallowing hard to keep her dinner down.

Sister Mary Anne had written the boy off. The rest of the trauma team hadn't. They saw hope, not tragedy. They saw the possibility of saving him. She saw only death.

It was her job to bring hope, to save people. But she had ignored her duty and run away. How could she be so stupid? Who gave up and walked out on a small child when they had the necessary skills and experience to help save their life?

"They're some our best doctors. Your son is in great hands. I'm going to check on a treatment room so we can see to your leg," she said meekly, not hearing the woman's reply.

Sister Mary Anne was racing down the hall, operating on instinct.

She turned the corner, colliding with the drunken, fat, sweaty man. He was too drunk to walk straight, and her mind was racing. She looked at him, the bastard who had nearly killed that innocent child. That innocent little boy.

Without thinking, fists started pounding him in the face. A white sneaker smashed into his testicles causing him to fall to his knees howling from the excruciating pain that somehow managed to cut through all the alcohol.

Her knee collided with his face, blood exploded from his nose. Her rage found a voice in a soul rendering primal scream.

Suddenly she was floating in the air. Somehow, she was being lifted off the ground and away from the target of her rage.

Suddenly, she found herself face down on the ground with her arms clamped behind her back.

"Sister Mary Anne, as a lifelong parishioner at Saint Michaels I can't believe I have to do this, but you are under arrest. You have the right to remain silent…"

***

Father Santini was sitting at his desk working on a Sermon when the phone rang. It was a number he didn't recognize, but he answered every call.

"Hello, this is Father Franklin Santini," he said formally.

"Frank, it's me, Sister Mary Anne," the voice of his favorite nun said.

"Hey, whose phone are you using? Where are you?" he asked, forgetting about his work.

"Well, I'm pretty sure you aren't going to believe this, but I have been arrested. I need you to help me figure out how to post bail," she said, embarrassed.

"What the… Really? Never mind, tell me about it later. Which jail do they have you in?" he asked rubbing his temples.

"City jail, over by the courthouse," she said.

"Ok, I know who to call, so sit tight, I'll be there as

fast as I can, please don't say anything to anyone without a lawyer present," he said as he disconnected.

Lord, I don't know what happened, and I can't figure out what is going on in this world. I hate to have to call this person for this kind of favor, but I guess we all have to do what is necessary to make a difference in this world. It's all for the greater good. Even if what we have to do is a little wrong to make things right.

The phone rang twice before being answered. Frank didn't wait for the person to speak.

"Dad, I need a favor…"

Chapter Three
Helping Sister Mary Anne

Barely an hour after getting off the phone Father Santini was climbing into one of his father's Jeep Wranglers. The man had owned at least two of them since Frank was old enough to notice such things at the very least, and probably much longer.

The family resemblance was impossible to miss, despite his father being in his mid-seventies and showing his age. He was still in good physical shape, all things considered, but he said many times, he wasn't as young as he used to be.

Father Santini was dressed in black pants, black shirt, black jacket and white collar.

"Thanks for coming so fast, dad. I wasn't exactly sure where to even start," he said as they pulled out of the rectory parking lot.

"No problem, Frankie. You know I will drop everything for family when called," Leonard Santini said.

He was Lenny to his friends, and Mr. Santini to everyone else.

"Well, all the same, I do appreciate it," Father Santini said.

"Besides, how often does someone get to bail out a nun for beating the crap out of some guy. I mean, I have bailed people out, been bailed out by people, but this is a first, even for an old goombah like me," Lenny laughed.

Frank let out a small laugh, "I guess I was so distracted I didn't think about it that way. Now that I think about it, this is kind of funny in a way."

"My guy is going to meet us there. He's a perfectly legit bail bondsman, and he'll have her out quick," Lenny said with a snap of his fingers.

"What do you mean, 'perfectly legit,'" Father Santini asked, cautiously. He tried to avoid any more information than absolutely necessary about his father's business dealings whenever possible.

"It means I have only ever used him to bail out people who weren't part of the...more grey areas of my business," the old man explained.

"Thanks for that," Father Frank said, relieved.

"Does anyone you work with know the true nature of my business?" Mr. Santini asked.

"Well, they know my last name, and I'm sure they know yours from all the press stories over the years, especially from that thing that went national when I was a kid. However, I doubt they have made the family connection. I am willing to bet all of that will change when the good Sister sees us together," Frank explained honestly.

He had never hidden his family connection from anyone, but he'd also never gone around volunteering that information.

"I know you have never been comfortable with the family business, but I would never bring someone out here to help the Church who wasn't completely outside of all that," Lenny explained, trying to put his son's mind at ease.

"Thanks, and just because I don't love the business you are in doesn't mean I don't love my family. It just means I wanted my life to go in a different direction. Besides, I know things have been shifting to be more legitimate in recent years. I am just glad you had the time tonight to help make sure this amazing woman doesn't spend one second more than *absolutely* necessary behind bars," Father Santini said.

"Hey, we all serve a purpose. Just so you know, even when we have some slightly less than legal stuff going on, it is always for some greater good. Sometimes the system doesn't work the way it should, when that happens somebody has to handle the situation, occasionally when we have to fix it we make a great deal of money as a result," Lenny said with a shrug of his shoulders.

Ever since he had become an ordained priest Frank had noticed that his father would attempt these rationalizations whenever they saw one another.

"Dad, it might surprise you to know, I agree we should all serve the greater good, and lately I have been thinking that should be done by whatever means are necessary to properly deal with the situation. Just so long as that is done within the guidelines of Scripture. In my opinion the laws of man cab be faulty, but the Laws of God are perfect,"

Father Santini said as they pulled into the police station parking lot.

"Sounds like there is more to that story, but we'll have to finish that thought over a meal soon," Lenny said with a quizzical look.

They parked and as they were walking up to the building a well-dressed man joined them.

Outside of weddings and funerals Father Santini hadn't seen people wearing business suits, with neck ties this late on a Friday in a long time. For his father this was typical, but for anyone else it seemed odd, but there was serious business to take care of, and Frank supposed professionalism mattered at times like these.

"Good evening, Mr. Santini, is this your boy, Frankie?" the man said as he opened the front door to the station for them.

"Yes, this is my son, but he goes by Father Franklin Santini, of the Catholic Church, not Frankie. His mother and I are the only ones who call him Frankie now," Leonard corrected. "Have you got it done yet, or are we going to be waitin' around for a bit?"

"Everything except the signatures. It was no big deal, and in the long run I think they are gonna drop all charges. For tonight, they are gonna release her to Father Santini here. It was easy, two good Catholic clergy, one signing for the other. The only condition is that she will need to keep Father Santini here appraised of her location until the formal arraignment hearing on Monday," the man said.

Father Santini found the reception area at the police station to be surprisingly small. It was a few feet wide, maybe ten feet long, if that, and had four uncomfortable looking hard plastic chairs along the wall across from an officer sitting behind thick, protective plexiglass. The moment the trio entered the reception area a uniformed officer came through the security door to meet them carrying a clipboard full of papers.

"I am going to take a guess that you are Father Franklin Santini," the officer said with a smile, being sure to gesture toward the priest's collar.

Father Santini smiled, glanced at the nameplate on the man's uniform, "That would be a good guess, Officer Marshall."

"Ok, well, if you could just sign by all the little arrows, we will bring her out. Don't worry, she was never fully processed, all we did was get her information and fingerprints. Since we heard from your bail bondsman almost immediately, she has been just sitting in an office while we filled out a giant pile of papers," the officer said as he handed over the clipboard and a pen.

"Really? That's it? Almost seems a little too easy," Father Santini said in disbelief.

"Not exactly," the officer said with what looked like a well-practiced wink. "By signing all of this you become legally responsible for her behavior between now and her arraignment hearing. That means, if she does anything to get in trouble between now and then you might be held legally responsible. Also, she *must* show up for that arraignment on time or it could result in a warrant being placed for your *and* her arrests. The details for that hearing are on the last page of the paperwork and you will leave here with a copy of all this," the officer said as he left the reception area with the clipboard of freshly signed papers.

"I don't know what I was expecting, but despite those little details, this seems much easier than I thought it would be," Father Frank admitted.

"Chuck here is the best bail guy on the North Shore," Lenny said with a smile.

"Must be," Father Santini said as he continued to sign documents, "Chuck, I do appreciate your help. If there is ever anything I can do for you, feel free to call me."

Officer Marshall quickly re-appeared with a folder full of papers and Sister Mary Anne who was still wearing her medical scrubs and a cold weather jacket.

"Frank! Thank you! I have no idea how you handled this so fast, but thanks," she said.

"If she spent any more time here there might have been a few Catholic converts in the back office," Officer Marshall joked.

"Oh, if I know her there is at least one already," Frank turned to his favorite nun, "Sister, it was really my father and Chuck here who are responsible for the speed and efficiency of getting all of this handled."

"It was no problem at all, and my pleasure," Chuck said, shaking hands with Sister Mary Anne.

"It's far from Chuck's first time here," Officer Marshall quipped.

"Frankie, this isn't a big deal. She is going to walk away without much more than a small lecture, I'm gonna see to dat," Lenny said.

"I already tried a lecture, apparently it didn't take," Father Santini joked, causing Sister Mary Anne to smile at the inside joke about their exchange in the confessional.

Officer Marshall handed Frank the thick folder and retreated to the interior of the station without another word, and the four of them exited to the parking lot.

"Dad, how exactly are you going to make sure she just walks away?" Father Santini asked cautiously.

"Now, now, don't look at me like I'm the Leonard Santini of old. I'm just gonna send *my* lawyer to the arraignment with her. She'll be fine," Lenny said.

"Just double checking," Frank said chuckling while holding up a hand to get his father to stop.

"No problem," the older Santini said.

"I'll explain all of this later," Father Frank whispered to Sister Mary Anne.

"Oh, I'm pretty sure I got it," she grinned.

"I like her. Now, take it from me on this. I know what I'm talking about. Take her to get some food, make sure she gets some sleep and deal with all of this in the morning. Tonight, emotions are going to be running high for everyone, and you won't accomplish anything anyway," Leonard Santini instructed.

"I am hungry," Sister Mary Anne admitted.

"Ok, we'll do it your way, dad," Father Santini said.

"Sister, I have heard a lot about you, and it is great to finally meet you, I just wish it was under different circumstances. My son has always spoken very highly of you. Here, Frankie, take my Jeep, we'll talk tomorrow. Chuck here will give me a lift, I have some more work to do tonight on another matter anyway," Lenny said as he handed his son the keys and a wad of cash.

The clergy members climbed into the Jeep after watching the two men walk away.

"Um, Frank, was that *the* Leonard Santini, 'suspected' mob boss?" Sister Mary Anne asked.

"Yeah, but to me he has always just been dad, and some of that mob boss stuff has been blown way out of proportion by the media on slow news days," Father Santini explained, trying to down-play the family business.

"Wow," she said. "I never noticed it before, but now I'll never unsee the family resemblance."

***

Frank and his favorite nun walked into a local

breakfast joint. It was very "New England," with some small tables for two, a few booths that would fit four or more, and a counter along the back facing the open kitchen for those who just wanted to be in and out quickly. With it being early on a Saturday morning there were not many patrons, only a few families sprinkled around enjoying breakfast together and lots of empty space.

It was an easy place for them to grab some breakfast and talk with a parishioner who might be able to give them some useful information about the situation.

Frank waved back at the man trying to get their attention from a booth by the window. Physically he was a small man but had a massive set of job responsibilities as a detective in the nearby township of Lawrence.

Father Santini sat down and scooted over to make space for Sister Mary Anne, "Jonathan, thanks for taking the time this morning. Have you ever met Sister Mary Anne?"

"I know of you by reputation, but I don't believe we have ever met. I'm Officer Jonathan Pierce," the man said, extending his hand.

"Jonathan here is a plain clothes detective in addition to being a parishioner. He is part of my men's prayer group and has been on the force for a little more than fifteen years," Father Santini explained. "I figured if you had any questions, or even if you just wanted to openly vent about what happened you might want someone who is more familiar with this kind of thing, so I called him, and he jumped at the chance to help."

"Yep, even if you want to complain about the cops in general, or even talk about the fall leaves I'm always happy to help the Saint Michael's spiritual crew," Jonathan smiled.

"That's very nice of you. Honestly, I don't really care what happens to me as a result of all this, but there is one thing I'd really like to talk about. I volunteer over at Holy Family Hospital. Mostly in the Emergency Room," she said.

"I actually knew that. I have a cousin on staff over there, and I know everyone really appreciates what you do," Jonathan said.

She blushed a little, "Well, everyone that works there is very dedicated. Last night's shift was just heartbreaking all around. It all started when three patients came in after an auto accident caused by a drunk driver. One of the people in the vehicle that was hit was critically injured," she explained.

"Yeah, I know one of the officers that was on the scene last night. He said it was a very young boy. Something like four, maybe five years old. I didn't get many details, but it sounded horrible, I really don't know what I would do if it was one of my kids," he said, seeming genuinely disturbed.

"I was there when he came in..." she folded her hands as her lips twitched and she was unable to find the right words.

"I am sorry you had to see that. I haven't heard much

but what I do know about it is just tragic," Jonathan said sympathetically.

"Have you had a chance to decide?" the waitress interrupted.

Everyone ordered a light meal with coffee. The waitress almost instantly delivered three steaming mugs.

"Bless you, I love the coffee here," Father Santini said to the waitress.

"The coffee here, coffee across the street, and any other cup you have ever seen," Sister Mary Anne joked trying to lighten the mood while discreetly clearing a tear from her face.

"Ok, fine, I admit it. I love the stuff," Father Santini admitted.

Sister Mary Anne smiled and turned back to Officer Pierce, "Anyway, my big question is, what's gonna happen to the drunk driver? I heard him admit to the officers that were with him in the ER that he had knowingly driven drunk before, he even bragged that it improved his driving, but I don't know what ever came of that. How do I help make sure he is punished enough this time so that he doesn't do it again?" she asked, her eyes filling with hope.

"Sister, I hate to be the one to tell you this, but honestly, I doubt there is much that anyone can do. In fact, my job prevents me from referring to him as anything other than an 'alleged drunk driver' until he is found guilty at trial. Based on my experience with other such cases he will have some high-priced lawyer who will plea bargain the case down to involuntary vehicular assault or something else that holds no real repercussions. If his lawyer is any good, they will likely get any mention of alcohol stricken from the record. If he goes to prison at all, which is not likely, he will be out in a few months. If experience tells me anything, he is probably going to pay a small fine and go about his life like it never happened. I know it sucks, and I wish I had better news for you, but that is how the system seems to work these days," the detective explained.

"That's it? Are you kidding?" she asked, shocked.

"I'm afraid so, I wish it wasn't the way these things go, but it is," Jonathan said.

"I see. I think I need to be alone for a bit. I'll just walk back to the Church, and I promise, I will stay out of trouble along the way. Enjoy your breakfast, you don't need to drive me back," she got up to leave, looking like she was ready to vomit.

Officer Pierce spoke up, stopping her in her tracks, "Sister, if there is anything at all I can do for you. If you need to talk. I would be happy…" he stammered seeing how distressed the woman was, and unsure how to help.

"No, I just need some more sleep," Sister Mary Anne said as she left the restaurant, avoiding eye contact with anyone.

Frank let out a deep sigh as the nun stormed off, frustrated with the state of the world and his pounding headache, "Ok, Jonathan please tell me more. How many more people, or better yet, what other kinds of crimes do people just get away with?"

"Gosh, where to start. You know Father, if you really want to learn more, just come by office on Monday and I'll get you out in a squad car with a patrol officer for a few hours," Jonathan offered.

"Really, that is an interesting idea," Frank said.

***

Father Santini arrived for lunch with his father a bit early. It would be nice to spend some time with him, before last night's events it had been a while, and he wished the circumstances bringing them together had been different.

His dad had chosen an Italian place owned by a friend of the family with a nice view of the ocean. It was someplace Frank had been a few times over the years and always found the food to be as spectacular as the view.

He found himself lost in the view when his father surprised him by pulling out a chair to take a seat, dressed in another phenomenal pin-striped suit.

"Hey, Frankie, how is the good Sister today?" Lenny asked.

"She's ok. Really, she's mostly pissed off that the guy she attacked is basically gonna walk away from the damage he did while drinking and driving," Father Santini explained.

"Yeah, I get that," Lenny said.

The priest let out a sigh, "Well, I suppose in the end he will face God's justice."

"That is one way to look at it," Lenny said.

"Hey, Mr. Santini, I haven't seen you in a few weeks," the waitress said.

"Rachel, great to see you. This is my son, the priest I was telling you about last time I was here, Father Franklin Santini," Lenny said.

"I heard a lot about you, your father here is very proud of you," she said with a smile.

"Well, that's my dad. He does love to talk," Father Santini said, returning the smile.

"Honey, can you please bring some of those baked oysters and lobster ravioli for us to share along with a bottle of that red wine I like? I need to chat a little with my son here," Lenny said.

"Sure thing Mr. Santini," she said, departing their tableside to arrange for their order.

"Thanks again for all the help last night, dad," Frank said.

"It was my pleasure, and anytime you need to call me for help, or just to shoot the shit, you know you can. So, Frankie, what besides your favorite Nun's troubles is bothering you?" the father asked the son, obviously concerned.

"That obvious?" he asked.

"Only to those of us that know you as well as I do," Lenny said.

"Well, it is just a ton of work problems I suppose. While I can't give you any specifics of things said in the confessional, I guess I can explain it in general terms," Father Santini proceeded to tell his father his frustrations with repeat confessors, society losing its moral center, rising crime, all of it. He came as close as he could without violating the confidentiality of the confessional. He wanted to tell him about Lisa specifically, but he let it go, speaking in the most general terms possible.

"Frankie, I know you took your vows to try to make the world a better place. I know you want to protect people but sometimes just using words won't get da job done. Just trying to talk people off the ledge doesn't do it all the time. Some people are just bad people, and nothing you say to em is gonna change that," Lenny said.

"I know that's the world you live in dad, but I live in a world of faith, faith in God, faith in humanity, faith in people," Father Santini said.

"I know that, but don't you also believe in evil? In Satan? And isn't it just as possible that evil walks among us? I know I have seen evil in my business dealings over da years," Lenny said.

"Yeah, I guess I don't fully understand the family business," Father Santini said.

"Lemme give you a little history lesson. Back in the 1860s Sicily became a province of Italy. Chaos and crime were the norm as the government was still tryin' to become established. Then in the 1870s someone had an idea. Roman officials asked a

Sicilian 'mafia' family to help them go after the dangerous, more independent and far more violent criminals. In exchange for that, officials would look the other way when the mafia engaged in its various businesses. This worked out pretty good because the mafia could take out criminals that the actual authorities couldn't get enough evidence on to do anything about but they knew who da guilty party was. Now it seems like every single time society takes a turn for the worse, dey lean on us Sicilians to come sort out the mess the rest of society made. So, while that sort of business may be frowned on by some, it is necessary on occasion. Now, my business isn't the Sicilian business of old, but our family can be traced back to those very original members. These days, we mostly just own and manage some legit businesses, but sometimes we gotta help out our friends to keep business moving along in the right direction," Leonard Santini said with a wink.

"So, the family protective instincts go back a long way," Father Santini said.

"Yeah, they do. But remember we always did it for the greater good. Now, I know you'll never be in the family business, and that's fine, I just hope you know that we don't do da kinds of things the news likes to talk about. I really am mostly just a legitimate business guy who happens to help people who are in trouble. Besides, at my age I'm mostly retired anyway," Lenny said.

"Ok dad, I get it, the secret is safe with me. Someday you'll have to explain a lot more of this historical stuff to me. If for no other reason than I am fascinated by that part of the family lineage," Father Santini said.

The waitress returned with their oysters and discreetly slipped away.

"For that, you gotta come by da house, we can talk in the library. I got some books," Lenny said picking up an oyster.

"Yeah, we gotta find a time for that. But let's eat, I have something I gotta take care of tonight so we'll have to figure out a time I can come by the house one-night soon," Father Santini said, happy that his headache was finally receding.

Chapter Four
Faneuil Hall

Lunch with his dad had convinced Father Santini that he had to take more aggressive actions in order to properly protect the innocent. It was a family tradition, and on top of that protecting the innocent was supposed to be a large part of his service to the Lord.

A married person confessing to violating their marital vows a ludicrous number of times had to be stopped, no matter what his personal sacrifice. The world was failing him, and it was failing God. Father Santini would no longer permit himself to fail the Lord. It was time for some Old Testament justice.

This woman had committed so many sins there was no real option. It had to come to an immediate end. She was violating her marital vows, the intent of the Confessional, and on top of that there was her attempt to pervert the Confessional and use it in an attempt to further engage in Sinful activity.

As a priest, he was meant to protect the innocent. He was meant to be the sword and shield of God, actively protecting the faithful from evil.

Father Santini knew he had to find her. Luckily, he remembered just where she said she would be and when she would be there. Her volunteering that information had to be a sign from God that he was *meant* to find her and take whatever actions were necessary to stop her poorly chosen course of action.

Why else would she have come into confession? To taunt him? To flaunt her indiscretions and her lack of moral fiber? Surely, she had not come in just to hit on him. It had to be God's influence that put her in that Confessional when he was working.

He had chastised her so often for this same sin that she *had* to know what was going to say before she set foot in the confessional. Then her disclosure of a list, and her attempt at getting him to engage in the act in direct violation of his vows. That was too much. She had attempted to corrupt him – a priest.

It was supposed to be Frank's responsibility to protect *all* the innocent people of the world, that included her husband. Her repeated violation of the Sacrament of Marriage had to be stopped, and he couldn't violate the privacy of the confessional. That would go against everything he believed. This burden was his and his alone.

She was neither innocent, nor repentant with any fiber of her being. Some people may feel that his coming downtown to find her might be going a step too far, but some version of this had been on his mind ever since she stormed out of the confessional. He knew no other way to stop her.

There was far more at stake than her husband. She was harming the souls of an untold number of others through her actions. It was impossible to know how many souls were being corrupted by her influence as they became witness to her evil behavior and use it as justification for their own behavior, using her "I can get away with it by confessing" mentality. How many others might follow her example.

Frank's head was pounding. It felt like someone was constantly pummeling him with a hammer from inside his skull in an attempt to escape.

It wasn't just her actions. It was her attitude that was the real issue. It was becoming all too commonplace in people her age.

He was on this Earth to stop evil.

This was a new Holy War.

In the long run this was just one step in the long-term goal of protecting all of mankind from evil. It may be a small step, but it was a vital one in the Cleansing of this world.

This world that had been a gift from God, and it was clearly not being respected the way it should.

He pulled into a parking lot that took cash and parked the Jeep. Just a few blocks later he was walking into the Black Rose, one of Boston's more popular Irish Pubs frequented by tourists, college kids, and more than a few locals.

Father Santini was dressed in jeans and a polo shirt. He had no desire to look like a priest tonight.

The place had a huge rectangular bar with high bar stools and a mirror behind the hundreds of liquor bottles on display. Every conceivable inch of wall space was covered with Irish flags, jerseys from Irish sports teams of one kind or another, and pictures of

Irish scenery. Every single beer on tap was, of course, Irish.

While Frank didn't know exactly where she would be, he decided hanging out in the main bar area so that he could have a view of the front door and the staircase leading to the upper level seemed like the best choice.

Father Santini remembered being in this very bar a few years back for a wedding reception of sorts, following a very small ceremony he had officiated. The place had not changed much, if at all in the intervening time.

He sat down on one of the empty bar stools, ordered a pint of a dark ale and prepared to wait.

At one point in his life sitting around for forty-five minutes listening to fragments of conversations had the potential to be entertaining. Tonight, he was finding it infuriating. It was a mix of people complaining about jobs, which was to be expected, but mostly it was people bragging about things they had "gotten away with."

It was similar to, and in some cases worse than what he had heard in the confessional. His head was pounding, and there was nothing he could do to make it stop.

While taking a sip of ale he saw her walk in wearing high-heeled, knee-high boots, an emerald-green miniskirt, and a ludicrously low-cut black top showing as much cleavage as she was physically able. She instantly noticed him, smiled, waved, and strutted across the room.

"Hey, Father, *please* tell me you are here because you changed your mind?" she asked, leaning over the bar showing off even more of her cleavage.

"No, but I think you should sit and talk to me instead of continuing on your poorly chosen course of action," he said offering her a spot to sit and hopefully a path to salvation.

"Ahhh, crap, not this again," she said, rolling her eyes. "I'll have one of whatever he's having," she told the bartender who reached for the closest tap to pour her one.

"No, not this again, this still, but let's change how we approach this subject for a minute. You have been married for a while now and hopefully there was a point when you weren't checking items off your 'list.' What pushed you to do this?" he asked, trying to dig into the root cause of the problem.

"That's a good question actually. You see, I used to, and still do, take mixed martial arts classes. See, I love adrenaline. It gives me a rush unlike anything else in this world. Even when I was a kid, a little bit of that stuff oozing into my veins, ooh, I just love it. Anyway, those classes offered a little danger because when we would get to the sparring I knew I might get punched in the face. But it wasn't long before I got pretty good at it and the rush went away. Then, I realized sex is one of my favorite things, so why not do something that I love in a way that is a little dangerous? Only makes sense, and it fulfills all of my needs at once," she explained with a shoulder shrug.

"Why not find a new way to get that same rush? I

mean, other than cheating on your husband," he suggested.

"Because this is so much fun. I mean he loves his job and makes more money than anyone else I know, so why not do something I love to keep things exciting while he is off at work doing what he loves?" she asked.

"Does he have any extra-marital...activity?" Father Santini asked.

"Ha, no way. He's always at work in some classified facility someplace, doing who knows what for some government program," she laughed.

"So, you believe that *this* is your only way to fulfill your...needs? What happens when you finish up your list?" he asked.

"Funny thing about that, I was looking at my list and I realized there was some stuff I forgot to put on it originally, so now I have *way* more than just the one left. But priest is still number one, if you want to help a woman out," she said flirtatiously.

"What? Lisa, seriously, do your marriage vows mean nothing?" he asked angrily, rubbing his temples.

"Not really, it's just a silly ceremony. I mean I guess they did at the time, but whatever," she said with a dismissive shoulder shrug.

"You guess? Ok, let's explore that. What do you mean by 'I guess?'" he asked, hopefully.

"Well, I mean he's cute, in a dorky kind of way, and makes a lot of money. That's clearly the second most important thing in the world!" she said, the excitement in her voice reaching a new level of exuberance.

"If money is second, what is the most important thing?" he asked, hoping he wouldn't be sorry.

"Sex, of course," she said with a wink.

He rolled his eyes and took a drink, finishing the ale.

"Where is God on your list?" he asked, fearing the answer.

"Oh, I guess, maybe, like in the teens?" she said. "I mean no offense, it works for you, but for me, I believe in God, but all these rules. I mean, why? When we can just go to confession and get into Heaven anyway without having to worry about all the little stuff like vows or whatever."

"Again, that isn't how confession works. Scripture is very clear on this," he warned.

"Oh, so you can't just forgive me right now?" she asked with a smile, bending over the bar a little more, attempting to draw his attention to her breasts.

"Not at all," he said. "It isn't a joke, it isn't just words, and I'm not kidding when I say that one must be truly repentant for their sins in order to be forgiven," he explained again.

"Ok, so let me ask you something. If you were to fuck me tonight, would you be sorry afterwards," she asked seductively.

"Yes," he said honestly, with an eye roll.

"So, why not do it, and then go to confession?" she

asked.

He let out a heavy sigh, "Because I take my vows seriously, and I know what you are trying to get me to do is wrong. By the way I am sure I have mentioned that *I take my vows seriously*."

"Yeah, like you never thought about it, especially when it comes to the idea of doing it with me" she said, leaning over again.

"Well, I am human, so sure I think about it from time to time in a very general sense, but I am not tempted to stop being dedicated to the Lord," he said.

"Don't you take time off? There has to be some part of the day when you aren't fully dedicated to your work?" she asked.

"I guess," he said, rubbing his temples, not sure where she was going with this line of questioning, but certain he wasn't going to like it.

"See, so you can spend some of that time fucking me, and it will be juuuuusst fine. Besides, maybe if you help me finish off the original list, I'll throw away the rest of my new list and just be done with it all," she said, putting her hand high up on his leg.

"Stop that. Listen, how many times have you come in and confessed to this sort of thing?" he asked, removing her hand from his leg.

"I dunno. A bunch, who really cares," she said with a dismissive shrug of her shoulder pretending to pout.

"See the problem here? Someone in my profession might refer to that as evil," he said.

"Lucifer gets a bad reputation, and it isn't, like, totally his fault. Didn't God create him?" she asked.

"Sure…"

"So, even if Satan sent me, it's almost like God sent me," she said.

"Look, honestly, is there anything I can say that will change your mind?" he asked keeping focus on the problem, instead of her diversion to the Dark Lord.

"Nothing you can say, but there is something you can do *to* me, and the rest of my list just magically goes away," she said putting her hand higher up on the inside of his thigh this time.

"Fine, let's go. I promised myself one way or the other I would stop you," he said, waving for the bartender so he could pay the tab.

"Really? What? Where are we going?" she asked flirtatiously.

"To a motel, this has to end, fast," he said, the frustration obvious.

"Hopefully not too fast," she giggled.

They left the Black Rose, headed for the parking garage.

"Is this really the only way to stop you?" he asked.

"Like I said, God put me here to do this," she said.

"*If* we do this, your list is *over*, and you are done violating the laws of God," he said, matter of factly. "God put me here to do *that* prevent evil from destroying this world. By any means necessary," he said.

"Whatever," she said dismissively.

They climbed into the Jeep and left the parking garage. He was sure even if they had sex she wouldn't stop. Her claiming that those being sent by Satan were essentially sent by God made him angry beyond description; and solidified what he must do in his mind.

"Can I ask a question?" she asked.

"Sure," he said.

"To whom will *you* confess this sin?" she asked with a giggle.

He let out a genuine laugh, "Any other priest can hear my confession," it was the last question he expected her to ask.

"So, who is the sinner *now?*" she asked.

"We are all born sinners. Some of us just keep it under control. In this case I am making a sacrifice to prevent you from doing these things in the future," Father Santini explained.

He was certain her soul was rotten and beyond any form of absolution he could offer. There was no demon present in the woman that could be exorcised, this was something else entirely. After years of interacting with her in the confessional there was no longer any doubt in his mind.

Father Santini was firm in his belief that the Savior would one day once again walk among mankind, but not before the world was ready. He also knew that with the current state of the world the Return was needed more now than it had been in a very long time. However, lacking a return of *the* Savior, a messenger of His would have to do.

The process of preparing the world was going to start with this woman.

This was clearly a situation for Saint Peter to sort out.

He was more sure than ever that his approach to stopping Sin needed to become more hands on.

The Cleansing of this wonton society would begin here, tonight, with this woman.

Yes, he was deceiving her with his actual intent. But he had to do what was necessary in order to solve the larger problem. He had to do this as part of his service to the Lord. He knew he must do what some might perceive as evil to restore goodness to the world, but those people didn't know what his real mission was. How could they? It had just recently become clear to him.

God was the ultimate authority on justice, and it was part of Father Santini's job to deliver that justice.

"I'm curious what you want to do. I mean sure, just bang it out, but I like more than that. In this case, I'm gonna bet you don't have too many ideas," she said while running a finger around her breast, slightly exposing an erect nipple. "Should I make a few suggestions?"

"You know, just because I am a man of God doesn't mean I was born like this. It doesn't mean that I have no understanding of, no experience with, nor fantasies about the pleasures of the flesh. Besides, in the confessional people tell me all kinds of things. Sometimes they describe their sins with loads of detail. You know, once in a while I think some of them are coming in so they can safely brag about their sexual improprieties to someone," he said.

"So, come on, tell me! What do you want to do to me? Don't keep it a secret!" she said, obviously excited by the notion of what was to come.

"Well, if we are going to get you on the right path, and I am going to have to go to confession anyway, we may as well do this right. What I want is to bind you to the bed with your hands and feet secured to the four corners. I will then cut the clothes from your body. My tongue will slowly descend from your breasts. Finally, when I am convinced that you are exhausted by orgasm after orgasm originating from my fingertips and tongue, I will thrust my manhood inside you. When I climax, I will spread my seed across your breasts," he lied.

"My, my, you are a naughty boy. Normally, I am not a big fan of being tied up. But by a priest, now *that* is kinky," a hunger emanated from her eyes as they pulled into the motel parking lot.

"Here, if you could please check us in, it wouldn't do well for me to be seen," he said, handing her some cash.

"Oh sure, I get it," she said with a wink as she jumped from the Jeep, quickly checked them in, came back with a huge smile and a key.

He parked just a few feet away from their assigned

room. They leapt out of the Jeep, opened the door with the plastic key, and they entered the small but serviceable room. No one would ever mistake this for a high-quality room, but it had everything necessary for what was about to take place.

Frank shoved her on to the bed in way he hoped would come across as playful.

She reacted with a deep sultry moan.

He had come prepared for things to end up going in this direction and pulled some leather straps out of his jacket pocket. He tied her to the bed and checked to make sure she couldn't slip free. If that were to happen, his ultimate goal would be far more difficult to achieve.

The further things progressed, the more Father Santini's headache subsided, and he experienced a growing sense of calm.

With her physically unable to move from the bed he reached into his inner jacket pocket for the six-inch, razor-sharp hunting knife he'd had since he was a teenager.

He swiftly cut the clothes from her body.

For a brief moment he wondered what she had planned to wear home, but she seemed to be enjoying things, so he let it go.

In time, her lack of clothing would be completely irrelevant.

He realized he'd forgotten an important step. He showed a ball gag in her mouth. It would be necessary to control any noise. Her eyes went wide, and she let out another moan as he tied the straps tightly behind her head. Her arousal was evident, not only in her eyes, but in the way she wantonly squirmed.

Frank was truly disgusted by the way this evil woman was enjoying herself. She had failed in every way possible to show even the slightest bit of remorse. Instead, evil was permeating from every fiber of her being.

With her fully prepared, he looked at her naked body. He could not help but admire the primitive nature of her curves. It must stoke a raw animalistic lust in most men.

It was the epitome of female physical attractiveness, which was the exact vessel Satan *would* choose. She had come from Hell, and to Hell she must return.

He tightened his grip on the knife and stretched the muscles in his neck and shoulders.

She looked at the knife in his hand and her excitement slowly turned to confusion.

Confusion quickly turned to panic.

She pulled and pulled in a useless attempt to free her arms from the straps that held true. The ball gag muffled any attempts at screaming.

"Lord, remove this heretic from earth," he clenched the knife in both hands and plunged it at her chest.

She rocked her midsection to one side.

He hadn't counted on her reacting this way. The

knife that was intended for her heart missed the intended target. All he managed was a deep cut down the right side of her torso.

Blood began to flow, leaving a deep red stain on the white sheet as she thrashed wildly. Father Santini wasn't sure if it was from pain or desire to be free.

Suddenly, the headboard snapped. The leather straps were too strong to break, but the cheap bed was not. She had one free arm.

She delivered a vicious blow to his solar plexus. It knocked Frank back against the wall, stunning him.

Father Santini was coughing and trying to stay on his feet as she freed her other limbs and made her way to his side of the room.

An experienced knee to the face sent him tumbling into the wall. Blood began quickly flowing out of his nose, down his face and onto his shirt.

He managed to get to his feet and brandish his knife, leaving a small cut on her forearm.

The cuts had to be painful, but a grin crossed her face anyway. She was obviously feeling that adrenaline rush she had spoken about in the confessional with lust in her eyes.

She had talked about having taken martial arts classes, but he hadn't prepared for that. He assumed this would be simple, and he had been wrong. He cursed himself for failing to prepare for all eventualities.

He lunged in a second attempt to get the blade to

find her heart. He missed completely as she spun out of the way, grabbing his arm, and in the process throwing him to the ground, knocking the air out of him for a second time.

He was confused, flat on his back, gasping for air. Part of his rattled brain told him to stay there and figure out how to get the pain to stop.

Suddenly a different, softer, deeper, yet far more insistent voice told him to get up.

He had barely reached his feet when she leapt across the bed at him. Somehow, he managed to get the knife up in time.

He almost lost his grip as the knife penetrated through her breast and deep into her chest.

He pulled the knife out and she staggered around the room, blood spouting from the wound in time with her weakening heart beats, she uselessly pressed her had to the chest in a feeble attempt to stop the bleeding. As she breathed in and out, he alternatively heard a very wet hissing and sucking sound coming from the wound.

She looked back at him questioningly, surprised, confused, like she wanted to ask why but the ball gag was still securely in place.

Saint Peter would have to explain it to her, if he wanted to take the time on such an evil soul before sending it to the depths of Hell for Lucifer and his minions to deal with.

He thrust the knife into her chest a second time, twisting the blade before quickly extracting it.

Blood came from the new wound like water from a hose and Frank knew he had hit her heart.

She fell to the floor in a heap, letting out just a few more weak faltering breaths before all life left her body.

Father Santini made the sign of the cross and performed the Last Rights.

He finished the ritual and stared at the body. It was a process he had never seen unfold. Watching a human being as the soul left was a new feeling. He wasn't sure what to make of it, but he was certain he would remember it forever.

It had been easier than he thought, although he admonished himself for not being better prepared for the more physical aspects of the evening. In one swift motion he had released a twisted soul from the physical body and removed this one bit of evil from the world.

Frank quickly grabbed a towel from the bathroom and wiped down every surface he had touched to eradicate his fingerprints or any other potential DNA, using a second one to catch the blood still flowing down his face.

Mere moments ago, she had been a beautiful woman, now she was a pile of blood covered meat on the floor, and her soul was having a discussion with Saint Peter about the way she would spend the rest of eternity, which would be unpleasant.

It had been relatively easy. Society was now a cleaner place.

With one last look, he left the room quickly praying that in this neighborhood the police wouldn't spend much time investigating. These sorts of things happened far too often around here.

He climbed into the Jeep, wiped the sweat from his forehead, then cleaned the rest of the blood off his face with the last of the clean towels he had taken from the motel room and pulled out of the parking lot, headed for the highway.

He needed to change his clothes and destroy what he was wearing, then get to the Church and pray.

The opening salvo in a new Holy War to reclaim God's Earth had been fired.

Chapter Five
The Morning After

Father Santini blinked as he tried to focus on the image in the mirror while rubbing his stiff shoulder. His entire body was sore. In his forty-five years of life he could not remember ever having this many aches and pains at once. It didn't matter, he had to push through the pain. He had to perform weekly Services and he would not permit himself to miss the chance to lead the congregation in prayer.

He looked closely in the mirror, searching for any sign of visible bruising on his face. When trying to fall asleep he had been concerned that if any developed overnight he would have to come up with some kind of reasonable explanation. He would be in close contact with hundreds of people by the end of the day, and he didn't want to have to answer any uncomfortable questions.

He breathed a sigh of relief and thanked God for his Italian heritage. It had blessed him with dark olive skin tone which had always hidden bruises.

His nose had swollen up just a little. Thankfully it was so slight that he was positive no one outside of his parents would notice, and they didn't attend Services at this Church.

He ran his fingers through his hair, showered, shaved and dressed in formal robes.

As he walked from the rectory to the main Church, he thought more about what had happened. It had been relatively easy. God had been watching over him and been the guiding force through it all. She had found the absolution she had been seeking, but not in the way she had expected.

Somehow, she had gotten the upper hand in the physical altercation, and only through God's intervention had he prevailed and sent her quickly on her way into the afterlife. Perhaps her soul could be saved, but that was up to Saint Peter.

Everything in the Church was in place and ready for the 8am Services. His Sermon was written, he could deliver it from memory, and hopefully with passion.

Father Santini's mind was not as focused on these routine tasks as he would normally have preferred. It was focused on the next steps that needed to be taken in the Cleansing of this world God had gifted mankind.

Cleansing, he liked that word to describe his mission.

So many people in this world had gone beyond absolution that there weren't remotely close to enough clergy to even *begin* to attempt to offer effective solutions for all of them. The Earthly plane had become so littered with twisted and tortured souls that Lucifer had either spewed into existence or perverted in some way, that drastic actions had become necessary. Something big needed to happen, and the time for this was now.

Some could be saved, others would not. This fight was for the whole of humanity. It would be challenging, but somehow, some way, the influence of the Lord had to be expanded.

He was thinking about all the worst things he had heard in the confessional over the years. Things were becoming clear. His reason for becoming a priest, the reason that woman had been put in his path, all of it suddenly made sense.

The routine parts of the Service went by in the blink of an eye, and suddenly it was time to address the congregation.

Father Santini stepped to the front of the altar, "Today's Gospel is a reading from the Book of Exodus.

"If men strive, and hurt a woman with child, so that her fruit departs from her, and yet no mischief follow: he shall be surely punished, according as the woman's husband will lay upon him; and he shall pay the judges determine. And if any mischief follows, then thou shalt give life for life, eye for eye, tooth for tooth, hand for hand, foot for foot, burning for burning, wound for wound, stripe for stripe."

He paused, closed the bible, and took a deep breath before continuing, "Today's reading is one of the most quoted, yet least understood, and as a result gets thrown around conversationally under the assumption that those using it fully understand the meaning. We might be able to argue that in some literal form it should be implemented far more often than it is in our world today. It *could* also be argued that an actual eye for an eye is a step too far, but even in our modern world this passage can find use.

"Can we, in our 'advanced civilization,' find a less barbaric way to implement the concepts of this passage without actual eye-gouging? I bet as an enlightened society we can. In a way we may have failed in our duty to the Lord. Perhaps by not applying the basic lessons of Scripture, including this one, I believe that we have failed ourselves, and failed God."

"What do I mean by this?"

"Think back to when our k-12 students all over the nation were not doing as well as people wanted on the annual standardized tests, for instance the SAT. We could have chosen to improve teaching methods, we could have focused on ways to improve performance, but instead the test was made easier. This artificially inflated the test scores and made everyone feel better because of the new altered outcome. In essence the entire process was dumbed down and standards were lowered because the kids weren't doing any better, they just appeared to be doing better."

"As a society we, decided to implement a well-intentioned, yet short-sighted 'solution.' But perhaps now, using this same methodology, we choose too often to make things easier by lowering standards, and not just in our education systems.

"I believe this portion of the Scripture is either missing from our daily lives or has been dumbed down far too much, in the very same well-intentioned fashion as our standardized tests.

"I think we can all agree that our criminal justice

system has been witness to a similar decline in standards. Now, don't get me wrong, I believe everyone should have a shot at forgiveness, I am a priest after all, a strong desire to forgive comes with the robes," he paused while there was a soft, scattered laughter among those in attendance.

"These days, if someone is actually found guilty of the same crime multiple times our court system ignores the repetitive nature of their crimes and has a tendency to merely levy a fine against the guilty party. This is done for a host of 'reasons' we have been given and stands in stark contrast to many different parts of Scripture, especially this one. I believe it also stands in contrast to the intention of those great men and women who formed this nation.

"*Perhaps* there is another way. *Perhaps* we modern day thinking people should find a better way. *Perhaps* if someone commits the same crime, or Sin, multiple times we could make the punishment more severe with each offense. *Perhaps* we should stop making excuses for those who do evil things. Perhaps we should have *actual* repercussions for those not making the most of their lives and give them a hand-up rather than a hand-out which seems to have resulted in the perpetuation of this seemingly endless societal downward cycle we are witness to, day after day. Maybe we should show those guilty parties that their actions have negative impacts on others. Then, perhaps, they will reach for that outstretched hand, rather than looking for shortcuts.

"Those guilty parties should be made to see that those impacts can be more far-reaching than some people understand, and it is *our* job as servants of the Lord to help them understand the situation fully. It is our job to show them that living your life in the Light of the Lord leads to eternal blessings," Father Santini concluded.

He purposefully kept his sermon short and to the point. He was pleased to see more people looking up and paying attention than normal.

Perhaps this world had not gone beyond the point of no return, as he had feared. Perhaps it could be saved, if things started to turn.

The people in this congregation were hard-working, Spiritual people that deserved a better world. They deserved better than the type of society that gave out free passes to evil doers.

Sure, they believe in forgiveness, but they also understand the ongoing battle between good and evil.

Evil deserved, no *needed*, to be punished. It needed to be banished to Hell where it belonged.

Lucifer himself was once an Angel who led a rebellion in Heaven and had been punished with the task of running the underworld for all eternity.

Evil acts deserved to be punished, and if they were evil enough that punishment could last an eternity. If enough sinners were punished, some might start to question their own actions and make different choices with their lives.

The Earthly plane *could* be saved, it *could* be made worthy of a return of the Holy Spirit, and Father

Santini prayed he was up to facing God's challenge to become an instrument of that change. He had to remain diligent, he had to stay focused. Perhaps someday other members of the clergy could join him on this mission, but for now he must work alone. It was his burden to carry.

Father Santini knew he had to be methodical, flawless, in his Cleansing process. He had research to do, preparations to make. Things had to move faster, there was a great deal of work to do, and enough time had been wasted.

Chapter Six
The Precinct

Given his recent nocturnal activities he knew that many people would consider him insane for what he was about to do. Their opinion was unimportant to him, he knew the truth. Father Santini was not the least bit nervous as he walked into the local police precinct in search of his friend and parishioner, Officer Jonathan Pierce.

He was ten minutes early for their meeting, but this was all a part of his official duties to the Lord, and it would be inappropriate for him to be late. Especially with his expanding mission. He must be even more regimented in his duties than ever before.

As the automatic door closed, he found himself in a larger reception area than they had at the police substation where he bailed out Sister Mary Anne, but it was similar in ways. It had the same type of hard plastic chairs along the walls as well as down the center of the room. The focal point of the space was an officer sitting behind thick bullet proof glass at the far end of the room next to a physically hardened security door that Frank assumed led to the working area of the building.

He glanced around the room at the half dozen people waiting. Some were staring at their phones, some filling out forms on clipboards, and one was just staring blankly out into space.

As Father Santini made his way over to the duty officer, one by one those waiting turned to stare at him. This was not uncommon when he ventured out in public with the collar silently announcing his chosen profession. Without it, typically no one would give him a second look, and with it on, people not only stared but it seemed like they always sat up straighter, which he never understood, but always found humorous.

Father Santini walked over to the officer who lazily half-looked up from whatever he was doing on his computer screen.

"May I help you…Father?" the man said as he sat up and blinked a few times to become alert and look attentive upon realizing he was speaking to a priest.

Frank suppressed the urge to laugh as the man almost fell out of his chair.

"Good morning. Officer Jonathan Pierce asked me to come by and see him. Can you please let him know that Father Franklin Santini is here?" Frank asked.

"Sure thing Father, please have a seat. I will let him know you're here, and he will come out whenever he is able," the desk officer said a little less lazily than his original greeting.

The desk officer looked like he was in desperate need of a good night's sleep as he picked up the phone and slowly pushed a few buttons.

Father Santini wandered towards an empty chair and stopped to look at some of the notices on a bulletin board. They ranged from the famous F.B.I. "most wanted" list to the more mundane public notices about upcoming auctions of seized goods. He was taking a closer look at the individuals on the F.B.I. list when Officer Pierce opened the door.

"Father! Great to see you," Jonathan said with a huge smile as he extended his arm to shake hands.

"Good morning, Officer," Frank said, taking the offered hand.

Jonathan being a plain-clothes police investigator was dressed business casual with khaki pants and a blue, button-down shirt. The officer motioned to the hallway on the left as Father Santini made his way through the door.

"I appreciate you coming by. There are a few different patrol areas I wanted to talk to you about before your big night out. But, before we get to that, I wanted to say that most of the patrol guys I spoke to jumped at the opportunity to have someone in the car to talk to, especially since many go out without partners anymore on a Monday night due to budget cuts. Having someone in the car really helps to break up the monotony," Jonathan said as they made their way down the hall.

"Before we get to that, I know of your love for all things coffee related. One of the very few perks of this job is that we keep it available hot, fresh, and free of charge twenty-four seven. We have a large self-service area down here on the right, and you can help yourself anytime you are here," the officer explained with a smile.

"Seriously?!? For free coffee I may have to swing by every morning just to say hi. Maybe I can give the squad cars a daily blessing," Frank said, rubbing his hands together with glee.

Father Santini poured himself some of the steaming hot liquid into one of the available disposable cups. Being a man of pure tastes, he always drank it black, the hotter and stronger the better. He took a sip and found it to be almost perfectly suited to his tastes.

"Right here, Father, this is the reason I invited you to come by this morning instead of just doing this over the phone," the investigator gestured to the large flat-screen display mounted on the wall. "This is our crime map. We put it right smack in the middle of the hall because of the foot traffic caused by the coffee. This is really just a much larger version of what you can get on our local PD smart phone app which can be downloaded for just about any mobile device. With this larger version stuck right here in the middle of everything it helps everyone to keep the bigger picture in mind."

"Interesting. Staying as informed and up to date as possible is always a good thing. If I could ask a dumb question, what do the different colored dots mean?" Frank asked.

"Not a dumb question at all. Each color represents a different kind of crime. The yellow dots are vandalism reports; nothing big, just kid level stuff. Orange dots are burglaries. Red dots are violent crimes, things like rape, armed robbery, and assault including domestic violence. I personally think we need a special category for domestic violence because they tend to be repetitious, not to mention more difficult to deal with because of the level of emotion, and I'd really like them to stand out in some way from than the rest. The different categories of crime always seem to cluster together. Those clusters help us figure out how frequently to put patrols in an area and which officers to put in what part of town. Some of our people are just better at dealing with certain types of calls, and we try to take that into account when making patrol assignments," Officer Pierce said.

"Can I assume that the more dangerous or heavily clustered areas are patrolled more frequently?" Father Santini asked.

The officer nodded as he sipped his coffee and said, "Yes, Father, something like that, well there is a little more to it, but basically, you are correct. Humorously, every once in a while, the news will do a story claiming that we patrol the more expensive areas of town more often, but that just doesn't reflect the reality of the situation at all."

"Well, if we are gonna do this, let's do it right. I wanna go out tonight, and in the area with all the red dots," Father Santini said as he pointed to the heaviest cluster of violent crimes.

"Father, are you sure? Maybe you should start in the orange area. Get your feet wet, so to speak," Jonathan suggested.

"If you only knew me, or about my life before I was a priest you wouldn't be so concerned," Father Santini said with a chuckle. "Besides, when you wear the collar, even the most hardened criminals treat you nicely, just in case. They don't want the Big Guy to be angry with them on the off chance they get to meet him in person, spiritually speaking."

Father Santini's mind was rushing from one thought to the next as the discussion continued. He was having trouble focusing. The information flow was helping in ways the officer could not possibly comprehend. When planning his future Cleansings, he would have to study crime maps. Keeping that app on his phone seemed like a good place to start. If he ever came under suspicion, he could easily explain the app's presence as a result of his relationship with Officer Pierce and his concern for the local community. Future Cleansings would require privacy if things were going to go according to plan that was starting to take shape.

It became clear to Father Santini he needed to become very involved with the local police, in any way they would permit him to be. If *any* suspicion ever fell upon his shoulders, it would help mitigate these future problems.

God must be responsible for this wealth of information coming his way.

What other unexpected gifts did God have in store for him?

"Father, I do admire you for jumping in at the deep end. Be sure to keep my cell number handy, just in case. Give me a coupla hours and I'll find you a fantastic officer to ride with," Jonathan said.

"Sounds great," Father Santini said.

"Father, before you take off, can we talk about something that might be a little unpleasant? My office is right down the hall, and we can have some privacy," Jonathan said, looking grim.

Frank swallowed, hard, as he followed the man down the hall to the private office. He entered the room and sat in the office chair convinced they had somehow loosely connected him to the "crime" scene.

That couldn't be right. There was no chance God would permit that to happen. His mission had just gotten started, and was too important to the future of humanity.

It took him a moment to realize that Officer Pierce would have never discussed police operational details if he was under any kind of suspicion. What was he worried about? God was on his side.

"Father, we got a call this morning from the Mattapan P.D.," Officer Pierce said, in a subdued voice.

Here come the handcuffs! Was dominating Frank's consciousness.

Suddenly a soft, comforting, almost angelic voice in his head told him to have patience, and to not worry.

Jonathan's voice got quieter, and he spoke slowly, "They found one of our residents murdered down there. Apparently, they have no shot at solving this one on their own and have asked us for help. They have no leads and are asking us for anything we might be able to tell them about the victim that might help them figure out if anyone had a motive. The only reason I bring it up is she was a parishioner at Saint Michaels," Jonathan paused, staring down at his desk, searching for the right words.

A voice in Father Santini's head was screaming at him to remain calm. It was so loud his head began to throb.

Lord, I love you, but please, can you speak to me later and allow me to focus.

The screaming vanished, and the throbbing instantly stopped.

"That's terrible! Did this person have a family?" Frank asked, breathing carefully in order to maintain an outward appearance as normal as possible.

"She was married, her husband is a parishioner as well, but they had no children. I actually met her briefly at a Church function once, and she seemed nice enough," Jonathan said. The officer was obviously troubled by the situation.

"Wow, someone active in our Church? The violence seems to get closer to home all this time. What was her name? Has her husband been informed?" Father Santini was certain someone just learning about the situation would ask these questions.

"He had reported her missing, and we have someone on the way to talk to him right now. Her name can only be released once we get his permission, which we may not, but there is something about this situation that really bothers me," Officer Pierce said quietly.

"What is that?" Father Frank asked cautiously, not sure where this was going.

"I just don't get it," Jonathan said as he got up and started to pace around the office. "She was apparently in a super-cheap and sleazy motel, in a really rough part of town, but her husband makes a butt load of money. No narcotics are on the evidence list, she had never been arrested, she had on some very real and very expensive jewelry, all of which was left on the scene. The investigators found some evidence of a struggle, but she may have had some ritual cuttin' on her torso, so one or more of the injuries may have been on purpose, but she died of a stab wound through the lung that would have likely been fatal, and another one through her heart," the man rambled, seemingly confused by how all the details fit together.

Frank took a deep breath, relieved, and calmly said, "That doesn't sound like what is really bothering you."

"It isn't. I guess it isn't this victim in particular, but a larger overall concern. My problem is that I have a fear is that there is a rough sex pervert out there that has gotten gradually rougher over time, who may now have a taste for blood. Maybe she liked it rough, but he got a little rougher than she wanted, they fought then he stabbed her in the heart? It just doesn't make sense. I guess I could just use some prayers that this is an isolated case because I don't want to see anyone else end up like her," Jonathan said.

"I will absolutely help you out there. I will ask the Lord to do what He can to ensure this stays a one-of-a-kind incident," Father Santini said as he made some mental notes. If it were necessary to Cleanse another woman there would be no more "sex scenes" used to hide what was really happening.

She had been a problem for years, and was now gone forever, but he didn't know when another such woman would cross his path, although he already had a clear target in mind for his next Cleansing.

"Father, I love my job, I live to protect and serve, but if a woman like her is going to put herself in a situation this dangerous for no other reason than a cheap thrill, how can I, a mere human, sworn to protect the public, possibly keep someone like her safe? She should have known better than to put herself in this kind of situation," Jonathan said, the situation clearly causing him to have doubts about his career.

Father Santini knew he was looking at a pure and honorable man. He wanted to help him through his moment of doubt, but he couldn't reveal what he knew, even though if the truth were to come out it would help the man.

"Jonathan, remember that even Jesus had his moments of doubt. I have those moments myself, occasionally on a daily basis. There will always be situations we face that will make us want to give up hope, and there will always be things in life that will test our faith, or at the very least stretch it almost to the limit. In those moments, I think about the crucifixion and what Jesus went through for us. Then I look for the good in the situation. Perhaps in this case we can say the good is that, assuming her husband didn't kill her, and he wasn't aware of what she was doing, that he no longer has to deal with an unfaithful wife. It is a small victory, but if he is a good man, perhaps it will help him in ways we aren't aware of as part of God's greater plan for the future," Father Frank said.

Officer Pierce waved a hand dismissively, "The husband has an airtight alibi. He was on an airplane at the time coming back from some business trip. Maybe you are right, and this is for the best."

"Maybe we should talk about this over a beer sometime," Father Santini suggested.

"That sounds like a good idea," Jonathan said.

"What time should I be here tonight?" Father Santini asked.

"About seven thirty should do it."

"I will be here with my thermal coffee mug in hand," Father Santini said with a smile.

"See you then," the Officer said.

They shook hands and parted company.

Chapter Seven
The Arraignment

Sister Mary Anne took up position in the security line with the rest of the people trying to enter the courthouse to a mixture of stares and whispers from many of those waiting in line. This reaction was not at all unusual when dressed in traditional nun's clothing. She rarely wore the most formal of attire anymore, mostly because to claim it was uncomfortable was an understatement. On top of that there was the old joke, which had some truth to it, that it made the wearer look kind of like a human-penguin hybrid.

None of that mattered today.

Today called for formality, and maybe a little Divine Intervention if things were going to go as they should. Besides, her clothing couldn't possibly make things worse than they already were, and if there was even the slightest chance it would help, then it was worth the discomfort.

At least one good thing had come to light in the last day. Benjamin would survive, and even almost fully recover, which could only be described as a miracle.

Her emotions had suffered greatly in the time since she had urged the doctor to stop treatment, which would have *certainly* doomed little Benjamin to die *long* before his time.

Then the news of his likely recovery had come out, and the extreme guilty for her actions hit her hard. She was thankful, so thankful for the rest of the medical team that she struggled to find the appropriate words to describe the emotion.

She had been unable to set foot back in the Emergency Room since that night. She had tried to walk through those doors twice but each time she came close, nausea had set in, and it was all she could do to fight the urge to vomit. One thing was certain, if she had become so inept as a trauma nurse that her emotions could impair her judgement and cause her to screw up so badly it could have cost that child his life, then perhaps it was time to detect that part of her career over.

That didn't change the fact that Benjamin should *not* have been in the hospital in the first place, and that was the fault of just one man, and his habit of routinely over consuming alcohol and driving.

Benjamin did not deserve any of what happened to him. He should be spending his time on a playground, not in the rehab ward trying to learn how to walk again. He should *not* be dealing with the physical pain that recovering from those horrific injuries were going to entail.

She finally made her way through the metal detector and gathered her things from the x-ray machine conveyor belt when a well-dressed man approached her.

"Are you Sister Mary Anne Margaret?" the man asked.

"Yes, very good guess. Can I help you?" she quipped.

"I am Samuel Russo, Mr. Leonard Santini's personal attorney," he introduced himself while handing her a business card.

"Yes, hello. Did you get all that paperwork I e-signed? I am never sure if that stuff goes through," she asked.

"Yes, I did. I hope you don't mind but I took the liberty of getting down here a little early to see where things stand with your situation," he said.

"I don't mind at all. How bad is it?" she asked, timidly.

"Not bad at all. It turns out I already managed to get all the charges greatly reduced or completely dropped. There will be a small fine and forfeiture of your bond, but other than some paperwork we are basically finished," he explained.

"That's it? Some paperwork and a fine? How much is the fine?" she incredulously.

"Don't worry about it. Mr. Santini is going to cover any costs incurred by this little incident," he said with a wave of his hand. "It's one of his ways of showing support for the Church, and he really liked your protective instincts."

"I see. Can you thank him for me? Or, better still, let me know how I can reach him so I can thank him personally?" she asked.

I will give him your contact information. Is there

anything else I can do for you?" he asked.

"Just tell me where to go and sign the paperwork," she said.

"As your attorney of record, I can handle all of that for you, so basically you are finished here," he explained with a polite smile.

"I see. So, who all did you have to get to agree to drop or reduce the charges?" she asked.

"Local law enforcement was willing to say you were acting out of character due to the stress of the situation, so they dropped those charges. Mr. Nathan Brown, the man you had your little confrontation with, was the only other one. He needed to do that so he could use it as a bargaining chip in his plea deal in an attempt at wiggling out of his own problems. But honestly, even if he hadn't agreed, we could have bargained everything down anyway. That's the approach his lawyers are going to take if they are any good," he said.

"Seriously, so if I understand this correctly, I'm not really needed here at all?" she asked in disbelief, and at the same time disturbed that she might have inadvertently played a part in helping *the drunken idiot* escape repercussions.

"Nope, I have it completely under control. I will call you later today with a status update," he said.

"Ok, well thanks. Can I assume Mr. Brown is here dealing with his issues today as well?" she asked.

"Yes, he is about to go into a hearing in a courtroom upstairs," Mr. Russo said.

"Well, I appreciate all of your help," she said shaking his offered hand.

"It's my pleasure," he scurried off down the crowded hallway.

She made her way upstairs, found the correct courtroom and took a spot in the back where she would be out of the way. Somehow it wasn't at all what she had pictured. According to the sign in the hallway the hearing involving Mr. Brown was scheduled to start any minute, and the room was virtually empty. There were only five people present: the defense attorney, the prosecuting attorney, a bailiff, a court reporter, and herself.

She was the lone occupant of the gallery area.

Not even the boy's mother was present. Why wasn't she here? Didn't she care about what was going to happen to the person who almost killed her baby boy?

The lack of even the smallest bit of public outrage made the situation even more depressing. Where were the reporters? Someone must care about the situation enough to be here. Surely, drunk driving accidents with critically injured kids had to still be newsworthy! There wasn't even a local crime blogger anywhere to be found.

Was this kind of thing becoming so common an occurrence that it had faded completely into background noise?

Voices could be heard in the hallway and the door suddenly opened. The formerly drunk man from the hospital was escorted in by a deputy sheriff loosely holding onto his upper arm.

The escorting law enforcement officer was wearing a uniform and looked just as she would have hoped had she thought about it. His clothes were pressed, his shoes were shined, his badge shone in the light, and his hair was perfectly in place. He was the absolute picture of professionalism.

The defendant, Mr. Nathan Brown, was wearing an expensive looking suit and tie. His hair, suit, tie all screamed wealth. The man could have easily been walking into an executive boardroom rather than a courtroom to face criminal charges.

Then she noticed something, and her face flushed with anger. The man wasn't wearing any handcuffs! He wasn't restrained in any way. The look on his face was like he felt he was being unnecessarily delayed on his way someplace more important. It was as if being here was an annoyance.

Her anger flared even hotter as more realizations came to her attention.

The defense attorney was well dressed, pressed, and polished at least as well, if not better than the defendant. The man could have easily been about to walk into a photoshoot somewhere as a model for an expensive clothing line.

All of this was in stark contrast to the prosecuting attorney who needed a shave, haircut, and was desperately in need of an ironing board for his disheveled suit.

The bailiff spoke loudly, likely out of habit or tradition as there was no noise for him to be heard over, "All rise!"

The scarce few people in the room that weren't already standing got to their feet as the judge quickly entered to start the proceedings.

"Take your seats," the judge said impatiently. His every action, the way he walked, the way he sat heavily into his chair, even his tone of voice indicated that, like Mr. Brown, he felt he had better things to do with his time than dealing with this situation.

While her legal challenges appeared to have vanished into thin air, she had hoped that was due to her being a first-time offender and because the overall situation making her actions justifiable. However, she was starting to lose any hope that Mr. Brown's punishment would fit his crime, and that was making her angrier by the minute.

The judge was in the upper half of middle age and looked as though he had been on the job for far too many years. He looked tired, or maybe it was annoyed, and certainly didn't appear as though he had any desire to deal with these proceedings in any way other than quickly. The only real interest he demonstrated was in the stack of papers on his desk. He was continuously flipping through them, stopping occasionally to scribble something on one page or another. These pages appeared to interest him far more than the people in the room.

"Mr. Prosecutor, what do you have for me?" the judge asked without looking up.

"Your Honor, we are charging Mr. Nathan Brown with driving under the influence, and reckless endangerment. On Friday last he departed a restaurant after having consumed too many alcoholic beverages, got into his vehicle, drove, despite his intoxicated state, and struck another vehicle. The occupants of the vehicle he struck were hospitalized with injuries ranging from superficial to critical," said the rumpled man, sounding as though he had said a close variation of these words hundreds of times and was bored with having to say it again.

"How do you plead?" asked the judge in a bored voice, still not looking up from his papers.

"Not guilty, Your Honor. Additionally, we would like to reiterate our request for bail, which was previously denied, and that an expedited trial date be set so that we can put this matter behind us and allow Mr. Brown to get back to his normal daily life without having this matter hanging over his head," the well-polished lawyer responded.

"Mr. Prosecutor, do you have anything further?" asked the judge, who was now furiously scribbling something on one of his all-important papers.

"We request that bail not be permitted in this matter. This is yet another event in a long and disturbing pattern of behavior, and we believe that if Mr. Brown is released, he will offend again, perhaps killing someone next time," came the timid reply from the prosecuting attorney who sounded like he was reading from a script.

The judge had still not looked up since entering the

room to see who, if anyone, was actually in the room as he flipped through a few more pages, "I see no prior convictions, therefore no pattern exists in the eyes of the law. Bail is set at twenty thousand dollars with trial to commence three weeks from today," he struck his gavel.

"All rise," the bailiff announced as the judge picked up his papers and left the room without another word.

"Let's go get some real food, not da crap dey have here," the lawyer said. "Funny, dis was faster than da last time I was here. This judge really doesn't give a shit anymore."

Sister Mary Anne sat in disbelief as not another word was spoken. Everyone involved in the proceedings just picked up their belongings and unceremoniously left the room, seemingly happy it was over so quickly.

Tears started rolling down Sister Mary Anne's face. She had assumed there would be more to it. She had hoped that the justice system was still capable of defending the Benjamins of the world.

One thing was certain, she was more determined than ever to find a way to ensure that justice was served. He had to pay for his crimes. *Somehow*, she would make sure it happened.

Maybe it was just time to retire, not just from nursing, from everything. She didn't feel as though she was making a difference in the world anymore.

Chapter Eight
The Bar Fight

Being out on patrol was not at all what Father Santini expected. He had not anticipated just how monotonous driving around town with no specific destination in mind was, and it gave him a new level of appreciation for law enforcement professionals who did this sort of thing night after night for years on end. He had somehow expected something important to be happening almost nonstop. The saving grace that kept him from falling asleep was the company of Officer Ray Jackson. Not only was he a great conversationalist, but he was also a rich source of knowledge about the problems facing the community. So far, the night had been crammed full of useful information and remained blessedly free of crime.

"Father, I am glad to see the Church getting more involved in the community. Some people around here could use a little old-fashioned religion in their lives, if for no other reason than to have some kind of positivity in their day-to-day lives," Ray said.

"I have a question about that. I see a ton of negativity on social media about law enforcement. There are some horrible things being said about people in your profession. I know there are *some* challenges, and certainly not *every* officer is a great guy, but I believe that by and large police are good people doing a hard job. Do you think social media adds to some of the challenges you face when dealing with the general public while on the job?" asked Father Santini.

"Some, but probably not as much as you think. I have been at this a really long time, and we saw a lot of the same problems even before social media became the driver for seemingly every conversation around the world. The attitude toward police has always been driven by pop culture and traditional media as much as anything. It doesn't really matter what happens. No matter what, when we show up on the scene some people will blame us for what is going on rather than their own life decisions. But, on the other side of that, there are plenty of times when we show up someone on the scene is happy if not visibly relieved or even ecstatic to see us," the officer explained.

"I bet!" Frank exclaimed. "When I spoke to Officer Pierce about tonight, I specifically asked for this part of town because of the violent crime statistics. Please don't take this as me hoping to see anything bad, or expecting some sort of shooting or something, but can I assume your night isn't always this peaceful and quiet? Not that I am complaining. I just really want to better understand what is happening in and around our little part of the world. That way I can determine what, if anything there is the Church can do to help improve our little corner of the world."

"Well, it is barely nine-thirty, so it is still a little early. Usually, nothin' really crazy starts till around ten, and sadly the day of week don't seem to matter too much. Something always seems to happen right around that time. Sometimes it is a simple robbery, sometimes it is much much worse, and we end up having to call in emergency medical teams. In this part of town, it usually falls in the 'worse' category, nothing much to steal around here. We also seem to get very busy around three in the mornin', but that tends to be more of a weekend thing. You can never tell though, it could stay this quiet all night, or the radio could start any second and not stop until after I go off duty, just kinda' depends on the day," Officer Jackson explained.

They continued making small talk as they patrolled up one street, down the next. Then the process would repeat, over and over and over again. Just before ten o'clock the radio came alive with more than the typical chatter, which up until that point had mostly consisted of officers calling in details about routine traffic stops.

"We have a call about a sexual assault or attempted sexual assault in progress at Third Street and Route Twenty-Eight in the bar parking lot. I need any available car to respond," said the calm, dispassionate male voice on the radio.

Ray grabbed the microphone, "Officer Jackson responding. I am just a few blocks over and will be on the scene in approximately three minutes." He flipped on the emergency lights and siren as he stepped hard on the accelerator. With a well-practiced series of motions, he had switched from routine patrol mode to action mode. Father Santini was impressed with the rapid and complete change in the man's focus.

"Thanks Ray, let me know if you need backup," came the same bored sounding voice on the radio with an audible sigh.

Father Santini couldn't help but wonder how often these types of calls happened if the dispatch operator the radio was truly as bored as he sounded.

The police cruiser raced around the corner and slid to a stop at the edge of a parking lot, packed with a crowd of people that was mostly male. They were cheering and holding up cell phones to take pictures or videos of something while chanting "*More, more, more!*"

Father Santini had only ever seen such behavior at sporting events, and something told him this was going to turn out to be something other than a pickup football game. Surely this couldn't be a sexual assault, the radio operator must have been wrong about that.

Ray grabbed the microphone, "Dispatch, this is Officer Jackson, I need *two* backup units *NOW!* There is a mob here, this could turn into a riot. I'll do what I can to get this under control, but I am going to need help!"

The officer jumped out of the vehicle, keeping one hand near his pistol while shoving people aside with the other. Father Santini was supposed to stay in the car but got out as fast as he could and followed staying right on the man's heels. Despite the officer's shouts to "make way" or "disperse" the people in the crowd barely gave him space to squeeze through.

One by one people realized a priest was on the scene and started to quickly turn and walk away. Frank had seen this kind of thing before and always just assumed it was on the off chance he had a direct line to the Big Man.

Two squad cars could be heard in the distance coming from different directions.

Help was on the way!

Father Santini finally pressed through the front row of the crowd.

Frank stopped in his tracks. Sure that his eyes were making things up just to mess with his brain.

This couldn't be real. It had to be a dream, it had to be his subconscious playing tricks on him.

Right in front of him, in the middle of the parking lot, two men were sexually forcing themselves on the same woman. Her clothes were in tatters and Officer Jackson was trying to pull one of the men off the front of her as a second man continued to violate her from behind. This second man seemed oblivious that anything out of the ordinary was happening.

The woman was trying to scream for help and fight them off but was clearly nearing exhaustion.

Father Santini grabbed the second man and pulled as hard as he could in an attempt to free the woman.

Thanks to the help from Officer Jackson and Father Santini she managed to wiggle free. Scrambling away, she was attempting to cover herself and regain some sense of modesty. Reaching a space between two parked cars she collapsed with her back against a tire and began crying hysterically, doing her best to remain hidden from the view of any onlookers.

Father Santini was finding it almost impossible to keep any kind of grip on the man he was grappling with and shifted his complete attention away from the escaping woman and solely on the fight for control.

Both of the rapists were in their mid-twenties and physically fit, but heavily intoxicated. Father Santini considered himself to be in good shape, and despite being older, was completely sober, giving him a significant edge.

The young man slipped free of Frank's grasp more than once, not due to his superior strength, merely as a result of erratic drunken movements. Frank finally managed to get him in a firm headlock after a few blows to the drunk's stomach. The man was starting to give up the struggle when Officer Jackson came up from behind to help with the situation.

"I'll take it from here, Father," Officer Jackson said as he handcuffed the now docile young man.

"You seem to have subdued him pretty well. I don't think he has any fight left in him, and by the look of things he may need some medical attention. You were supposed to stay in the car but I'm honestly glad you didn't. I don't think I could have handled this alone, and she didn't have time to wait for backup. Can you check on the young lady? See if she needs any kind of first aid that we can give her with what I have in the car? Backup should be here any second, and EMS will be shortly behind," Officer Jackson said, while trying to catch his breath.

Father Santini looked at the two young men, now handcuffed, face down on the pavement, officially in custody with their legal rights being read to them. It all happened so fast, almost instantly transitioning from routine patrol, to total chaos, then to what could only be described as a cleanup operation. Two people had done that. Two people had made all the difference. All it took was two people dedicated to the service of helping others to go from chaos, back to order.

Frank cautiously approached the victim, trying to not appear threatening. She was still scared almost to the point of hysteria, "Young lady, good evening. My name is Father Franklin Santini, I am a Catholic Priest, and I'd really like to help you. I am not going to harm you in any way. Helping people is sort of a job requirement in my profession, and something I take great care to do properly, no matter what the situation. Please take this," he removed his overcoat and cautiously handed it to her.

She took the coat and put in on seemingly comforted as much by the warmth as by the modesty it provided.

"Thank you, Fathwer," she slurred her words almost to the point of incomprehensibility between sobs. She was keeping her distance from him, trembling like a frightened animal.

"I am very sorry about what has happened to you. My friend, Officer Ray Jackson over there has those two men in custody, handcuffed, and completely under his control. They can no longer do any physical harm to you or anyone else," he said softly, attempting to calm her while hoping he wasn't saying or doing anything to make matters worse.

She managed to fully cover herself in his coat and was sobbing hard, although no longer hysterically. The panic seemed to be slowly leaving her body.

Officer Jackson called from his position twenty feet across the parking lot, "Father! Two ambulances are coming this way as fast as possible. At least one of these guys is going to need some medical attention, and I don't want her and them in the same emergency vehicle."

"Did you hear that, Miss? I'm sorry I don't know your name," he said hoping she would fill in the blank.

"Awmadshwa," she slurred drunkenly, finally looking Father Santini in the face.

The woman was so intoxicated that he was having difficulty understanding anything she said. He prayed what he was about to say was correct.

"Well, Amanda, there is medical help on the way, and it will be here soon. I will make sure that no more harm comes to you while I am here. Not on my watch. Would you like to get off that cold cement?"

He extended his hand to help her off the ground in what he hoped was an unthreatening manner, "Those two men are restrained now, what is left of the crowd is way over on the other side of the parking lot. Most people have already gone, and we have a warm, not to mention comfortable police squad car you can sit in until the ambulance arrives."

She cautiously took his offered hand with her uninjured arm and slowly, with a great deal of pain, got to her feet. Father Santini put his arm around her shoulder to guide her as well as to offer support if she needed because of her injured and drunken condition as they made their way to the waiting squad car. He took a route through the parked cars that would avoid any possibility of eye contact with the attackers.

Another squad car screeched to a stop in the center of the parking lot and a female officer jumped out. The uniformed woman immediately took over the job of consoling Amanda who was now in the front seat of Officer Jackson's patrol car.

Father Santini returned to Ray's side, standing near the two men in custody. The men were still face down on the pavement, handcuffed and docile with their pants around their ankles.

A third squad car pulled into the parking lot and turned off its siren, leaving the emergency lights rotating, adding a new element to the already bizarre pulsating lighting display illuminating the area.

Officer Jackson looked at Father Santini out of the corner of his eye, "Thanks for your help, Father. That was really *far* above and beyond for someone who was just coming along to observe for the night. Just for the record, I have never seen a crowd scatter like that. Usually someone, or some group of onlookers wants to stick around and give me a hard time even if they are just shouting some kind of nonsense. You weren't kidding when you said that the collar makes people behave a little differently. When we first got here, they scattered like freaking *insects*. I may have to bring you out on patrol more often, but officially, and for the record I have to remind you to stay in the car next time," he winked.

"Shouldn't we cover them up, or put their clothes back on them or something? I can't imagine how that cold ground feels on their, well, you know," Father Santini suggested.

"Probably, but I think leaving them with their nuts exposed to the cold concrete for another few minutes won't kill them. After what we saw I'm not inclined to give them any comfort beyond what is required by law," Ray said. "Maybe we'll get lucky, and some ants will take an interest in their junk before the medical teams arrive."

Frank thought that would be a good start, "What else can I do to be of service?"

"Not much, once we get some more help here on the scene, I need to start getting some statements from people inside the bar, but if experience tells me anything I won't get much, if anything useful. I respond to this place more often than you might think, and 'I didn't see nothin' is gonna be about all I hear. I do have a bodycam, so based on what that thing shows we probably won't need much in the way of testimony. Video makes things much easier for the prosecution once things go in front of a judge. Even with that we may need your eyewitness testimony, unless these two plead guilty," Ray said.

If Frank hadn't seen it with his own eyes, he might not have believed it. How could a society, an advanced society, a so-called peace-loving society have degraded to this point? How could this have taken place just a few miles from where he lived and worked? Nothing made sense.

Father Santini couldn't believe what he was about to ask, "Have you ever seen anything like this before? People just cheering on a gang-rape without anyone trying to help the victim. I mean, it was like some kind of game to them."

Officer Jackson let out a sigh, "This is a new one, but honestly, I'm not *that* shocked. I have seen some strange things in the last few years. This is up there, but sadly it is really not that surprising. Especially from this place," he said as he gave the bar a dirty look.

"What else goes on around here that I don't know about?" Frank asked to no one in particular as the sirens from the arriving ambulances drown out his voice.

A few moments later the two assailants were being picked up off the ground. One was headed for a squad car; the other was being placed on a gurney with a team of EMTs examining his injuries. Father Santini stood alone as a spectator to all the action, outwardly calm in the middle of chaos.

This was a crisis of humanity. God *must* see this as unacceptable. This could not have been the intent when He created the Earth. Someone had to act, why not a priest? It made sense, in a way.

He waved to Officer Jackson while jumping into the back of the ambulance with Amanda.

"Hello again," he said warmly.

Amanda was on a gurney with a young-looking female emergency medical technician examining her injuries.

"How is she?" Father Santini asked the EMT.

"Some minor lacerations, bruises and likely a broken arm. They will do a more complete exam at the hospital, but from what I heard about this incident, it could have been far worse," the EMT explained without looking up from her work.

"You see, Amanda! You will recover," Father Frank said enthusiastically.

She had stopped crying and finally seemed fully aware of her surroundings.

"Thanksh for your hewlp," she said concentrating hard in an attempt to form words correctly, but her level of intoxication was making it difficult.

She finally focused her eyes on his white collar in the center of the neckline of his black shirt. Even though he had introduced himself as a priest in the parking lot she finally seemed to realize it.

He supposed she had been in a state of shock, combined with an enormous amount of alcohol in her system, so it wasn't surprising that it took time for some details to stick in her brain.

She opened her mouth as if to speak, then closed it,

unsure of what to say.

"It's ok, I am a servant of God, not God himself. No need for anyone to fear me, nor should any good person fear God for that matter. I am not here to judge you. My job is to forgive people for their sins. Besides, from what I saw those two sinners from the parking lot need to be ready for me to mention them by name during a prayer later today asking for the Lord's justice," Frank said with his warmest smile.

She smiled back, just a little, but it was a small step in the right direction.

"Are you reawy a priesht?" she slurred drunkenly.

"Yes, I am!" he exclaimed proudly.

She offered him her good hand. He reached out and clasped it in his own.

"I am nawt a Cathowic though," she said timidly.

"Oh, who cares about that. Look, Amanda, I have no way of knowing what you are going through emotionally or spiritually at the moment. To make things even more frustrating, I have no way of knowing what the coming days will bring for you in terms of emotional pain, doubts and inner turmoil. No man can. I do know someone who might be able to help. A nun by the name of Sister Mary Anne Margaret. She is an older woman, and a wicked awesome poker player so don't ever bet against her if she ever goes all in. Would you like for me to arrange for her to meet us at the hospital so you can talk with her?" Father Santini asked.

Tears were slowly but steadily rolling down her face.

"That would be nish. Couwld you alsho cawl my moter and ashk her to mweet us thewe?" she asked.

"Certainly!" he said reaching for his phone so he could call both women.

Whatever the exact mission God had given him would bring to his future, helping this woman had to be part of that plan. God had obviously put her in his path for a reason.

Chapter Nine
The Interview

In the days since the bar parking lot fight Father Santini had become a well-known enough public figure that whenever he went into public people would stop him and ask to snap a picture together. Based on the number of views some of the online videos of the now famous fight had gotten, he assumed it would be the same almost anywhere in the country.

Even before the event he would routinely post something on social media about Scripture and how to apply it to everyday life. The day before those videos hit the internet, he had a few hundred followers and rarely had anyone comment. Now he was approaching a million followers, and the comments would come pouring in almost instantly after hitting post.

First on his agenda for the day was a live television interview, then runover and visit with Amanda at the hospital.

At long last Father Santini was exhilarated by his work. Work had always humbled him, he had never once second guessed his decision to become a priest, but it had never been truly exciting, until now.

He was no longer just a passive member of the clergy, standing on the sidelines watching as society crumbled around him. He had been chosen by God to achieve something great and was not going to permit himself to fail. It didn't matter where this mission would lead, or what might be asked of him along the way.

Frank made his way to the kitchen and poured himself a cup of coffee. He let the aroma waft into his face before taking a sip and heading for his father's jeep to make his way to the television station for the interview. Apparently, a local priest wrestling with a drunken man in an effort to break up a brutal sexual assault in progress was newsworthy. Everywhere Frank looked there seemed to be people watching and commenting on a continuously looping video taken by cell phone cameras from every conceivable angle.

After a short drive he pulled into the television station parking lot. He parked in a visitor space and made his way into the reception area. It had a few comfortable looking chairs with a security guard behind the desk.

"Good morning, I'm Father Franklin Santini and I'm here at the invitation of Julie Cross," he said.

"Oh, hey, you are *that* Priest, the one from the video! Cool, let me get her, if you could just sign in on the tablet," the man pointed to an electronic tablet mounted on a pedestal.

He hadn't even finished signing in when a professionally dressed woman appeared, "Hello Father Santini, I'm Julie Cross."

"Hello, Miss Cross, I have been watching your

segments for a long time. I am a big fan!" Father Santini said.

"I am also a fan of yours," she said turning on the charm. She motioned for him to follow her.

"Well thank you. I only did what others who were there should have," he said.

She was all business, "I'm sure of that, but you actually did it. Remember, we will be live this morning, as a result remember only answer the question that was asked. Time will be limited. Answer from the heart. We only have a few minutes on air, and it will go by much more quickly than you realize."

They turned a corner and Frank saw the news studio he had seen on television hundreds of times. She motioned for him to sit in one of the chairs in front of the intense lights.

"The anchor is over in Studio A doing the majority of the broadcast and will throw to us in about fifteen minutes. Until then just get comfortable in the space. Don't think about the cameras, pretend this whole thing is just us having a conversation," she said.

The reporter and the priest sat exchanging small talk as they waited. The majority of her questions were about why he had chosen to become a priest, which he declined to answer saying it was very personal. She was oddly curious about his parent's opinion of him joining the priesthood so much so that he wondered if she knew who his father was. The man had been talked about on the news plenty of times, but Frank always avoided the subject whenever possible.

Father Santini came to the conclusion that she had vamped like this with hundreds of people and didn't really care about the answers. Finally, a crewmember holding a piece of electronic equipment he didn't recognize warned them they had ten seconds to air.

Julie sat up a little straighter, smiled into the camera and waited. The red light on the camera came on and she remained silent, but nodded every few seconds, until finally, "Thanks Erica. I am here with Roman Catholic Priest Father Franklin Santini."

She turned to look at Frank, "Father, thank you for agreeing to join us this morning."

"Thank you for having me."

"Now, our viewers are familiar with the rising crime rates and other problems facing our nation. But instead of just watching from the sidelines you decided to get involved and try to help out here in the Boston area. We just showed our viewers of you putting a stop to at least one particularly heinous crime. I'm sure you know which video I'm talking about; it now has more than three million views on YouTube alone. After seeing it some people are calling you a 'hero' while others have called you 'the vigilante priest.' Do you agree with either of these descriptions?" she asked.

"I personally think 'hero' is a grand overstatement of what really happened, and I am certainly no 'vigilante,' it wouldn't go with the ceremonial robes very well. In reality what happened was Officer Ray Jackson and I were patrolling through town. I was really just along for the ride to try to see for myself what the police experience on a nightly basis to try to understand what the church can do to help out when a call came over the radio about a sexual assault or attempted sexual assault in progress, the dispatch officer wasn't sure which it was. We happened to be the closest available patrol vehicle. When we got to the scene, we found two men in the process of raping a woman in public, surrounded by onlookers cheering them on. Officer Jackson, Ray, went to work trying to stop one of the men, all I did was lend a hand in stopping the other one," he explained, trying to give the most accurate description of events possible.

"From what we saw on the video there were plenty of people on the scene. Are you telling me that no one else, not a single person in that crowed, tried to help that poor woman? I mean, did the video miss someone who was actually trying to help?" she asked. Like any good, well-disciplined reporter her facial expression turned to one of equal parts curiosity, shock and disgust.

"For the most part those in the crowd were doing exactly what the video shows, cheering things on, thirsty for things to keep going," he said with disgust.

"That's terrible! What has come of this world? Cheering for something like that?!?" she asked, the disgust clear in her tone of voice and body language.

"I'm really not sure, but I for one think it is high time we had a serious discussion in this nation, and world really, about values and morals. I don't care if the discussion focuses on Catholic values or just basic human values, but it must happen, we must take action, it can be put off no longer, no matter how uncomfortable it is to discuss. Being responsible for our actions and helping thy neighbor is a good thing. I am almost certain I read that somewhere in a book we have laying around the Church someplace," he quipped with his most charming smile.

"Have you spoken to either of the men or the woman since all of this happened?" the reporter asked.

"I have not spoken to either of the men, but I have spoken to the victim. She needed someone non-threatening to speak with, so I as well as another member of the church have been happy to be there for her. In fact, once we are done here, I am going to pay her a visit. She has had some questions about the Catholic Faith I have been answering for her," he said.

"I am sure she was happy to have you there for her this past Monday. I had a chance to speak with her off camera and she has referred to you as her savior. It may surprise you to learn, and this is a quote, she thinks you 'may just be the second coming of Christ, come to deliver the world from evil,'" the reporter said.

Could God have told Amanda to say these things?

Could it be true?

Was he the second coming, was his body being inhabited by God?

Certainly not.

Maybe?

It couldn't be.

"Well, I am sure that I am not. I am just a simple man of faith, and an imperfect one at that," Father Santini said, trying to put the notion out of his head and stay focused on the interview.

"We have also spoken to the lawyer for the two alleged assailants. He claims you attacked the man without provocation. He apparently suffered two broken ribs and a fractured arm in the altercation. His attorney has said they are planning to file a lawsuit against you, and the Church," she said.

"Well, it was certainly not unprovoked, and to claim otherwise is just silly. There was a struggle, and I did everything I could to help a victim of a shockingly horrific attack, that was all. I certainly did not show up there that night intending to cause harm. I do think we can claim beyond any doubt that he intended to continue to harm that poor woman," Father Santini said.

He realized he was rambling. Could the adrenalin have gotten the better of him? Was it God? Was God wielding justice through him? Were the injuries part of this man's punishment for his sins?

"Well, Julie, all I can say is that God works in mysterious ways. I will pray that he recovers quickly from these injuries. I will pray he seeks help for whatever it was that drove him to this despicable act, and that he never, ever commits such a sin again," he said.

"Father, I agree with you, we will hope he has learned the error of his ways, but I hope he spends time behind bars. With that, we are out of time. Erica, back to you," she said into the camera.

The red light turned off, ending the on-air discussion.

"Thank you for taking time for us today, Father. This story really seems to have captured a lot of attention," Julie said.

"Thank you for having me," Father Santini said.

"If I can give you some advice. Take this opportunity to become more active on social media. You have momentum, and if you can maintain a large enough following it is really a great way to influence change in a lot of people quickly using your own unfiltered voice. Trust me when I tell you that you don't want someone else taking your story in a direction you may not appreciate," she said light-heartedly.

"That is a fair point. Thank you again, and if you ever want me back, never hesitate to call," he said.

"I may do just that," she said.

***

Father Santini was walking through the parking lot when his phone vibrated. He took it out of his pocket to see an email from his dad.

Frankie,

Remember when you told Sister Mary Anne to stay out of trouble. I am going to have to give her a call and see what she is telling you now.

Saw you on the news. Proud of you for getting your hands a little dirty. But don't get a big head. You were just in the right place at the right time. Don't let these fifteen minutes of fame distract you. Stay focused on the bigger picture.

Don't worry about the lawsuit, I will make sure it goes away.

Love

Dad

Frank didn't want to think about how his dad was going to make that happen. He took a deep breath and got on the road to meet Amanda.

Chapter Ten
The Congregation

"Let us go in peace to love and serve the Lord," Father Santini said to the congregation.

He had spoken these words many times in the past but felt a greater connection with them today than he had in many years. Perhaps more than at any point since taking his in his life.

Proceeding up the center aisle of the Church he listened to the uplifting hymn and felt an overwhelming sense of love coming from those around him. Maybe that feeling had always been there, but today it shined brighter, and he felt it more than ever before.

Once at the back of the Church he took up position by the main exit so he could shake hands and exchange pleasantries with anyone who desired a few moments of his time.

No sooner had the hymn ended than a line of parishioners materialized in front of him. It seemed like every single person in attendance wanted to shake his hand.

"Father, I know you believed in hard work and getting your hands dirty, but I never thought you would get your hands *that* dirty," said Mrs. Ashford smiling while clutching his hand.

"Oh, it was just another day at the office, Mrs. Ashford," he said with a warm smile wondering what she would say if she knew how dirty those hands had gotten on a different night. But that was between him and God.

The second she released his hand someone else took her place.

"Father, I saw you on the news. Way to go!!!" exclaimed Mr. Bigelow as the human tidal wave continued.

"What are you going to do as an encore?" someone shouted, he couldn't tell who it was, the crowd was too thick.

His mind was racing. Euphoria was the only way to describe how this level of support for his unorthodox actions made him feel. It was unlike anything he had ever experienced. He was happy in ways he never thought possible.

He wondered how much more they might support and admire him if the parishioners only knew what he had done in support of the larger mission. Would they understand why it was necessary. It would be amazing, but those actions were between him and the Lord, at least for the moment.

"Father, if you keep this up, things will really start to turn around for our little town. If even our priests will come out and *literally* fight back, the criminals will have to back off. Are you coming to the Fall Festival this afternoon?" Mrs. Chase asked, refusing to let go of her iron-like grip on his hand.

"Of course, I would never miss it. I just need to finish up here and get changed into something more appropriate," Father Santini said.

"I will look for you. My family wanted to say a special thank you for helping that woman, maybe we can have you over for dinner again soon," the small woman offered.

Father Santini knew that wasn't an invitation, from this tiny woman it was an instruction, "I would be happy to join you!"

He exchanged small talk and handshakes with another dozen or so people, then made a mad dash back to the rectory to change clothes into something more practical than his ceremonial robes. His black pants, black shirt, and white collar would do for the afternoon.

With a quick glance at his watch, he decided he had time to re-read an email from the Cardinal, if for no other reason than to be sure he hadn't imagined it.

Father Santini,

I saw you on the news, and I have heard a great deal about the work you are doing. It is, to say the least, impressive for a man as young as yourself.

As I think about the situation you have put yourself in, I am reminded of Ephesians 6:10 – 6:18.

6:10 – Finally, my brethren, be strong in the Lord and in the power of His might.

6:11 – Put on the whole armor of God, that you may be able to stand against the wiles of the devil.

I have always interpreted the armor of God to be the members of the Priesthood, as it is obviously those of us called into His service who are meant to protect the innocent from evil. It appears that in your case you have put that belief of mine into physical as well as spiritual action. The older I get, the more I feel we must protect the innocent by whatever method God has determined is necessary. While we must not condone violence in a general sense, sometimes force must be met with force. In your case you were very obviously defending the defenseless. You are indeed one of God's warriors in action.

6:12 – For we do not wrestle against flesh and blood, but against principalities, against powers, against rulers of darkness of this age.

Your work is certainly doing this for us. The darkness is everywhere, and the Church has not necessarily met it as head on as we should. Perhaps in the future we can be more proactive in our dealings with evil. Perhaps we have let the scandals of the past make us timid in our response to the modern day needs of our parishioners.

6:13 – Therefore put on the full armor of God, so that when the day of evil comes, you may be able to stand your ground, and after you have done everything, to stand.

6:14 – Stand, therefore, having girded your waist with truth, having put on your breastplate of righteousness,

6:15 – and having shod your feet with the preparation of the gospel of peace

6:16 – above all, take the shield of faith with which you will be able to quench all the fiery darts of the wicked one.

You obviously have Faith, and no fear of darts, or anything else it seems from the news reports. The wicked one, God's fallen Angel, may be what is causing some of the problems we face, but with men like you on our side we have hope that he may someday permit us to live in peace.

6:17 – And take the helmets of salvation, and the sword of the Spirit, which is the word of God

6:18 – praying as always with all prayer and application in the Spirit, being watchful to this end with all perseverance and supplication for all the Saints.

I shall continue to keep you in my prayers. I also took the liberty of forwarding some highlights from some news articles to His Holiness. He responded personally and said you are to be commended and suggested that one day soon you should come to visit him in Rome.

Yours in Christ,

Cardinal O'Neill

His Holy Father, the Pope, knew his name. He had not set out with this intent. He had merely set out to do what he felt was justified in the name of the Lord. His Service to the Lord was being noticed and discussed at the highest possible levels on Earth. Was this all a part of God's greater plan?

He began feeling somewhat guilty because this sort of thing could lead to ambition and temptation, which he was starting to feel.

His head began to hurt. The pain behind his eyes was relentlessly stabbing at him.

Heavenly Father, I apologize for my moment of ambition. I will strive to remain humble and meet those challenges to the best of my abilities. I will leave this community a better place than I found it, and ensure Your Glory is reflected.

Ambition and temptation were not positive traits for a priest. It is meant to be a life of Service, a life of Service to something greater than one's petty little personal desires. It was simply not possible for an ambitious person to give themselves over fully to God. An ambitious person would place their own desires in a higher position than their worship of the Lord, and that went against Scripture.

The headache was back. He rubbed his temples. He shoved aside the ambition, refusing to feel that emotion, and forced himself to be fully thankful for the challenges in his path, putting his full trust into God's plan. He promised himself that he would never again go down that path and the pain in his head began to subside.

Pushing the pain aside he took a deep breath to think for a moment. This email certainly validated his mission. It clearly justified his actions in a substantive way. If he considered these Scriptures referenced by the Cardinal in the way they were intended when written, it was easy to justify his actions. The Cardinal had even offered justification without having firsthand knowledge of his other actions in support of God's vision for the future. Clearly the Lord had a hand in crafting this message with these Scriptures, not to mention the interpretation given by a man this importance and theological expertise. Frank felt reinforced that he was on the correct path in his Service to the Lord, and he would not falter.

He fastened the final two buttons on his shirt, tightened his collar, checked his appearance in the mirror one last time, and left his room heading for the Fall Festival. The moment he stepped outside he found Amanda waiting in the parking lot.

"Father Santini!" she called from a row of cars away. "I hope you don't mind me surprising you over here. I don't know anyone over there, and it seems like a really large crowd," her voice trailed off at the end.

"Oh, it's perfectly fine. We can walk over together, and I can introduce you to some people I think you will enjoy meeting, that is if you feel up to it," he offered with a smile.

He knew from their talks that she had an

understandable newly found fear of venturing into a group of people she didn't know. It was impossible for Father Santini to find fault with that based on her recent experience.

"You will find that these people here are good, caring people who just want to live their lives in peace. They don't like what has been going on in the world around us these days and believe that if you obey the laws of God, you should be able to live free and without oppression. They love their families, their friends *and* the Lord. They make every attempt to let that love come through in their daily lives, but they won't beat you over the head with it. This whole event isn't some kind of old-time revival tent meeting, its so that kids and families and anyone else who wants to join them can have at least one wholesome day outside, having fun, before winter hits and we all run inside to try to stay warm for the next few months," he explained.

Father Santini realized with great relief that as he spoke about the Lord and his congregation that the pain in his head had completely vanished.

"It looks like there is a lot going on over there." she said nervously.

"Well, we have some typical carnival type games, bingo of course, food, which will include my favorite snack...kettle corn," he said along with some yummy noises as they continued to make their way toward the crowd.

"Oh! I love that stuff! It tastes great and smells so good as they pop it," she exclaimed, starting to relax a little.

"Anyway, like I said, the whole point of today is to come together as a community and enjoy one another's company and forget about the problems of daily life for a little while," he explained.

"Sounds like a slice of Heaven," she said.

"Well, I am kind of in the Heaven and Hell business, and I do have a certain preference for Heaven," he said, smiling broadly.

She laughed as they crossed the street to the schoolyard where the festival was taking place.

As they walked around the events, he introduced her to everyone who approached to shake his hand and make some comment about the bar parking lot video. He would only give out her first name, but little else other than she was curious about the Catholic Faith and considering converting. No one needed to know who she was, and the viral video never showed her face, or anything that would reveal her identity, which Father Santini considered a small blessing in the wake of such a tragedy.

It was soon clear that Amanda was becoming overwhelmed. He led her over to get some kettle corn then to a picnic table with just a few of the older parishioners sitting near the edge of the festivities.

"Amanda, I want you to meet Don Hinkle, Jonathan Pierce, Jonathan's wife Robin, and last but not least, Heather Sanchez who enjoys arguing with Don. May we join the four of you?" Father Santini asked.

"Please, sit down, join us. Father, hopefully you can

keep the moment in the spotlight to yourself and not include me in the media madness," Don Hinkle chided.

"I will do my best to not let it splash on you, Don. Amanda here is thinking of converting to Catholicism, so she came to join us today to learn a bit more about what brings us together every week," he explained.

"That's great," Don said. "If you want the old-timer's opinion you are making a good choice. I grew up in the Church, so I may be a little biased, but I know it has given me a lot over the years. Far more than I could ever give back to it."

"So, what's the hot debate today?" Father Santini asked as he took a seat.

"Honestly, there isn't one. Sorry to disappoint you Father," Robin said.

"Seriously? Well, I'm sure some sort of argument will come along at any moment," Father Santini joked with a dismissive wave of his hand.

Heather sighed, "No, we actually all agree this time. I was just saying how much my kids have been looking forward to today. They are just under so much pressure these days to grow up faster than ever before. One of the things that really bothers me is the over-sexualization of younger and younger kids. My daughter had a friend over the other day and this little brat was shocked that my eleven-year-old daughter didn't have a boyfriend. This kid asked her what she was saving herself for! I wasn't sure what to say. I mean, when she was six these sorts of things were innocent, but this wasn't that. This little girl was serious, so I asked a few other mothers and apparently it wasn't just this kid talking that way, and several kids in that age group had been caught their daughters making out with boys either their age or older."

"Oh, I know what you mean. I can barely send the kids outside to play anymore. During the day if I go out with them it can be ok, but that changes around four in the afternoon or so, and it gets worse the later, and darker it gets. Like the other day, I wasn't outside, and this car pulled up in front of the house and someone tried to sell our fourteen-year-old son drugs and when he refused, they tried to get him to sell some to his friends. When he told them his dad was a cop they sped off while threatening that he better keep his mouth shut," Robin said.

Don couldn't help himself, and with his typical Bostonesque philosophical style, "Halloween is coming up, and when I was a kid all the good stuff happened after dark. Now, even if I go with my grandkids, they can't go out and have fun after the sun goes down. These days about all you can do is go to the mall and see if any stores are giving away 'free candy with purchase.' Or if someone is feeling energetic, they set up a Trunk or Treat at the local school, but even that is questionable these days. It's too bad really, scaring the crap out of friends was always the best part. I remember when my brother was like ten or eleven, I scared him so bad he pissed all over himself," Don laughed so hard he almost dropped his iced tea.

"Not to add any fuel to this fire, but we had a junior high principal in the office the other day. I can't say which one of course, but he told us that many students are starting to view drug and alcohol rehab as some sort of badge of honor. Going more than once is becoming kind of a status symbol for some students," Jonathan added. "There is even some kind of online group that keeps score with a leader board to see who has gone the most verifiable number of times, with teams and everything. I would not be surprised to find out they had some kind of betting on the so-called winner going on."

"Well, let's not worry about any of that today. Let's just focus on the amazing weather, and the food. I must run over and help out with a third-grade skit, so please make Amanda here feel welcome, and Amanda don't let Don suck you into one of his long discussions on what's wrong with the Red Sox," Father Santini warned as he got up from the table.

"I promise I won't. Thanks for everything, Father," Amanda said with a wave and a giggle.

Frank was confident that he could now lay claim to having saved one more soul. This woman was now obviously on her way to becoming a devoted follower of the Lord, and certainly on the right path to achieve eternal Salvation. Making her an official member of the Church was irrelevant, her life was on the correct path, and her eternal soul was now saved, hopefully for all eternity.

Chapter Eleven
The Future of Cleansing

Growing up Father Santini had always taken the world-class Boston public library for granted. It was one of those things he would just pass by without a second thought on his way to somewhere more interesting. Now he was fully aware that it was not only an impressive bit of architecture, but an amazing research tool. Academics came here from all over the world for access to what this building had to offer.

Walking up the front stairs he was surrounded by impressive marble architecture. Everyone around him was so distracted by the building it offered him some anonymity despite his recent social media "fame." Especially as he was avoiding eye contact with everyone and keeping to himself.

Research and privacy were his only desires for the afternoon; therefore, he had chosen clothing that would not give him away as a priest. He had on kahki pants, a blue long sleeve shirt, a Red Sox jacket and ball cap. Dressed like this he would blend in and appear to be nothing more than the local he had been his entire life.

He and Sister Mary Anne had discussed Catholic history many times over the years, and recalling one of the chats had given him an idea that if he could learn more about the tools and techniques the Church used back in the thirteenth century during the Inquisition, then maybe he could adapt them for his modern-day mission. He had read a little about it over the years, but not nearly enough to satisfy his need for specific knowledge and understanding.

He knew that the Inquisitors were tasked with extracting confessions from suspected heretics and to try to get the sinners to return to the Faith through a shockingly painful process to encourage repentance, which could put them on the road to absolution.

Somewhere around the year 1250 things became especially brutal when Pope Alexander IV encouraged Inquisitors to absolve one another of any wrongdoing that occurred during these confession extraction sessions. Then these same Inquisitors, a select number of priests, were free to go forward and do whatever they wanted without any spiritual concerns. Father Santini found the entire policy a perversion of the intent of Holy Scripture in some ways, but in others it was an interesting and potentially adaptable concept that could be applied to his current situation.

There was a line that could absolutely not be crossed. As long as that rule was obeyed without fail, his actions would remain within the boundaries of God's laws. Some of the techniques used by the Inquisitors might help him come close to the intent of an eye for an eye in his mission to let Saint Peter sort out the details of their ultimate penance once the soul in question made it into the afterlife. He had to be sure that only those who were *truly* beyond absolution became the subject of his Cleansings.

But what exactly should happen to the sinners once they were determined to be beyond absolution? It would certainly depend on the severity of the Sins that had been committed and how often they had committed them. Researching the individuals on his list would have to be part of the process, and verification of their sins had to be detailed and accurate.

He found a half dozen books on the Inquisition along with a few on medieval torture and settled into a private study room. He wanted to take some notes but didn't dare check the books out for fear of leaving a paper trail that could lead back to him should he ever come under suspicion.

It was important to fully understand the historical reasons someone would have been declared a heretic. Like most things it began with some very specific reasons as determined by the Church leadership, then continued to expand until it evolved into whatever the Inquisitor wanted it to be on that particular day. Essentially the Church leadership failed when they allowed the Inquisitors to stray from the fundamentals and didn't step in quickly enough when things became bloodthirsty.

Officially a heretic was considered a "dissenter from established religious dogma." At the heart of the matter was the Ten Commandments. Father Santini had decided that if he didn't stray from those basic rules the continuation and even expansion of his Holy Mission would be acceptable in the eyes of God.

Father Santini took a deep breath and turned his full attention to the Inquisition tools and techniques. The original intent of the Church and these "torture" devices was to bring sinners back into God's good graces. The number of heretics, then as well as now, was so high and their offenses were so extreme that in some cases only in the afterlife could their worthiness for absolution be determined.

Only those beyond absolution on the mortal plane of existence would be Cleansed. That would enable those worthy to live in peace.

Applied properly these techniques could lead to sinners becoming truly penitent. When that happened their eternal soul would be spared from damnation and if that happened anything that happened to their temporary mortal bodies was irrelevant. If a Priest, the armor of God, was the one using the tools. If the tools made the sinner repent, they would spend eternity at peace in the Silver City. The mortal plane was no longer relevant.

He reached for a book from the dusty stack of reference material.

He flipped through some pages and came across a device known as an iron gag designed to stifle the screams of those being interrogated, as the screams could be distracting to the inquisitor. It had a simple iron ring and a metallic box. The ring was large enough to be worn like a dog collar while the iron box was forced into the mouth. The box had a hole large enough to allow for the passage of air, but small enough to be blocked with a finger. Blocked for a prolonged period of time the wearer would suffocate. None of the Sinners he had in mind had any chance of surviving what he had planned, but they would suffer as they had made others suffer.

An eye for an eye.

He found several devices that were annoyingly interesting but would require more privacy and time than he was likely to have for a specific Cleansing he had in mind. One was a truly delicious form of punishment, a pendulum covered in razors. It was a great idea that would likely leave evidence behind that could lead back to him.

Water torture piqued his interest as it was easy to do and difficult to trace. Force enough liquid into the stomach and it would rupture, causing extreme pain. He took detailed notes on how to perform this one. It was a bit tricky, but seemed to have been highly effective when employed.

He found the subject fascinating and many of the tools potentially useful. He read about the heretic's fork, the pear, breast ripper, garrote, and something called a head crusher. His favorite potential device for some types of sinners was called the anal eviscerator, and from the pictures looked like it would live up to its name.

He pushed back from the table to stretch and think for a moment. There was so much work to do that he decided that he would have to develop a triage process. The hope was that while the worst sinners were being Cleansed others would see the error of their ways without a visit from God's chosen Holy Warrior.

One thing was certain, the punishments must fit the crimes. If he didn't prioritize in some fashion things could become overwhelming and there was no margin for error, not in God's War.

Father Santini looked at his watch and realized he had been at it for hours and was hungry. It was time to put away the books, get some dinner and think about what he had learned, as well as the next steps.

***

He was enjoying dinner and flipping through social media to see who had tagged or commented on his account. In the process he noticed that following was growing quickly.

On one platform he was at almost a quarter of a million followers. Once word got out that the "vigilante priest" not only had an account but would respond to some questions, things had grown like crazy.

The questions and comments were on everything from religion to crime and people were commenting from all over the country and even some parts of the world. Some of them were certain that he went to the bar parking lot that night looking for someone to hurt, others were convinced he was a highly skilled martial artist masquerading as a Priest, which had zero truth to it. Some women were obsessed with his "good looks" more than his good deeds and lamenting that he was unavailable.

He took a sip of beer and sighed.

Focusing on religious questions had always seemed like the right path. Since this whole moment of fame began, he had been trying to answer questions for anyone he could that was showing interest in the Catholic Faith.

The one he found most interesting was from someone with the handle @FightingPriestFan12. It was a simple question with a complex answer.

How long has God blessed you with the ability to instantly, and so accurately judge right from wrong while guiding you in the right place at the right time to jump in and rescue someone from trouble?

How could he explain that it is easy to do when two people were caught in the act of raping a woman, but far more complex in the confessional? How could he explain that it wasn't always obvious at a glance who was evil and who wasn't? He sat writing a series of posts explaining this while eating his chicken when he noticed that a number of high-profile reporters from both sides of the political aisle were now among his online followers. That caused him to be extra cautious on how he phrased his answers so it wouldn't be spun in some strange direction to fit some political argument. God was above politics.

Ten minutes after finishing his post, and deep into watching a discussion on ESPN his phone vibrated with a text message from his dad.

Lawsuit has been dropped. Nothing to worry about. Love, Dad.

Father Santini responded with a simple,

Thanks, talk soon

and decided to not ask any questions about how. He texted Officer Pierce.

Hey, can we go grab some coffee or a beer soon?

The reply came quickly.

Sure thing, Father, just name the time and place.

Chapter Twelve
The Lawyer

Several people had cautioned her against getting any more involved with the situation than she already was, but the more people tried to talk her out of it, the more Sister Mary Anne was determined to make sure that the man who hurt little Benjamin was harshly punished for his crime. It had taken almost twenty phone calls to figure out who the prosecuting attorney would be, and blessedly it wasn't the man she saw at the fifteen-minute preliminary hearing. A few phone calls later and she had an appointment where she planned on offering to be of whatever assistance she could to ensure he was found guilty so he would pay for his crimes and had little intention of taking no for an answer.

She arrived at the District Attorney's office for her appointment a bit early and had been asked to wait. The small reception area had furniture that may have been comfortable at some point in time, but those days were long gone. Even the reading material was out of date, not to mention it was covered in a thick film of dust.

There were so many conversations coming from the interior of the office it was difficult to make out anything specific from her position. It was permeating the waiting room as a shifting level of white noise.

Another ten minutes went by before a stressed-out looking young man in khaki pants and a button-down shirt with the sleeves rolled halfway up his forearms poked his head out, looked at the three people waiting and said, "I hope I have this right, is there a Mrs. Margaret here?"

"That's me, but its Sister Mary Anne Margaret," she said with a smile as she got off the couch. The nun had dressed in formal attire today, clearly that of a nun.

"I do apologize, Sister, if you follow me, I will take you back for your appointment now," the young man said.

"Don't worry about it, people make that mistake all the time. Can I ask your name?" she inquired.

"I'm Jerry, Mrs. Hernandez's intern," he said.

"Great to meet you Jerry," she said.

He offered her water or coffee which she declined. They made their way past several rows of cubicles and more stacked up boxes full of file folders than she could count on their way towards a row of offices along the back of the large open work area.

"She's in that second office on the left and is waiting for you," he pointed as he ducked into a messy cubicle.

"Thank you, Jerry."

Sister Mary Anne knocked on the doorframe of the tidy office with the open door containing an oversized desk covered with huge stacks of paper,

"Hello, I am Sister Mary Anne Margaret, we spoke on the phone."

"Yes, Sister, please come in, have a seat, I'm sorry to have kept you waiting," Mrs. Hernandez said, waving at a chair without getting up or offering to shake hands. The lawyer was all business and didn't seem the least concerned with pleasantries.

Sister Mary Anne was a bit taken aback by this, but decided to let it go, maybe the woman was just having a bad day, "Like I said over the phone I am here to offer my assistance in the case against Mr. Nathan Brown. I was on duty in the ER when he and the other people from the car accident arrived by ambulance, and I heard him clearly admit to the police that he had been drinking and decided to drive anyway. In fact, he told the police officers he felt he drives better after he has been drinking."

"Oh, I am *very* familiar with everyone's activities from that night, including yours," the lawyer snarled, clearly not pleased.

"Well, what can I do to help?" Sister Mary Anne asked, not sure why the word very had been emphasized so heavily.

"Absolutely Nothing," came the blunt reply.

"Sure there is something I can do," Sister Mary Anne protested.

"I mean there is nothing you can do and the less you do, the better off we are all going to be. Let me explain the legal situation to you, and why it would *not* be improved if you stuck your holier than thou self-righteous nose into the process any further than you already have. As a legally registered and highly experienced nurse you made an attempt to get the medical staff to abandon treatment of Benjamin because you were of the belief that he was beyond hope. That was before you went and physically attacked Mr. Brown in front of not one but two police officers, one of whom you apparently bit, hard enough to not only leave teeth marks but draw blood. Do I have these highlights correct so far?" the lawyer asked, speaking quickly.

"Well, yes, but…"

Mrs. Hernandez was clearly not going to let Sister Mary Anne explain the motivation behind her actions, "When the doctor leading the medical team kicked you out of the treatment room, the *rest* of the original team continued working, along with other highly qualified *doctors*, one of whom has a great deal of experience treating head trauma, which you are not. After the *doctors* in the room removed emotion from the equation, it was discovered that the rod did not penetrate the skull, and the real problem was the bleeding coming from other parts of his body as well as a slight, but controllable swelling of the brain. Then, for some reason, you proceeded to come *back* into the treatment room along with another person who wasn't masked properly, and in the process, you massively increased the risk of infection for Benjamin. Do I have that correct as well?"

"Yes," Sister Mary Anne said, sounding defeated, slumping down in her chair.

"I spoke with the boy's mother a few moments ago concerning Benjamin's injuries, as well as about what *she* would like to see happen in detail, and do you know what I learned?" the lawyer asked with a sense of angry sarcasm dripping more and more with each passing word.

"Not really," she said, speaking at no more than a whimper. Sister Mary Anne braced herself for what was coming next.

"I learned that Benjamin has a nasty concussion, but he will fully recover from the head wound. His broken bones will cause what is expected to be a temporary loss of gross and fine motor skills, but with physical therapy across the next six months to a year he is going to recover with little, if any, long term impact. However, his hospital and therapy bills are expected to be amazingly high, astronomical was the word I heard used by multiple sources, and this single mother has no medical insurance. Therefore, she has only one realistic way to pay for it all. Do you know what that is? Should I explain it to you?"

"No," Sister Mary Anne said in a small voice, part of her knew what was coming, she just didn't want to believe it.

"Mr. Nathan Brown has graciously offered her enough money as a settlement to pay off her house, and cover Benjamin's medical as well as physical therapy bills, plus some extra. On top of that he is voluntarily entering into an alcohol addiction recovery program. But all of this is only if we cut a deal that does not include jail time, otherwise deal is off. Benjamin's mother has begged me to make that happen. So, if we do what you want and throw the man in jail for a very very long time, their future is bleak. So, if you really want to help that child and his mother from this point forward you will stay completely out of it," Mrs. Hernandez said bluntly.

"So, he will pay some money and go home? Then this whole thing basically just goes away? He just gets to go about his life like it never happened," Sister Mary Anne did not want to believe it.

"Sister, this situation is no longer any concern of yours, and I would strongly urge you to let this issue go before you get yourself back into trouble. Now, if there is nothing else, I have a very busy day," the lawyer said while beginning to focus on other sets of paperwork on her desk

"Thank you for your time," the nun said, holding back the tears. "I'll show myself out."

***

Sister Mary Anne had been sitting in the Church praying for so long she had nearly fallen asleep. When Father Santini came up behind her and placed a gentle hand on her should she was so startled she almost fell to the floor.

"I am sorry, Sister, I didn't mean to frighten you. Is there anything I can do to help you with your challenges, or even just sit and offer a sympathetic ear?" he asked.

"I don't think anyone, except maybe God, can help me with this situation. Sadly, to make things worse, I'm not certain He is listening to me much these days," she said looking older, and far more tired than normal.

"Oh, I am certain He is listening, but often He wants us to solve our own problems using the hints and clues He has left behind. Why don't you tell me what's wrong, and perhaps together we can find a way to get Him to listen, or even figure out the clues He has left behind for ourselves," Father Santini offered.

She took a deep breath and passionately told him the story of Benjamin, some of which he knew. Sister Mary Anne included everything from the moment he showed up at the hospital through the meeting with the infuriating lawyer. He sat listening quietly, nodding along as she spoke.

"Honestly, Father, I haven't been able to work as a nurse in any capacity since that night. Not only could my actions have resulted in the death of that innocent little boy, and today I found out there will be no justice for him, just a pile of *money*. That money is supposed to make everything all better. Which means this man, this sinner, is going to go right back out there and do it again. This evil man is going to keep using his wealth and power as a shield over and over, and he will not care who he hurts along the way. He even bragged about on the way out of the courtroom, he told his lawyer to pay whatever it took to make this go away," she said, tears freely flowing down her face.

"Well, I am confident that in the end Saint Peter will make sure this man, what did you say his name is?" Father Santini asked.

"Nathan Brown, he is some big wig lawyer whose main office is down in Boston but lives up here with another satellite office here in town someplace," Sister Mary Anne said, tears still flowing.

"I know it isn't a big help but, in the end, we both know that Saint Peter will make sure he faces God's justice. It is my belief that he, and those like him, are given special attention in Hell when they meet God's Fallen Angel and his demon minions down below," Father Santini offered as consolation. He was unsure if anything he said was helping but he was hoping to get her to see things as a woman of faith, rather than as a medical professional whose protective instincts were obviously still in high gear.

"I know that ultimately he will pay the price, but the entire situation just makes me re-think my place in the world," she explained, the tears finally coming to an end.

"Are you thinking of making a drastic change of some kind?" he asked.

"Well, I can't imagine myself working as a nurse ever again. I have been thinking of retiring from everything. Maybe put in an application to go to Rome and do some research in the archives for the remainder of my days," she said, thinking out loud as much as anything.

"Let me ask you a question before you make a massive change you may someday regret. Did helping Amanda with her emotional and spiritual challenges make you feel good about your work here?"

"I suppose," she said, sitting up a little straighter.

"Why don't you take a month off, go to Rome, I can call the Bishop and make the arrangements, do a little research while you are there, and in the process take some time to think about the future. After a month, if you feel Rome is right for you, you'll already be there, and we will figure out how to make it permanent. If it isn't right, come back here and focus more on the ministry and victim recovery side of things," he suggested.

"Visiting Rome does sound nice. Maybe all I need is a break from everything," she said sounding a little better.

"Ok. Why don't you go get some sleep? I will stay here and pray to the Lord that this Nathan Brown character receives some measure of punishment. Let's see if I can manage to get some action from up above," he offered with a wink and a smile waving his finger in the air.

Sister Mary Anne slowly got to her feet. She had been sitting so long her legs needed a moment to wake up, "Ok Frank. Let's talk again in the morning."

"Let's meet for breakfast in the rectory. I'll even cook," Father Santini offered. "Maybe we can even use my fifteen minutes of fame to do something about this kind of situation. Perhaps an anti-drunk driving campaign of some kind with a new twist brought to you by the 'vigilante priest.' Along the lines of you better hope the cops get you before I call God," he said with a smile, trying to lighten the mood.

She laughed a little, "That might actually go someplace."

"Perhaps," he said.

He was already trying to figure out the best way to Cleanse this Mr. Nathan Brown from the mortal plane, sending him someplace more appropriate.

***

Once back in his room Father Santini turned his attention to social media. He had a few posts he wanted to put out before going to bed.

The Church can be a guide when things seem hopeless. Not just through the Word of God, but through the friendships and mentors available at your local Parish. Be active!

Remember if you are out drinking, friends or Uber are a great alternative to drunk driving. Stay safe! #DontDrinkAndDrive

Remember God does not punish those that repent for their Sins. He is forgiving and not to be feared. #GodLovesAll

He watched for a few minutes as people started to respond. Many wished him well, some prayer requests, even a few saying God didn't exist and religion was all fake.

He'd have to come up with some way to respond to that sort of person. They seemed to be finding a way into his responses at the top of the list every time lately.

Soon alerts started going off indicating new followers. New followers meant more questions. The more questions he received, the more he gained insight into just how misunderstood the Church was.

The Church had lost their way over the years. He needed to put both the perception and the reality back on track, even if in just some small way.

He turned off his laptop and prepared for bed. He needed rest and some time to think about how to deal with his next Cleansing. This one would require a special kind of attention in order to meet the intent of an eye for and eye.

Chapter Thirteen
Old School Justice

The traffic on I-93 southbound headed into Boston was as predictably slow and congested as ever. During the work week there was simply no "good time" to make the journey.

"Frank, I don't know how you pulled this off so fast. I really didn't expect to be getting on a plane just a few days after barely considering the notion of a trip halfway around the world. I mean, actually going to Rome, staying in Vatican City, it is a dream I have had even since before taking my vows," Sister Mary Anne said with a gleam in her eyes that hadn't been there in a long time.

"It turns out with all the press attention lately I seem to have a little bit of pull. What good is it if I don't use that 'popularity' to get a favor or two, from now on I guess you should call me the godfather," Father Santini said doing his best Marlon Brando impression while focusing on the bumper-to-bumper traffic. Getting to Boston's Logan Airport always involved this little "pleasure."

"Just thinking about getting away for a little while, I am already starting to feel better. Thanks for everything from the suggestion to single-handedly making it all happen, I will find a way to repay you for the kindness," she said.

"It was my pleasure, think nothing of it. Do you have a research topic in mind yet?" he asked, wishing he could go with her.

"I have a few ideas kicking around, but I think I am going to focus on the Archangel Raphael, God's healing force," she said.

"Interesting choice, and sounds right up your alley," he said pulling off the highway. You have a direct flight, so this should be an easy trip. I couldn't get you anything better than a business class ticket, but I hear on international flights it is really comfortable. Maybe if you ask at the gate, and there is an empty seat in first class you can get an upgrade."

"Honestly, I don't care about the seat. I am so excited I wouldn't care if they tossed me in the luggage compartment," she said with a smile, sounding happier than she had in years.

"Just a bunch of hours on a plane, what I am told is a short drive across Rome, and you'll be there. I really wish I could go with you, but I will have to pull a little extra duty without you here. Maybe in a few months I can sneak away and follow in your footsteps," he said, already trying to figure out when he would be able to go and plotting a way to meet with the Pope, if even for only a few short minutes.

Perhaps His Holiness knew the details of his mission, perhaps he wasn't the only clergy member touched by God in this way. If anyone knew, it would be the Pope.

"If anyone deserves some time off, it is you," she said.

They exchanged small talk for another few minutes as he worked his way to her departure terminal, parked and helped her unload her meager luggage.

"Have a safe flight," he said as she disappeared into the crowd.

Father Santini jumped back in the borrowed Jeep and headed north. There was some dirt that needed to be Cleansed from the earth.

***

He had been sitting outside the smaller legal office of Mr. Nathan Brown where the man was known to spend his afternoons working for three hours when he saw the lawyer come out and get in his car. Frank put his vehicle in gear and followed the man being sure to stay several cars back to avoid being noticed.

The sun had gone down, but the streets were lit well enough that he had no trouble following the man. The lawyer was in a luxury sedan that was so new it still had temporary paper license plates. Father Santini figured the man wouldn't tolerate driving a car that had ever had the paint scratched, much less been in an accident.

The fat man was waving his hands as he drove. Frank assumed he was using his time in the car to bill someone an obscene hourly rate for the conversation. A few miles down the road he swerved into the parking lot for an upscale steakhouse, parked and went inside.

Father Santini pulled to the far side of the parking lot near what he assumed were the employee vehicles. At least these were the only ones in the parking lot that didn't look expensive enough for their drivers to be here on a random Tuesday without a special occasion, and they likely wouldn't have parked this far away from the entrance if that were the case.

He jumped out, looked around to see if anyone was paying attention, stabbed a hole in two of the man's tires, jumped back in the Jeep and started to wait. Two hours later the lawyer staggered out, obviously drunk based on the way he was, Father Santini supposed it could be called...walking.

"Hey buddy!" he shouted across the parking lot. Now that he saw the lawyer up close, he knew there was no way he would be able to carry him, so the anesthetic dart gun in his pocket was out of the question for the moment. Besides, dragging an unconscious man across a parking lot would attract attention, arguing with a drunk guy about not driving themselves home would be forgotten moments later.

"What? Who da hell are you?" the drunkard said, clearly annoyed.

"You look like you have had a little too much to drink, how about I give you a lift?" Father Santini offered, trying to talk him into the Jeep without a struggle.

"I don't know who da fuck you are, and I can drive myself. I been drivin' carsh shinch I was fifteen. Now go awaysh before I schlap you," the lawyer slurred with spittle flying out of his mouth as he spoke.

Frank sighed and waited patiently. The man turned his back to Father Santini and almost fell over twice before getting to the driver's side of the car.

Seeing the flats, the man yelled as he kicked the tire, "FUCK! A week old and two fucking flats! Hey, you, asshole, gimmie dat ride."

"Sure," Father Santini said calmly. "Let me get my Jeep, and we can be on our way. I can get you home in no time at all."

Climbing into the high riding vehicle was so difficult for the drunken lawyer that Father Santini had to lend a hand. It was a step up for most people, and someone of his size, even sober would have had challenges.

"There ya go. Just buckle up, now where to?" Frank asked.

"Jusht drive dammit, I'll tellsh you where da fuck ta turn," he snapped, droplets of spit hitting the windshield as he waved his flabby arms.

Father Santini became more convinced as the man spoke that what he had planned might not be harsh enough. He had caused so much suffering that it was clearly justified.

An eye for an eye.

After a half a block of being constantly berated for everything from the air temperature to the bumpy ride Father Santini stabbed the man in the neck with a hypodermic needle, injecting him with a general anesthetic. He had no desire to listen to the tirade any longer, and the injection would be necessary as soon as the man realized he was not being driven home.

"Be quiet and just go to sleep, we'll be there soon enough," he told the surprised drunkard.

Mr. Nathan Brown, Esquire, slumped against the passenger door. If Frank understood what he had read about the drug, and assuming he had estimated the man's size properly, he had about ninety minutes. Maybe a little longer due to the excessive amount of alcohol the man had consumed.

Frank calmly drove towards the coast. There was an isolated area with private homes that he knew were rarely, if ever, occupied. Their super wealthy owners tended to use them only for the occasional weekend getaway.

He stopped before making the final turn onto the deserted street and thought for a moment. As a teenager he had been in this area many times and knowing how to figure out at a glance which houses were empty was common among the crowd he hung out with at the time. They would come here to do things they didn't want to be caught doing. Sometimes it was a beach party, other times it was to engage in some petty theft, occasionally it was to be alone with a girl. It was a true miracle he had ever become a man of God and was amused that his path somehow led back here. Life was making a full circle.

There was to be no earthly redemption for this

disgusting pig of a man, and Father Santini didn't want to waste any time. Everything had to be in place before he regained consciousness. There was no margin for error with this Cleansing. Last time he had gotten lucky. Tonight was about executing a plan, there would be no half measures or improvisations this time.

There were three houses on the street that were of specific interest, all next to one another. They were known to belong to certain organized crime members of a family out of New York. Father Santini had come to the area yesterday to look for any security cameras and found none. He guessed the owners didn't want any records of what went on here that could be used against them in a court of law.

He pulled the Jeep to the very end of the end of one of the driveways, the only one that was both a vacant and allowed him direct access to the beach without having to go through the house or a locked gate.

It was a very dark night and none of the houses he could see had any sign of human activity. The only sound he could hear was coming from the tide. The conditions were perfect, another gift from God.

He made sure to park the vehicle on the concrete so there would be no tire tracks to help the investigation that was sure to follow. He got out and went to the back of the Jeep to change clothes. He brought some clothing along that would be destroyed when everything was finished, and just to be extra cautious bought a new pair or very common bargain brand sneakers that were a size and a half larger than his feet as he knew he would be leaving footprints all over the sand, which would ultimately be called a crime scene. But no real crime would be committed this night, at least not in the eyes of God, which was all that really mattered.

Father Santini took a deep breath and opened the passenger side door. Had it not been for the seat belt the fat man would have fallen to the ground in a heap. It was impossible to reach across to unbuckle him due to his size, so Frank went in through the driver's door, pushed the button and let him fall to the ground with a thump.

He made his way around to the passenger side to look at the stinking pile of flesh in the expensive suit on the ground. There was no way to carry him to the sand, so he rolled him like a doughy log. Even rolling him was difficult, and by the time Father Santini got the piggish lawyer in position near the water, he was covered in sweat despite the cold temperatures.

With the man in position, Father Santini went back, grabbed his duffle bag from the back of the Jeep and jogged back to the sand where he paced off the spacing for his wooden stakes, being sure to position them for maximum spread of the man's arms and legs. He pounded the stakes deep into the sand to eliminate the chances for the Sinner to free himself. With that task complete he chained the lawyer's hands and feet leaving him spread, face up on the sand.

Everything was ready, but the man needed to be awake for what came next. It was necessary in order for the eye for an eye principal to be achieved, or the punishment would be far less than what the man deserved. Besides, Father Santini needed a few answers first.

The research leading up to this Cleansing had uncovered so many evil wrongdoings on the part of Mr. Nathan Brown that Father Santini was amazed the man was walking around free from any kind of criminal conviction. It was just further proof about how bad the world was at dealing with criminals. Someone with a law degree or enough money could write their own rules. That had to end.

Father Santini sat down on the beach to wait and pray. He lost track of time in his one-way conversation with God when the man regained consciousness and was clearly not happy to find himself on the ground, and unable to move.

"Hey, fucktard, where am I?" he demanded.

"No need for profanity, Mr. Brown," Father Santini said calmly.

"Good, you know who I am. That means you should know that unless you turn me loose right now, I'm gonna sue your balls off," the lawyer threatened, obviously used to getting his way by intimidation.

"Funny you should mention balls, but we'll get to that in a bit. Before we are done tonight you *will* come to realize that I answer to a higher authority than the laws of man, and I do not fear any kind of legal proceeding that you or anyone else might bring," Father Santini said.

"What da fuck does dat mean? You should know, some of my clients could make you disappear," the man threatened.

"It means I am going to ask you a few questions, and then we'll see what happens next," Father Santini explained calmly and dispassionately.

The lawyer didn't say anything, instead he was spending his energy uselessly pulling against the restraints. Father Santini sat quietly until the fat man expended what little energy he had on his worthless struggles. It did not take long before he was out of breath and just lying on the sand, panting from exertion.

"Now that you are finished with all of that nonsense, I know you are the reckless man who injured Benjamin, a very young boy, as a result of your drunk driving habit. Have you paid his mother the money you offered as compensation for your actions?" Father Santini asked.

"Yeah, I paid dat stupid bitch da money for the worthless brat, who da fuck cares?" the lawyer asked.

"That's all I need to know," Father Santini said getting up from his comfortable spot on the sand.

"Great, now dat we got dat shit all figured out, get me da fuck outta here," Mr. Brown looked at Frank's face and his expression changed. "Hey, I know you. I've seen you online. Dat priest from da video in dat pahkin' lot with da rape. Dat bitch probably had it comin'. Maybe she even liked it and you fucked up her night. Hell, she probably asked 'em ta do it."

"That's me, and I assure you she was not there of her

own free will. Now I understand you like to drink. Let's see how I can help you with that," Father Santini said with a smile as he shoved a plastic tube on the end of a funnel into the man's mouth and deep into his body.

Father Santini hoped it was deep enough to reach the man's stomach. He had read enough about this procedure he assumed he was at least close enough for this to work. In time, it wouldn't matter, this was only phase one of the man's penance.

The fat man thrashed and thrashed, but Father Santini was stronger, completely sober, and not tied to the ground. As quart after quart of Holy Water went down, bizarre noises were coming from the man's body. Father Santini felt it sounded eerily similar to the plumbing in the rectory. The more water was forced down, the less the lawyer struggled until he started to cry, sounding like a whimpering dog.

Father Santini knew the moment the man's stomach ruptured. A very strange, muffled sound like a water balloon popping came from his abdomen and the man's eyes went wide as he tried to scream, bet the apparatus prevented it from coming out as more than a gurgle.

"Calm down ya big baby, we are just getting started," Frank said serenely, completely at peace with the situation. This was God's will, and he was God's weapon.

He removed the funnel with a quick jerk and shoved a gag in the man's mouth. Without it this Sinner would get loud as things progressed. They were far from any living person, but better safe than sorry.

Father Santini took out his hunting knife and removed parts of the man's clothing, tossing them to the side.

Father Santini leaned close the man's ear, "You are going to meet Saint Peter tonight, and from there it is up to the two of you if you are to be absolved of your Sins. In my...professional opinion you do not deserve absolution on the mortal plane, you have long since gone too far for that. Right now, I am going to sprinkle some crab bait on your nuts and will soon be dumping some rather large crabs into that same area. They haven't been fed in a while and are rather hungry. It is going to hurt, more than a little." While he wasn't enjoying having to do these things, he understood the utility. Cleansing the world, and protecting the innocent was his calling in life. If this was what God demanded, this is what he would do.

The lawyer's eyes went wider than Father Santini thought possible as he tried to scream in panic and pull himself loose, but he was running out of energy and the restraints had him too well secured. Things had been too well prepared for the man to have a chance.

Frank dumped out the crabs and they did what hungry crabs do. They ate the food on the sand, then they found the food on the man and started grabbing at it. The sound of their claws clicking was getting louder and louder. Sometimes the crustaceans got the food, sometimes they got a few extra bits of flesh, then more flesh as the food ran low. Sitting back out of the way, Father Santini watched as the crabs did their job, and the lawyer started to understand just how dire his situation had become.

Blood flow began to flood the sand, faster and faster saturating the area around the sinner.

Fifteen minutes of muffled screams and sobs later the man relieved his bowels. Frank knew things were coming to an end soon, the combination of smells was unlike anything he had ever experienced, or even imagined. He wasn't sure he wanted to put up with it much longer, but the crabs seemed to be invigorated by this new development.

"Well, Mr. Brown, I've had enough," he said as he plunged his knife deep into the man's bloated abdomen, twisting it a bit to hook some of the intestines, he proceeded to pull them out. The crabs quickly made their way up his body and ate like they would never be full. It took a few minutes for the minor struggles the man was capable of came to an end and the only thing that could be heard was the waves and the clicking of crab claws. The crabs were all over, climbing in and out of the gaping hole in his abdomen. Eating their fill of what used to be the internal organs and then once they were full heading to the ocean. Lines of new crabs and other scavengers could be seen making their way to the body to get in on the free meal. Soon the entrails had been pulled in every conceivable direction.

Frank was back home and peacefully asleep long before the feeding frenzy reached its peak.

He slept gloriously, knowing that the world was now a cleaner place, and no one else would suffer because of this evil man, ever again.

Chapter Fourteen
The Beach

Jeff jumped in the car for the quick drive down to the shoreline to get in his morning run. It was a twenty-minute drive, and his wife always gave him grief about driving somewhere to go for a run, but the beach at sunrise was always an amazing experience. Living this close and not taking advantage of the natural beauty was unthinkable. Besides, it gave him motivation to actually get out of bed and exercise, whereas the treadmill didn't have the same attraction.

He parked the car and stretched in preparation, enjoying the chilly morning air. It was cold enough to wake him up, but not so cold that it hurt to breath. Taking a deep breath, he started down the foot path leading to the sand at a brisk trot.

In this area every single grain of sand was part of a private beach. A client at his accounting practice owned one of the homes along the route and told him to name drop if he was ever accused of trespassing. The client said that all the owners in the area know one another, and the name drop would be enough to get anyone in the area to leave him alone to exercise and enjoy the scenery.

Just as the sun was making a full appearance over the horizon he noticed a flock of squawking birds surrounding a spot on the beach less than a hundred feet in the air a half mile or so away. This sort of thing happened from time to time so he continued around the bend, and he saw hundreds of them hoping around on the sand and pecking at whatever it was that had drawn their attention. He had seen things like this before when something died and washed up on shore. But he had never seen this many birds at once, so it had to be something larger than the typical fish carcass, maybe it was a shark this time.

As he approached, he realized just how loud the collective bird noises were. The clicking of beaks being slammed shut, the ruffling of feathers, the squawking, it all combined to create quite a cacophony. He had never witnessed such a frenzy outside of documentaries or horror films. Those directors had gotten it shockingly correct. Jeff decided he could have done without that confirmation.

He considered cutting his run short and turning back as the smell and noise was becoming unbearable, but he wasn't close to his halfway point. Besides, by powering through, he could have some fun scattering the birds, then he would try to forget about the smell, and he could satisfy his curiosity about what washup out of the water to get all the attention.

As he got closer to the frenzied flock, he noticed something was off about the smell. It was far more putrid than he had experienced in his life. There was also no overarching fishy smell component to the rancid rot, and he was starting to cough from the smell. It smelled more like an old leaky septic system after a rainstorm. Why didn't it smell fishy? Something wasn't right. Maybe it was a dog that had gotten loose and died.

The birds took flight, he stopped so quickly he almost fell face first onto the sand. Doing a double-take to make sure of what he was seeing he fell to his knees and emptied the contents of his stomach onto the sand.

He forced himself to stand and staggered a few steps backwards, thinking he should just leave, then realized his footprints would alert anyone that someone had seen this. A security camera or two along the route had likely captured his image at some point. Better to inform the police than to have him knock on his door and ask him why he had been here and not reported anything. Despite his desire to flee the disgusting smell and disjointed piles of flesh that he wanted to get away from, but he couldn't seem to stop looking at, he decided to do the right thing.

He pulled out his cell phone and reluctantly dialed.

"Nine-one-one, what's your emergency?" the operator asked nonchalantly.

"Uhhhh, my name is Jeff Romano, I am not at home…uhh I was jogging and found part of a human body on the beach. At least, I think it's human, but I truly hope I am wrong," he said then gave the operator his approximate location stammering through it all, trying to not freak out. He found himself unable to look away from the gristly mess.

"Ok, Jeff, I need you to stay on the line with me and keep as calm as possible. Let's see if we can figure this out together," the operator said in a bored tone of voice someone might use while ordering dinner.

"I guess I'm not going anywhere, but I may back up a little because of the smell," he said trying to calm himself, not sure if he was going to be able to deal with the situation without losing his mind.

"Ok, Jeff, you only gave me an approximate location, can you tell me anything else that will help us find you? Are there any landmarks? Is there a house nearby with an address you can see? Anything a patrol car can use to more easily locate you?" the operator asked.

"Just tell them to drive down the street I gave you and look for the birds, they'll know it when they see it. It is unlike anything I have ever seen and I have lived in this area for years. It is a flock of hundreds of birds just circling above the thing," Jeff said trying not to gag on the stench.

"Are you sure it is a human body, Jeff? You don't seem sure. Things do wash up on shore in that area from time to time and if birds have been picking at it the remains may be difficult to identify. A dolphin can be large enough to be mistaken for a human if the body is highly disfigured, and especially if it covered by birds. So, let's stay calm and not make any assumptions. We don't want to get people worked up for no reason," the operator said obviously trying to keep things under control.

"Let me try to describe it," Jeff said. "Hopefully I can do that and not throw up again. There are piles or globs of what looks like stringy meat surrounded by dark, weird colored, reddish sand. What is left of what I think is the body has the tattered remains of what may have once been a pin stripe suit that has been torn up and scattered around the area. It looks like the person was tied down in what was either a sexual or what could have been some sort of ritualistic sacrifice kind of way, or hell maybe it was torture, I don't know. This doesn't look like something that was an accident."

"I have multiple squad cars on the way, and they can now hear our conversation. One of the officers would like to know what you mean by ritual," the operator relayed, sounding much more alert, but remaining professional.

"Well, there are four, I guess they are large wooden stakes that are sticking out of the sand, they are fairly thick, and they are attached to what is left of the hands and feet by chains and shackles. Maybe it wasn't a ritual, maybe it was something else, fuck, I dunno I have never seen anything like this. On top of that, from what I can tell even from this distance it looks like someone sliced open his stomach and pulled out his intestines because they are all over the place. I don't think birds could have spread things out that far. It looks like twenty feet or so. Excuse me, I'll be back, I need to," Jeff dropped his phone and emptied his stomach acid onto the ground.

The gristly scene, the smell, and having to describe it was just too much. The dry heaves continued until

Jeff was physically and emotionally drained. His fight or flight instincts told him to run, while the logic centers of his brain told him to stay. The entire situation was making him go numb.

He wanted to go back to his spreadsheets and tax laws. This was not how he was supposed to spend his time. He was an accountant for fuck sake!

He was watching his stomach acid disappear into the sand when a high-pitched buzzing sound went by overhead. He looked up in time to see a midsized drone flying away, then stop, return and start to circle the area. It pointed directly at him for a few seconds then moved to the body and hovered with its camera focused on the scene.

"Is that drone with you guys?" he asked the operator, hoping it was a sign of help arriving soon.

There was a pause on the line.

"No, we don't have any drones that can get there that fast. Can you see the pilot?" the operator asked.

Jeff looked around, "No. I don't see anyone and some of those things have a pretty long range, but they could be anywhere. There are lots of little places to sit and not be seen around here. Wait, I can hear some sirens!"

He was relieved that help was getting close. Jeff suddenly realized that if a person could do this to another human, he shivered at the thought that they may still be in the area. Maybe the drone pilot was the killer admiring his work! He wanted to run, just leave, and not look back.

"There are two cars on the way, and very close now. If we need to I can get more dispatched as well. I need you to closely watch that drone and see where it goes. You gonna make it through this, Jeff? I'm right here, I'm not going anywhere," the operator said trying to calm him down.

"I just fucking hope whoever is operating that drone isn't whoever did this admiring their work. They saw me!" Jeff shouted at the operator.

"I doubt that would happen. But if what you are looking at really is a crime scene, whatever video is being recorded by that drone could be helpful, and might not be something we want publicly released," the operator said.

"Ok, I'll watch it, and see if I can tell where it goes," he said, wishing the cops would hurry. He could hear the operator tapping furiously on the keyboard.

A few seconds later Jeff thought he heard the operator say, "Oh fuck," very quietly. So quietly he thought he might have misunderstood.

"I'm sorry, what?" The sirens are getting pretty loud, I don't think I heard you right," Jeff said.

I apologize Jeff, I shouldn't have said that. Apparently, that drone of yours is doing a live feed streaming directly to social media, and it is getting a following very quickly. I can see what is left of that body. I'm going to send a CSI unit that way and a few more squad cars," the operator said, emotion finally in his voice.

"It sounds like at least one squad car is almost here,"

Jeff said relieved.

"Please just stay where you are. Everyone coming to help knows you are not a threat," the operator said.

"That doesn't make me feel better. Can you call my wife and explain I'm going to be late, she will never believe this," Jeff asked, starting to recover the capacity for rational thought.

***

"Dude, stop the streaming feed but keep recording, this video is gonna be worth a freakin' fortune and we shouldn't give it away for free. I'll keep the drone on location as long as we have enough juice in the batteries to get it back," Craig said, excited at the potential income from a video they had not set out to record.

"You really think we can sell it? Maybe we should just use it to increase our following?" Jack asked.

"Yeah, I'm sure. Check it out. There are a ton of cops coming this way, so this is gonna be news, maybe national news," Craig said, more focused on piloting the drone than normal. "Besides, we only have about ten minutes left before I have to bring it back."

"Holy shit. Did you see that cop barf?" Jack said with a laugh. "Have you ever seen someone projectile vomit like that? Must have gone ten feet, and almost hit that other guy who I guess was the person who found it."

"Well, good for him. If this does go national, we may actually be able to make some real cash. Then maybe we can finally get some better equipment for our channel," Craig hoped.

***

Father Santini stepped out of the shower, reached for the remote and turned on the local news while dressing. The hot topic of the morning was a body discovered on the beach.

He briefly wondered if there would be any information about the note he left when the phone rang. His heart skipped a beat, and he froze in place.

It hit him that no one coming to arrest him would call first. They would just appear on his doorstep, or more likely they would just come through the door unannounced.

"Hello, this is Father Santini," he said.

"Hello, Father. This is Julie Cross, we met when I interviewed you after the parking lot brawl," the caller said.

"Yes, I recall. Miss Cross how are you?" he asked his heart rate returning to normal.

"We are looking for an in-studio guest to come in this morning for a segment we are doing about violent crime and increased homicide rates in the Greater Boston area in light of this new murder out on the beach. Can you come in as our guest this morning?

This story is about to go national," she said.

"I can be there in about forty-five minutes. Will that work for you?" he said looking at his watch.

"We will see you then," she said with excitement.

Father Santini couldn't help but laugh. He was going to be interviewed for his opinion on violent crime, because of his Cleansing. If this wasn't God's handiwork, he didn't know what was.

Thank you, Lord, I needed the laugh this morning.

He put on his black pants, a black shirt, and his white collar. Grabbing his phone, he wanted to post something on social media before heading for the studio.

Violent Crime is getting out of hand. We need to see that punishments fit the crimes. No more free passes. See you on the news later this morning where I will be in-studio.

Chapter Fifteen
The Future

Father Santini walked into the police precinct with his head held high. His near daily visits had become so routine that most of the duty officers manning the front desk no longer asked him to sign the visitor log. Between the ride-along nights, and discussions with detectives about the parking lot incidents and just stopping by to say hello and fill his coffee mug he knew almost everyone in the building at this point.

He strode past the bored looking people in the waiting area and straight up to the duty officer, "Hey, Joe, I'm here for a meeting with Officer Pierce. Mind if I head back early for some of the best coffee in town?"

"No problem, Father," the officer said with a smile as he pushed the button under the desk to unlock the access door.

As Father Santini entered the working area of the station he was greeted with more than a few smiles and nods from the people hard at work as he made his way through the building to fill his thermal mug. It was time for him to reload his caffeine levels back to their normal operating capacity.

He was filling his mug when he heard his name called from down the hall.

"Father Santini!" Officer Pierce shouted above the

background noise.

"Jonathan, just the man I wanted to see. I am a little early, but your 'cop strength' coffee calls out to me," the priest said, turning to shake hands with his parishioner.

"Come on back if you want to get going early. I'm running ahead of schedule and free now, which is unprecedented," the officer said gesturing across the noisy, open work area towards his office in the back.

Father Santini closed the office door to block out the noise and they sat down across the desk from one another.

"I saw you on the news again, you were good. Urging people not to resort to violence is always helpful coming from someone like yourself. Even if you only reach one person it can save a life, and it means I have one less sleepless night investigating some preventable tragedy. I mean, that murder, part of me is glad it wasn't in our jurisdiction, if I had seen that firsthand, I'm not sure I'd ever sleep again," Officer Pierce said with a shudder.

"Yeah, when I was at the studio, I overheard a few details about the scene that they didn't broadcast. Sounded terrible. I keep getting asked about what else I know, especially online, and the only thing I can say for sure is that the victim obviously had enemies. Any idea on the video feed? Where did it come from, and how did it go out live?" Father Santini asked, with an ulterior motive.

"Yeah, it was a group of environmental impact amateurs who video the coastline around here all the time. They are looking for anything they can point at and try to claim it is as a result of climate change, pollution, erosion or whatever else they want to complain about. That morning they got a little more than they bargained for, but in this social media crazy world we all live in they might be enjoying all the attention for all I know. From what I heard about the crime scene I'm not even sure if the victim's fingerprints would have survived. This thing is going to have to go to DNA. Apparently, the crabs got a good meal, then the birds ate some of the crabs and continue to eat whatever else they could find that resembled food, so I guess those enviro guys are going to use it to boost their social media profile somehow twisting this into a way to get their message out. How it got out? That's a good question, most streaming services will censor certain types of content, but this all happened really fast, and I guess they didn't have time to respond, so it went out, and grew fast," the officer said with a shrug of his shoulders.

"I bet you are right, and I bet that streaming service pays more attention from now on," Father Santini said with an inner smile.

"Anyway, that's not at all what I asked you here to discuss," Jonathan said trying to get the meeting back on track.

"What's up, you sounded serious on the phone," Frank said sympathetically seeing something was clearly bothering the man.

"You remember me telling you about that female parishioner who was murdered in some dumpy motel while cheating on her husband?" the officer asked.

"I do. Did they ever find out who killed her?" Father Santini asked, calm as a cucumber.

"No, and they really have nothing on the investigation, it is completely stalled out from what I understand. That isn't the issue. Her husband is refusing to come claim the body, and the PD with jurisdiction asked for our help. Apparently, he feels betrayed and wants no part of anything where she is concerned. I was wondering if you or someone from the Church could go talk with him, then if he still refuses to claim the remains, we can say we tried and go to the more extended parts of the family without catching too much administrative grief, but if he decides to help us out, maybe you can give us a hand with some kind of service for her. She did have some friends that are offering to pay for everything," Officer Pierce explained.

"Of course. Typically, with this sort of thing we would send Sister Mary Anne, but she is on a little trip to get some rest and reset her stress level, so I will go over there and handle it myself," Father Santini said.

"Really? Where's she gone off to?"

"Rome, well really Vatican City. I pulled some strings and got her into the Vatical Library, including some parts that are 'permission only.' After the thing with the DUI and her arrest she really needed a break," Father Santini explained. He didn't add that it got her out of town for his Cleansing to give her an airtight alibi.

"Good for her, she really did seem to be badly in need some rest."

"Yeah, it's actually a cool trip. I kinda wanted to go with her given everything she has planned. But that's a discussion for another day. What can you tell me about the case with this woman? The more I know the more I can help the husband get through his emotional challenges."

Officer Pierce took a deep breath, "Well, you know most of it. This one is different from most and in ways it really bothers me. We have nothin' to work from, and I mean nothin'. This is the kind of case that keeps me up at night tryin' to figure out exactly what really happened. It is the sorta thing we are forced to call an 'open' case, but no one is going to do any more work to try to close it unless some new piece of evidence magically appears."

"Ok, well, I will do what I can. Just remember, you and I are basically in the same business. You protect the body, but I protect the soul. She was a member of our congregation, and I was supposed to be there to rescue her soul for all eternity, but it appears Satan beat me. We might both have to just let this one go, and maybe have a beer to commiserate our collective career troubles, then we can think about looking more at the big picture instead of this individual loss," Father Santini offered.

"That sounds like a good plan, and I always enjoy a cold one. Here, we prepared a file for you on the husband with some details and his contact information. Let me know how it goes," Jonathan said as he slid a file folder with a few sheets of papers inside across the desk.

"Certainly," Father Santini said as they shook hands to part company. "Maybe one night this week we can have that beer."

***

Father Santini sat down in front of his laptop to send a few emails and was not surprised to see he had hundreds of new messages on social media directed at him, and more inbound emails than he felt he could possibly read. Prioritization was going to be the key if he was going to make any progress.

Highest priority was an email to Officer Pierce to let him know the husband would come claim the body and proceed with end-of-life plans. It had been a difficult discussion, but after some discussion and lots of prayers, the man had agreed.

He then organized his emails by sender looking for any critical church business.

"Apparently being on television makes you kinda popular," he mumbled to the empty room. His most recent television appearance had gone out on national news. If he had thought about the ramifications before all this began he would have started a second email address for the public website, while keeping a private out for official business use, but hindsight was always 20-20. It was something to put on his to-do list.

He found one from a friend of his from Seminary School urging him to keep up the good work and teasing him for "hogging the spotlight." Father Santini smiled at the good-natured ribbing from an old friend and fellow priest.

There was one from the Cardinal in Washington D.C. and Father Santini clicked with excitement.

Father Santini,

I want to thank you for your hard work on behalf of the Roman Catholic Church. Because of your efforts we appear to be gaining ground in the area of public sentiment, something we could certainly use and is long overdue. If we had more priests with your drive, and your public image more of our pews would be filled each week.

There is a Bishop in your area that is set to retire. I would like to invite you to come to Washington so we can discuss the process involved in going from a Priest to a Bishop that they don't tell you in the rule books, and with a little help from God, we can get you in that leadership position and perhaps someday into the College of Cardinals if you have the stomach for politics at this level.

Yours in Christ,

Cardinal Wilson

He slowly pushed his laptop to the back of his desk and folded his arms.

Could he really become a Bishop? At his age? That would place him on the fast track for Cardinal. God had a plan, and who was he to question it.

Lord, I see you have noticed Your mission is being carried out. It appears you approve of what happened to the Lawyer. Wait until you see what happens next.

He managed to find the social media feed for the environmentalists and became a follower. He wanted to be sure to track their public statements and follow the comments on them just in case anything important resulted from their lucky break. They had around a half million subscribers now so he was just one of many.

Then it was time for the "vigilante priest" to make a few statements.

There was recently a brutal murder in the Boston area that has made the national news. It was captured on video and has made the rounds on virtually all social media platforms. Any guilty party is not a hero, and the deceased is not a martyr. Let the police investigators do their job free of any controversy or public pressure to rush to conclusions.

He found a fuzzed-out picture of the scene to post with his next statement. Frank was careful in how to word his statements. What happened on that beach was not murder, and with the correct messaging could spread God's word as an added bonus to the Cleansing of the world.

#Murder is not something that should take place in a civilized society. Anyone who is guilty of it should repent for their sins immediately or fear the price they will certainly pay the price in the afterlife.

Thanks to his main account having surpassed a million followers replies were coming in quickly. His favorite was simple:

Pray for us Father, pray for us.

He could certainly do that.

***

Jack had been responding to inbound messages for longer than he wanted to admit. It was nice to finally get noticed. Some of the traffic was even resulting in some pretty good environmental protection questions from people.

With a sigh he realized he hadn't eaten anything in almost seven hours. His diet had consisted of online discussions and coffee that entire time.

He grabbed his phone to shoot a text to Craig.

Dude, you hungry?

Yeah, I could go for something, came the reply.

Wanna go grab a burger? He asked.

Sure, meet me in twenty minutes at the place we went last time.

He stretched, grabbed his keys and headed for the bar. He had been waiting for ten minutes when Craig showed up.

"How many are we up to on Twitter?" Craig asked without saying hi as he sat down.

"Bout a half a million, up from five thousand just before the video. How about YouTube?" Jack asked. They had split up duties on different platforms.

"We are well into actually making some revenue, finally."

"Well crap, lets order some shots! Finally, we broke through!" Jack exclaimed.

"Took long enough. We have to keep up the momentum. Somehow, we have to get all these new people to understand the importance of conservation. Hopefully they will come for the murder and stay for the right reasons," Craig said, always the true believer.

"That's all cool and everything, but we gotta focus on making *some* money. We have been workin' our asses off with no kinda' return. Maybe we should get the drone out on more cop activities and use the money we make to fund the environmental side? Maybe split it in two different channels?" Jack asked, thinking out loud as much as asking a question.

"Not a bad idea, maybe some kind of limited series now that YouTube will put ads in our stuff. Maybe we should get a second, longer range drone with better optics," Craig suggested.

"Now that is a solid plan. Now let's get some food and make an equipment list that will be budget friendly," Jack said, not wanting to go nuts spending money just yet.

"Yeah, maybe we can find some of it used, and get some much-improved airtime. Right now, we are kind of limited," Craig said, thinking out loud.

"Yeah, imagine how much more we could have caught out at the beach before we had to bring it back in," Jack said with a sigh.

Chapter Sixteen
Information Flow

Frank was partway through the cool down portion of his daily workout when his phone rang, noticing the international number he answered suspicious of who it might be, "Hello?"

"Frank? It's me, Sister Mary Anne. Did you see the news? Someone killed him!" the frantic voice of his favorite Nun said.

"Hello! Ok, slow down. What news? Killed who?" Father Santini asked, despite being certain who she was talking about. He had been expecting this call since before she arrived in Italy.

"That drunken lawyer, the one that hurt Benjamin, he was murdered, someone staked him to the ground and tortured, then killed him. The police called me to ask if I knew anything, they even asked my whereabouts at the time of the murder, but I was here already when it happened. I had just landed about the same time someone killed him. I googled it and found a video someone had taken of the murder scene. Frank, someone did a real number on him. I watched the video and, what was left of him, it barely looked human! As someone who worked in the ER for years, I have never seen anything like that, ever. I knew he was evil, but who would do that to another living human is beyond me," she rambled, speaking very quickly, the shock of the situation obvious in her tone of voice.

"I saw that video on the news! They even brought me in and interviewed me for a television segment on violent crime. Was that really the same guy you were telling me about? The one on the beach is the one that you attacked over at the hospital? Are you sure? I haven't heard that the victim was ever identified," he asked, using couple of lines he had rehearsed in anticipation of her call.

"I'm certain, the officer I spoke to said they had DNA, and it was a perfect match for his. The police wanted to know if I was involved! I don't even know anyone who would be capable of doing the sort of things I saw! I'm not sure I can imagine what such a person who could do this kind of thing would be like. How could they think in a million years I would know anything about something like this?"

"Are you in some kind of legal trouble over this?" he asked, hoping he knew the answer already.

"No, but I was apparently listed as a person of interest. Even if it was just briefly. How could they even suspect I would do that sort of thing is beyond me," she said, starting to calm down a bit, more than a little offended someone would even suspect her of being involved.

"Ok, if you want, I will try to find out anything I can. I don't think the police will tell me much, but I would be happy to ask around," he offered.

"No, that's ok, I don't want you to go to any trouble, besides it's what a guilty person might do, and I really don't want to know more than I already do about this whole thing. I prayed that he would get what punishment he truly deserved, but I never would have wanted something like this. Maybe God had a hand in it. Perhaps this man had done things so much worse than what we already know about. But I'm not sure I want to know any more about any of this, it looked like something from a more brutal part of history, like something from a medieval history book," she said.

"Ok, I won't stick my nose into it. Now, quick, before the international call charges become insane. I know Rome is fantastic but tell me about the archives, I need to know about the archives. Are they everything I dream they are?" he asked, feeling like a school kid asking what it was like to meet a rock star.

"As a research tool nothing could possibly compare anywhere on the planet, and I have full access to everything besides the most restricted or secret areas. With all the time I have spent in them, I still I can't imagine what more there could possibly be in those areas. I'm told the items in that are off limits are just one-of-a-kind things that have had entire books written about them but are so fragile they dare not let anyone who has not been properly trained in their handling touch them. There could be a few secret or unpleasant things hidden back there I guess, but I could spend the rest of my life in the unrestricted areas and be happy. The entire thing is massive. The section on Angels alone is the size of the entire rectory back home. You really must come over and see it for yourself someday, it is truly stunning," she said, the stress gone from her voice. Her trip was obviously achieving its primary goal.

"I will make a point to figure out a time when I can do just that. Now, enjoy yourself, and hopefully you will not decide to just stay there for good. We would sure miss you around here," he said before they said their goodbyes and disconnected the line.

***

Despite Sister Mary Anne being in Rome and already being short-handed, the other priests he worked with agreed to cover the duties he would normally do for a few days so Frank could slip down to Washington and meet with the Cardinal. While he was there, he wanted to take advantage of the situation to see the museums in the area for a day or two.

When planning the trip, he could have flown, but taking the train was less expensive, offered him some time to relax, see the countryside and came with a stable Wi-Fi connection for him to spend some time focusing on his growing social media presence.

He had more than a million followers now, and that number grew dramatically whenever he spent time online and publicly responded to people. He was discovering that there happened to be a lot of misinterpretation of the Catholic beliefs and with his newfound public profile people were listening to what he had to say. The more he found ways to relate those beliefs to their daily lives, the more they seemed to respond positively. He couldn't have dreamed, let alone planned, for this kind of reaction to his public statements. At least some good came from the parking lot brawl.

He supposed the public at large twisting the Catholic beliefs was somewhat justified given the cover ups that had occurred following the sexual-abuse offenses committed by some members of the clergy. However, it was time for someone to start put things back on track.

As he thought about those cover ups, he concluded that was a Sin beyond all others. For a member of the clergy to abuse those they had been charged with protecting or guiding to the Light of the Lord and do so with a child disgusted Father Santini to even think about. No greater perversion of the laws of God could be imagined. Frank had not personally known any of the Priests involved and hoped to never meet one of those accused.

Then there were those with a driving ambition to be in charge, believing they were entitled to a certain rank, and perhaps they were not necessarily guilty of these perversions but how many of them were guilty of covering those things up in exchange for support of advancement in the leadership positions of the Church. The ambitious clergy members were not to be trusted for they didn't put God above all others, they tended to put getting themselves into a higher position then Service to the Almighty and this was not acceptable.

Since becoming a member of the clergy, he had left personal ambition behind, but the thought of becoming a Bishop, or even a Cardinal meant he could save more souls, positively impact more lives, and that could allow his Holy War to evolve into something different. This wasn't a promotion he had ever thought about in any way, but it was one that would allow him to serve God in new and more impactful ways, and that was all he cared about. He reasoned that he had been approached rather than vice versa, and that meant it had to have been part of God's greater plan.

He wanted this promotion. He would ensure that those who played political games to advance would be stopped if he were able to do so. Only those who followed God's plans should advance into the leadership.

If God wanted him to be a Bishop, then he would accept the honor, just as he had accepted his mission.

***

Sister Mary Anne woke up early, finding herself unable to sleep, and returned to the archives. She had been thinking about the murder of that horrible lawyer before falling asleep which caused her to have more than one nightmare. She vaguely remembered something from years before and had to find out if her memory was faulty or if the murder scene was a repeat of something out of Catholic history.

Somehow the video of the remains of the lawyer spark a memory from a book she had read about the

Inquisition from years prior when doing some research about old church practices. It was a fleeting memory, but it was driving her crazy trying to remember where she had seen it. Perhaps her mind was playing tricks on her, but she didn't think so. This was so specific, like she had seen it in a painting or sketch or something, it was so vivid that it couldn't be imagined or ignored.

She turned another page in the ancient tome, and there it was in black and white. Other than the involvement of the birds and crabs, the historical description and accompanying sketch was more or less, exactly what appeared to have happened to Mr. Brown, but in a much less messy way thanks to the absence of wildlife.

It was either a shocking coincidence, or someone with knowledge of the Catholic Inquisition had killed him using this bit of history as inspiration.

She thought for a minute that perhaps she should call the police and tell them about this discovery, or should she? With the Catholic tie in wouldn't that just result in her becoming a person of interest again?

Was the untimely death of this man really such a bad thing?

He had been an evil man. Perhaps this was God's justice taking the place of the imperfect justice of mankind. And being a servant of God, perhaps she should accept that his justice was done and not mention what she found to anyone. After all, she had no evidence, and it could just be a giant coincidence. In reality all she had was a suspicion.

***

Richard Hartke had been a crime scene investigator for more than a decade and in all that time had never had a case that deeply worried him, until this one. Something about it said there were more brutal murders to come, but on the other hand, given the history of the victim he almost didn't care as long as the victims were like the one he was looking at now. That was something he'd have to talk to the union's professional psychologist about at some point. He had a job to do, and a killer on the loose who needed to be found, that was where he forced his mind to focus, before this person struck again.

He sat, with the Chief of the Boston Police Department, in the State House waiting to see the Governor of the Commonwealth. That's how much attention this one case was getting due to the graphic nature of the situation, and of course the leaked videos that the nightly news, not to mention the voting public was now discussing ad nauseum. All of that with a new election cycle right around the corner.

"The Governor is ready to see you," the young woman who had politely introduced herself as Heather, one of the Governor's interns, said.

The massive door to the inner office opened, "Chief O'Malley, good to see you again. Mr. Hartke, good to meet you. I hear you have a rough one on your hands this time. Come in, tell me whatever it is I need to know," the politicians said.

"Mr. Governor…"

"Please, call me Charlie, given what I know of this case already we will probably be spending a great deal of time together, unless this guy just shows up and turns himself in," the politician said.

"Ok, Charlie," Richard said uncomfortably, "well, we have several things you need to know that brought us here today. The rest I am sure you already know. But these things are not public and the investigative team would prefer them to not become public, if at all possible.

"First, you should know, I have personally been involved in more than fifty murder investigations throughout my career, and this one is by no small margin the most brutal murder I have ever seen. Every indication on the scene was that this guy had no remorse at all about what he was doing, almost like he was, and I can't believe I am saying this, but almost like he was doling out punishment in response to some perceived crime, or maybe injustice is a better way to describe it," Richard explained.

"I don't understand, what brought you to that conclusion?" the Governor asked.

"The victim was tortured in shockingly painful ways before he was, for lack of a better term, put to death in another, and even more painful way," the investigator explained.

"Ok, I get it, and let's just leave it there and spare me the gory details I haven't already seen on the video,

I'd like to be able to eat dinner later," the Governor replied. "Besides the less I know, the more I can tell the press that it is part of a confidential police investigation that is being held only amongst the members of the investigative team and do so honestly."

"The second thing you need to know. To say that this was pre-meditated is the understatement of all time. This was scripted and researched in order to cause as much pain without leaving any trace back to the murderer as possible. This was done in such a way as to cause intense amounts of pain and to elongate the suffering the victim felt before death. Based on the methods used, I think that the killer is either Catholic or has intimate knowledge of religious history, and I don't believe that this is the last one of these we are going to see from this killer. Based on the evidence at the scene we can call this one a virtual certainty," Richard said confidently.

"Usually, only lobbyists are sure of things when they come in this office. You seem to be very sure, why is that?" the politician asked, trying to get to the point.

Chief O'Malley took over the conversation as he slid a folder across the desk, "He left a letter. In Latin and hand-written in a very artistic calligraphy, the contents of which are something you might expect to see in an ancient religious text. Really beautiful if you ask me. That letter heavily quotes from Scripture, and in particular the one about an eye for an eye. It continues to mention morality and laws being less meaningful than ever before in the modern world. Apparently, he doesn't like anyone being soft on crime, so some people here in the State House are not going to be on his Christmas Card list this year," the man attempted to end with a joke trying to lighten the mood in the room.

The governor flipped to the page with the English translation of the letter.

Dear Law Enforcement,

If you would do your job, I would not have to undertake this mission. And while I do not relish what must be done, my task has been given to me directly from the Almighty, therefore must be completed.

The laws of man originate from the Laws of God. Over time the laws of man have been weakened and watered down to the point where they have almost no meaning and would certainly not be recognized by the Almighty as coming from his influence as was the original intent. This must change, and if you are unable to do the right thing, I must.

God has told us many things to help guide us during our time here on this mortal plane. He has even spoken in the Scripture of an eye for an eye, although that passage should not be taken literally, it should be adhered to in spirit and that is simply not happening in our modern world. Currently it is not even used in any way other than as either a punch line or an after the fact lament when offering condolences following a mass casualty event when conjecturing about what should happen to those who commit such barbaric acts.

The laws of this world have become weak. Breaking the

laws of our society must begin to have consequences once again. Until then, the Soldiers of God will once again have to rise up and enforce the laws that man has chosen to ignore. The Laws of God are above those as man; therefore, my actions will only be judged in the afterlife, and I will be heralded as a Saint among men for all eternity and given a special place in Heaven.

I beg of you to start doing your job so that I can focus my efforts elsewhere and turn my sword back into a plow once again.

The Cleanser

"Ok, I see what you mean, you are right, this one is not going to stop here and is likely just getting warmed up, what's next on your list?" the Governor asked curiously as he read through the letter.

"This guy, the one who was killed, was a really bad guy. Sure, he was a lawyer, and we can make all the jokes we want about that. But the people he defended were exceptionally bad people. Known violent but rich criminals, real serious white-collar criminals, hedge fund managers who trade on dirty information, almost killed a young kid during what was not his first DUI. This time he basically bribed the mom with a huge settlement to not press charges. Somehow, he even got in a physical fight with a nun while in the hospital emergency room, which is the only other Catholic involvement we can determine with this case, but she was a nurse at the hospital the night of the DUI incident. She had apparently just come from treating a badly injured child from the other vehicle in the accident and it was actually her who started the altercation," Investigator Hartke said, speaking more quickly than he normally would.

"This guy was attacked by a nun?" the Governor laughed.

"Yeah, and I never thought about it, but that is kinda funny," the Chief said.

"Let me guess, you have no leads other than the Catholic angle, and you aren't sure you want any, because this victim was a really bad guy himself," the Governor conjectured looking back and forth between the two visitors.

"Yeah, if I am honest about this. Yes, I think he did us a favor and I think he is about to do us a few more in the near future," Mr. Hartke said. "Although, you are correct, some part of me doesn't want to find him if he is going to help remove the worst of society that we can't seem to obtain any actional evidence on, but I know we have to. He is only going to get more brutal, not less, if history is any guide. I don't want to use the word serial killer out loud, but I think we have one on our hands that is either starting their transition into that world, or he has finally become so arrogant he doesn't care if we know about his activities. Maybe this wasn't even his first killing, based on the nature of this situation and victim, I would almost bet real money on that. I would also bet we will never determine which of the unsolved cases running around are because of this one's activities. There was no sign of remorse in this case, indicating he already has experience."

"He's on our side right now, but only until he changes the rules and decides to go after not as bad people. This guy has to be crazy, and we can't let him walk around among us," Chief O'Malley said.

"Well, there is that, he will change the rules so suit what he perceives as necessary, that I can't disagree with," Richard agreed.

"Any possible connection to this new celebrity priest I see running around on the news? A lot of Catholic stuff all at once seems kind of coincidental, and I don't normally believe in any kind of coincidence," the Governor asked.

"I really don't think so, he's so busy working with the cops near his Church a few towns over from where this murder occurred that I don't see how he could be that many places at once, but he does work at the same Church as the nun. Plus, there is no physical evidence to suggest it was him, we can check on alibies, and talk with the cops he volunteers with, but I'm confident he'll come up clean," the Chief of Police answered dismissively.

Richard hadn't realized that connection, and his mind instantly jumped to that possibility. He couldn't believe the killer was a priest, especially that one, but given the situation, maybe? The letter seemed to indicate a religious and perhaps even a personal motivation in this case. But a priest taking a single incident like a DUI and going off the deep end like this seemed highly improbable.

The Governor audibly sighed.

"So, from what you have told me, we likely have a

new serial killer on the loose, but for the moment he is targeting people we would like to put in prison ourselves but can't for one reason or another. You two are here in case that news accidentally leaks, and I get questions that would be difficult to answer, which I appreciate more than you realize when it comes to the press. Those people always seem to find a way to blame me personally for anything taking place anywhere in the Commonwealth. Especially when it isn't positive.

"Gentlemen find this guy and quickly. Chief I know he is out of your jurisdiction but please be sure to help out in any way you can, and let's hope both of you are wrong about this situation and this is a one-off, but I agree that is probably not the case," the Governor said rubbing his temples staring at the photocopy of the original letter in Latin.

"Mr. Hartke, are there any other state organizations that would be helpful in this case? I'll call anyone you need me to call and light any fire I need to light underneath someone to get them to act," the Governor offered.

"Well, it isn't state level, but there are a number of FBI people who have experience with serial killers, and we don't have anyone here locally who has ever seen such a thing. It isn't a state entity but perhaps the FBI could be brought in," Richard said, not wanting to believe he just asked for the FBI to come in and take over, but it seemed like the thing to do given the circumstance.

The Governor walked to his office door, stuck his head out, "Heather, can you get me the director of the FBI on the phone please?"

***

Frank had been on his laptop answering public social media messages for a half an hour. They were all about violent crime and asking for prayers for someone who had been a victim of a crime. There was so much need for help he couldn't get over it.

While I do agree we need to be more pro-active in preventing all types of crime I think literal interpretation of Scripture is not the intention of God. Be careful when trying to draw direct correlations. If you have questions, any clergy-member from a local parish would love to discuss details with you, that's what we are here for!

He paused for just a moment and replies started to come in, stating that more needed to be done. Something he couldn't disagree with at all.

Maybe we just need to spread the Word of God in a more pro-active way. Invite your friends to come to your Church with you and introduce them to the Community of active parishioners in your area! That's what we are here for, to offer guidance in troubling times!

Frank couldn't believe that things had grown to the

point where whenever he posted anything responses would come in within seconds of him hitting "post." People were listening, and that had been his innermost hope! The plan, and mission were succeeding in bringing people back to the Faith!

Chapter Seventeen
The Cathedral

Father Santini took a deep breath as he pulled into a parking space near the Cathedral of the Holy Cross. If he were to become a Bishop, this or someplace like it would be where he would serve the Lord.

Downtown Boston was a natural place for such a grand structure, and it was not in the worst part of town, but it was not far from places it was ill-advised to go after dark. This was a part of town that begged for Cleansing of everything from simply sweeping the streets of the trash and discarded items blowing around in the wind, to the souls of some of those residents.

The meeting in Washington convinced him that he needed to do something to impress upon some of the other politically connected priests who would be part of the decision process that he was more than just an attention hungry, media savvy man who wanted name recognition beyond all else. He must show that he is for real, and not just enjoying a temporary moment of notoriety. The most influential names on the list of those he needed on his side worked in this very building. Ultimately the Pope could just make the decision, but Pop Francis was known to prefer a consensus whenever possible.

Structurally, the Cathedral, like most bearing that

title, was a massive stone structure. He loved his little Church, but the two did not even belong in the same discussion when it came to being impressive monuments to the Lord. He was walking around the exterior of the building looking at the stonework, dressed in his robes and collar, which earned him some highly predictable reactions from tourists which routinely flocked to the building for pictures and other touristy activities.

A few recognized him from either the viral video or his news appearances and asked for a photo, which he knew would quickly end up on their own social media feeds. It was interesting being a little bit famous, it wasn't something he sought out, it had just found him, but if it helped him in his mission, then he would use it as a tool. It was certainly aiding in his ability to spread the Word of God further and faster than ever before.

Frank was admiring the level of effort and artisanship it must have taken for each one of the statues to be created, and if they were considered together it had to represent decades of human labor. Not to mention representing an amazing amount of love for the Lord, as no one would exert the level of effort for a subject they didn't feel passionate about. On top of the statuary, if you also considered the stained-glass windows adorning this house of worship that also must have taken an army of artisans and cost a small fortune to build that beautiful portion of the monument.

The inside was somehow even more impressive than the outside. Frank had been here before, but the purpose of this trip, and his recently accelerated career path made him look at things differently. The artwork, the altar, the pipe organ, all coalesced into an image that truly was a place worthy of being called a House of God.

Frank had been here many times, but each time he seemed to discover something new. The mere thought that he might be serving the Lord someplace like this monument to the Almighty was humbling to say the least.

This visit was different than any before. Today he was here for work, and it seemed to heighten his senses. The Priests here heard confessions only a few days a week and it resulted in long wait times for the faithful who came in seeking absolution. Frank had promptly volunteered to come down and lend a hand, which was met with an enthusiastic response from the local clergy.

In his traditional pre-confession routine, he made his way to the front row of pews and knelt down in front of the altar, it was a massive altar at the front of the stone columns with huge archways across the top. The entire place really was a sight to behold. To think he may someday have someplace like this as his regular place of service to the Lord...he hoped he was worthy of such a blessing.

Dear Lord,

Thank You for the challenges You have put in front of me. I am doing everything possible to Cleanse this world of the filth put here by Satan to pollute the beauty of Your creation. There is much more to do, and I will continue to be Your soldier until my final breath. There is no margin for error when executing Your will. I will dedicate myself to Your goals and do so to the best of my meager abilities.

Amen

He made his way over to the confessional where there was already a line of the faithful waiting to confess their sins. He felt bad for making them wait while he prayed, but he felt it was necessary to be in the best mental state to offer absolution to those who were worthy.

Two hours, and many routine confessions later there was a break between those seeking forgiveness. It gave Father Santini an opportunity to think about things while taking a few moments to take care of an increasing need to release bladder pressure resulting from his coffee. Perhaps he had read the situation in this part of town wrong, maybe those who came to the Cathedral were really the truly Repentant and Faithful. As he sat back down in the confessional, he wondered which parish the worst confessors would be found attending.

The door to the confessional on his right opened and closed. The privacy divider was lowered, and he found himself face to face with a well-dressed woman in her mid-forties. She had lowered the privacy divider, which was the first time during this session a confessor had opted to not hide their face.

"Bless me Father for I have sinned. It has been one month since my last confession," she said with her eyes cast down, and hands folded.

"Tell me your sins, my child," he said expecting another routine interaction.

"Father, I am here because I am married to a man who regularly commits the same sin, I can't stop him, and if I am being honest, part of me doesn't want to stop him, although I know as a God-fearing woman I should. I am so confused, I don't know what to do, should I try to stop him, should I just let it go, and just that lack of being able to make that decision, and knowing the right thing to do makes me feel as though I have sinned," she said, obviously feeling guilty.

Father Santini slid to the front of his seat, paying closer attention to this woman, "His sins are not my concern right now, only yours. What do you mean you don't want to stop him? Not stopping someone else from sinning in and of itself is not a sin, and not knowing the right path is also not a sin. That is why I am here, to guide you upon the correct path. You can urge him to do the right thing, but I'm afraid I'm going to need more information before I can help you."

"Well, is it a sin of mine when his sins produce a level of income that we would not have any other way, and I do love the money. I tell myself he is just doing what he needs to in order to support the family, but that isn't right. We have so much more than other people, and I don't care, and if he must do something less than ideal to achieve that level of income, I don't know that I want to stop him. Does that make me evil?" she asked.

"Many people in modern society are putting money before God, worshiping it in a way, and that is a sin. One you should avoid at all costs as it flies directly in the face of one of the Ten Commandments," the priest explained.

"I would never do that, and we do donate a great deal to charity, including the Catholic Diocese. But I do enjoy having it in my life, and I know how he earns it is wrong, I just don't know what to do. Because technically, I'm not the one doing anything wrong, but I am enjoying the results of those sins, and that can't be right," she said.

Frank's curiosity was piqued, "How does he earn this extra money? Perhaps it isn't as bad as you think."

"It is not a good thing. I am not even sure if I should say exactly what it is, but it is something God would not approve of, in any way shape or form, I can assure you of that," she said, still avoiding eye contact and appearing ashamed.

"You have nothing to fear by explaining his actions to me, and as for you enjoying the money, if you are truly ready to receive absolution for your actions then, once again, you have nothing to fear," Father Santini said, not really addressing her concern but trying to get her to continue.

"Well, we live down on Cape Cod and he has a charter fishing business that does ok, but from time to time he does more than sunset boating with tourists and deep-sea fishing trips. He uses the boats to take some of the Boston elite and ultra-wealthy out on extended non-fishing or sight-seeing tours," she paused.

"None of that actually sounds bad, or evil, or even something I would call a sin, I mean a pleasure cruise can be relaxing, and the Boston financially well off that make up the more elite part of the social scene have a need to relax as much as anyone," Frank said trying to put her at ease and get to the part that was obviously causing her distress. There had to be more to this but trying to get her to open up he decided to take this tactic.

"These aren't just sight-seeing booze cruises. What he really does is take some of Boston's most wealthy and well-connected people out far enough to be in international waters so that laws here in the United States don't apply, and they can have rather violent sex with underaged girls without the challenges faced by the laws and fear of consequences that would be involved here in the United States. These things fall under maritime law which no one really understands, and he would probably never be prosecuted under, as long as everyone stays quiet, because of the high net worth of those who would instantly jump to his defense because they want to keep the party going. Not to mention the politicians who have gone out and would do everything necessary to keep this from becoming public," she said.

"Ok, that is bad, and very much a sin. We must think about this together. How does he find his clients?" Father Santini probed, with an ulterior motive in mind.

The woman sighed and some of the details of her husband's operation came flooding forth. Complete with how much he charged ad some idea on how to make contact.

He had come across another soul that needed to be Cleansed from this world. This was another truly evil souls that didn't deserve to walk this plane of existence.

***

It didn't take him long to figure out what the woman's husband looked like and their exact business name and physical address. The planning for this one was easy, and suddenly it was time for his next Cleansing. The lawyer hadn't been that long ago, God wanted him to work quickly, and there was so much to do he didn't want to hesitate given the nature of the Sins this man was continuing to commit. If he waited, more innocent young women would be hurt by this man's continued sinful path.

He had one chance to get this right. The man was down on the Cape and his wife, according to her Instagram account, was in Boston for a few more days of shopping and seeing old friends. In reality she was probably seeing old friends and drinking heavily at parties being seen by the movers and shakers of the Bat State.

Even when he found the right town his mobile app was having trouble finding the right street, a typical challenge Cape Cod. It didn't matter, he was patient, and God was on his side. He would find the man, that much was certain.

He didn't want to stop and ask anyone for directions because in these small Cape Cod towns, especially in the offseason, everyone knew everyone, and he would be instantly remembered as an "outsider" who didn't belong. Once the police asked around, which they would certainly do, his description would be given, and that would not be beneficial to the path God had put him on.

God deserved perfection.

The business' dock had a few boats of different sizes offering different levels of luxury. He had expected that. Anyone who grew up in the Boston area had likely experienced more than one trip to the Cape in the summertime and understood how these little businesses worked at some level.

He waited. A man with his wife out of town was unlikely to cook. He would be out at a local restaurant, where he would certainly know the owner and could be a while before coming home. Frank parked the Jeep where it couldn't be seen yet was still on the pavement to avoid any kind of tire tracks, and waited, then waited some more.

It was cold but he had a thermos full of coffee and didn't mind waiting if that was God's will. He stood sipping the wonderful beverage, leaning on his Jeep, and continued waiting patiently.

Finally, a lone pair of headlights turned into the little complex with the business buildings and dock on one side and a small home on the other.

Frank dumped out what was left of the coffee in his mug and tossed it through the open window and onto the passenger seat.

When the man got out of his pickup, Frank came around the corner of the shed, "Mr. Anderson!" he shouted.

"We're closed, come back tomorrow," the man snarled loudly before muttering, "stupid tourists."

Frank moved closer to the man before continuing. "Oh, I'm not here for the fishing. A guy I know said you arrange some very specific, and special party boats that go out into international waters from time to time if the money is right. The kind we don't tell our wives about, with some very...uh...young crewmembers," Frank said.

"Yeah, and you are right, those are expensive. It's fifty grand, cash, up front, before I get it setup, and another fifty the night we launch."

"That's all I needed to know," Father Santini said as he shot him in the neck with the tranquilizer gun.

The man was out cold before he hit the ground.

"You are going to meet Saint Peter today," Father Santini said as he got to work.

***

Richard Hartke had been in his office answering

emails for twenty minutes when the phone rang.

"Hey Chief, what can I do for you," he said seeing the name on the caller ID showing the name of the Chief of Boston Police.

"It turns out you were right; he wasn't done after the lawyer. Your guy struck again, and from what I was told, this one might just be worse than the Mr. Brown," the Chief said, not sounding happy.

"We don't have a call for a body anywhere. You sure? How can it be my guy and I don't have a crime scene in the area to go look at?" he asked.

"Yep. I'm not senile, at least not yet. You don't have it because it dropped all the way down in the central part of Cape Cod, and we just got the alert asking for some additional and specialized help," the senior law enforcement officer explained.

"You sure it's my guy? You sound sure. How are you so certain?"

"He left another note in Latin in that same artistic Calligraphy, and the cause of death was unique to say the least," the Chief said.

"What do you mean unique?" Richard asked, rubbing the bridge of his nose.

"You want the clinical version or the real one?"

"Just give it to me," Steven said rubbing his temples, not sure he wanted to know.

"I'm sure there is more than what I have been told so far, but the dead guy choked to death when his balls got caught in his throat, but that was after his dick was shoved deep into his own ass using the grip from a fishing rod as an insertion tool," the voice on the phone said rather quickly and bluntly.

"Given that our guy seems to be wanting to punish people for a crime, I am almost afraid to ask, what the fuck was this guy's crime we couldn't put him away for?" Richard asked rhetorically.

"Running underage girls out on boats to international waters for some very elite and rich guys out of Boston. At least according to some notes left behind by your guy, we heard rumors someone was doing it down there, but we didn't know who. I guess we either just found out or this poor bastahd got caught in the crossfire, and is just being blamed for it so that we get off the trail of the real perp."

Richard let out a sigh as he said "Thanks, send me what you have, let's hope whatever CSI team is down there has a stronger stomach than the one here had. Almost the whole team called in sick after that case."

"I will send it, but pack your gear and get down there yourself, we need you to go down there and see what they don't see," the Chief said.

***

Craig sat down at his desk looking at their number of ad impressions. It was nice to see some money coming in. The environmental stuff would always be his passion, but something had to pay the bills, not to mention help them recoup the new investment in drones and cameras.

He looked to see the trending topic list and saw a murder being discussed, and coincidentally was another one along a shoreline in Massachusetts.

Something about this sounded eerily familiar. He almost wished they had been the ones to find this one as well, it would do fantastic things for their following.

After looking into the details, he realized that the drone wouldn't have been helpful. The body had been found on a boat out on the water that had started to drift back into the maritime traffic close to the shoreline of the Cape.

Well, too bad, he thought, they could at least comment on it, and maybe get down to the Cape and take a few pictures of the area, once the dust settled a little. The scenery was always amazing down there. Maybe he could take his girlfriend for the weekend and do some work while enjoying the time together.

Quickly looking at the top few posts he saw the Priest whose fifteen minutes of fame seemed to be turning into twenty discussing God's wrath for the wicked.

He wondered if they should learn something from this guy. He certainly seemed to be able to spin a subject that probably wasn't his favorite, back into a religious discussion. They had tried that with crime going back into environmentalism, but that was proving to be difficult.

He had an idea, and decided it was worth an email.

Jack,

We found the first body that made this Father Santini the go-to talking head for these violent crimes, and I'm going to bet that the Commonwealth has a serial killer on the loose now.

We started out trying to make a living on environmental impact, but if the audience isn't there maybe we should shift over to crime and punishment. Maybe we should even go see this priest and do a joint live social media streaming event.

We could help him, and he could help us.

What do you think?

It couldn't hurt having on a semi-famous priest, I mean maybe religious people are interested in the environment. Anything to get eyeballs on the screen at this point dude.

Craig

Chapter Eighteen
The Investigation and Discussion

In all of his years as a crime scene investigator, Richard had not experienced a whirlwind series of events in the investigative portion of a case like had taken place in the past thirty-six hours. Part of him was excited to be on a team like this, part of him hoped shit like these murders never happened again. Maybe they could catch this one fast, maybe whoever it was would just quit, but that seemed unlikely.

Things had gone from his small lab with a team of three including himself to a massive FBI lab working the case with more than a dozen investigators with a wide range of specialties. They came from several different places, and they had equipment that he would never be able to get approval to purchase due to the budgetary constraints down at the local level. He figured that the Feds did have more of a need to use the stuff, but he couldn't help being a little bit jealous of the capabilities and how much more efficiently he could do his job, even on less high-profile cases, if all of this was back in his facility. But then federal budgets were by their very nature far more able to support such expensive state of the art gear.

Despite all his years of experience, he still felt like an amateur compared to some of the people on this team. They didn't have his case solve record, so that was something in his favor. But then again, they only got the really hard ones. They certainly had job titles and advanced college degrees on their side, and his cases almost always turned out to be a family member or friend of the victim in a crime of passion when a body was involved. Either that or some drug deal that had gone bad. He had never dealt with anything like this, he wasn't even sure if there ever had ever even been anything like this. Maybe it was a first in modern history.

There were two psychologists, a religious scholar, an artificial intelligence expert, and multiple forensic scientists, all with different and highly specific areas of expertise. Somehow, he was supposed to be a contributing member of this new team and not sound like an idiot, or maybe he was overestimating them just based on their job titles. His wife constantly reminded him that he undervalued himself. Hopefully this was one of those times.

Thankfully the meetings were intended to be relatively informal working sessions rather than formal reporting meetings, which meant this was supposed to be more in his comfort zone. The man in charge was an FBI Special Agent named Jim Ross who always wore a perfectly tailored suit with a tie but told everyone to just be comfortable in whatever business casual attire they were in. That was his claim. In reality, his working style was making it difficult for him to feel comfortable as a member of the team.

Special Agent Ross strode into their large, open workspace and assumed everyone was ready without asking for their attention, "First up, Hartke, I want to hear from you. Apparently, you were the lone voice that had this guy pegged for multiples back when he had only one known. You wanna tell us how you figured that one out when no one else could, or did you just get lucky?"

"It was a crime scene unlike anything I had ever seen. It was planned out in a way to that it looked like it took research and painstaking precision, in short it looked professional in ways unlike any other murder I have ever investigated. It took patience, premeditation, and not second guessing while everything was in process. It gave me the feeling..."

"We at the FBI are trained to understand that to catch one of these we can't care about feelings, they don't think like we do, just give us the facts, tell me what we can prove, and whatever information about the scene that you observed, not your reaction to it," Special Agent Ross interrupted him.

Richard took a deep calming breath as in his experience successfully solving murder cases was almost always about feelings, and this team was going to have to take more than a clinical by the book approach if this one was going to be caught. If he was just going to run the federal government sanctioned checklist this guy would be on the loose for a very long time.

"Ok, well, the first crime scene was too well thought out to be a crime of passion, it was something that had to be planned, step by step, and well in advance. It was more than planned, the entire thing was highly researched to cause a lot of physical pain, and to do so to a guy with strong ties to more than one criminal element that all of our sources say had no reason to want him dead. So, this could not have been some kind of repercussion or payback for doing a bad job or stepping out of line somehow. It was as if someone was sending a message to one of those criminal elements he was involved with, or maybe to punish this guy for something he had done, but not from his own crew, meaning this had to be external," Richard explained.

"What about the letter?" Special Agent Ross asked.

"At first, we worked under the theory it was left to confuse us. Almost as if it was meant to take up time so we wouldn't focus on anything else, why else would they do it in handwritten instead of computer-generated Calligraphy and in Latin? But after the translation and examination of what it said, it clearly wasn't meant to be confusing but as an explanation of why. It was in a folder also containing the victim's criminal history, at least the recent parts of it, some of which we couldn't make stick to him if we tried. Then, it said some things about the Laws of God being above those of man, and it was clear that through his actions he felt he was trying to help us out. So, judging by what was said in the letter, what we saw on the scene, the religious overtones, taking in the big picture it indicated someone on an idealistic crusade, and I assumed he would continue to do what he perceived as helping enforce right and wrong," Richard explained.

"We shouldn't assume anything in any investigation, but in this case, luckily it seems to have gone your way and you were smart enough to call for help. Ok, now let's open this to anyone. What else about this scene other than the letter screams Christian involvement of some type, or some kind of connection to Scripture, if anything? Is the perp an active Christian or part of organized religion in some fashion or is he just trying to throw us off the track," the Special Agent asked pointing to all the evidence hanging up around the room.

"The method of death is something close if not exactly what would happen to some people described as heretics during the Inquisition period. So, our criminal definitely has the knowledge base of someone very deeply familiar with the Catholic Church and its history, but I would be remiss if I didn't mention that this information is available online and in any library with a decent section on religious history," said Alex Steele, the expert on loan to the task force from the Georgetown University department of Religious Studies.

"So, it could all be done by anyone with access to the internet, and some deeply rooted religious beliefs, or the other hand it could just be someone with an internet connection and a score to settle, wanting to do so in a way that will keep us busy going down a rat hole that will ultimately yield us no useful information in identifying this particular psycho," said Special Agent Ross.

"I think it is just someone who grabbed a few images off the net and wanted to stage something that resembled a religious fanatic, and the letter only strengthens my belief. It is just too cliché to be a real religious re-enactment," said Alex Steele.

"One other possibility is that this is just someone who has a true fascination with the medieval period and decided to try something different. I mean after that movie about William Wallace from Scotland, I'm honestly surprised we did not start to see some types of copycat actions. Those depictures were pretty authentic if I remember correctly. I don't get involved in too many cases but personally it seems like everyone wants to leave their own signature, and do something bigger than the previous, most famous whatever it is you call this person," Steele continued.

Richard rubbed his temples in frustration and let out an audible sigh.

"You disagree Mr. Hartke?" asked the now obviously annoyed Special Agent Ross.

"Had this guy only struck once, maybe I'd agree, but given we have two dead bodies who were, for lack of a better term, punished while in the process of being killed, and those killings took time, I think this guy is very much Christian, maybe even specifically Roman Catholic as they have confession requiring the confessor to be repentant for Sins, and is possibly an individual known as a regular to the clergy. Which in the Boston area is still roughly two million people so it doesn't help us narrow it down very much," Richard explained.

"Why, according to your theory, must this guy actually *be* Catholic, and not just someone familiar with the history of the Church, especially during the inquisition? This could just be some masochist out for a thrill."

"I think based on the way these letters are phrased that he is giving out penance to the victims. It reads like he is a true believer, and a true believer would go to Church regularly, and more likely than not goes to confession on a regular basis as well. I do not think they would confess these things as Sins because I don't think whoever this is sees these actions as wrong in the eyes of God," Richard said, not believing he said the words out loud.

There were a series of eye rolls around the room and some nervous shifting in place by some team members.

"Ok, from this point forward this team only deals in facts. I will not tolerate any more conjecture or the person doing it will be off the team," announced Special Agent Ross.

***

Father Santini felt like he was starting to spend too much time behind the wheel, but he had promised to pick up his friend Sister Mary Anne when she got back in town. Waiting at the airport this time was a different experience than he had ever had before, even when in the past he had been identifiable as a priest versus wearing regular clothes.

This time, waiting near baggage claim, more than a few people recognized him. They wanted to shake hands or get a picture with the "vigilante priest."

More than one of them said it would get them new followers on their Instagram, and he supposed that was ok. Whatever made the faithful happy or caused people to consider a return to the Faith, or even spread the Word a little further than he could do alone.

He didn't care for that nickname, but it was interesting that he was being recognized. He had done a half dozen spots on the local new channels and somehow every time he did, that video from the bar started showing up again on a social media surge to remind people who he was. It was now one of the top watched videos of the year on YouTube and Frank just assumed it was all a part of God's plan.

People were flooding into the baggage claim area having gotten off their airplanes from all over the country, and a few parts of the world. In the middle of one of the human waves of passengers was his friend.

"Welcome back!" he called.

"Frank! Thanks for picking me up. I have a little surprise for you, and I wanted to break this one to you in person. As I was leaving a messenger brought this to me and told me to give it directly and immediately directly to you."

She held out an ornate envelope. The wax seal indicated it could only have come from the Pope himself.

"Really? This isn't a souvenir or something? It is really from him?" Father Santini asked completely taken aback.

"It is from him, the messenger said he was careful in how he wrote it. The messenger said His Holiness was measured in writing this, probably more so than when he writes letters to the various heads of state," Sister Mary Anne said beaming with pride in her friend.

"Well, let's get home so I can sit at my desk and give this the attention it deserves. This is no place to open such a thing," Frank said, holding the letter carefully, unable to pull his eyes away.

Heavenly Father, thank You for the opportunities you have given me. This is so much more than I would have ever expected. I will remain Your humble servant and execute Your will to the best of my ability.

Chapter Nineteen
Correspondence & Conversation

Frank sat quietly at his desk staring at the envelope. He originally had wanted to share the contents with Sister Mary Anne the moment he opened it but decided he should read it first. If this had something to do with his mission, it could be necessary to keep the contents confidential. But, if anyone else on this mortal plane of existence knew of his mission, it would be His Holiness.

He had been tempted to rip it open the moment he saw the Papal Seal while standing at the airport, but he waited until he was home and could focus. Not to mention he did not want to risk damaging the precious contents by accidentally dropping or wrinkling them.

He carefully split the wax seal, opened the envelope and withdrew the precious contents. The thick stationery had been folded precisely in half. He could almost see the Pope's hands making the fold, then placing the paper in the envelope. The quality of the paper was amazing. It was the first time Father Santini had ever received a personally written letter from someone so important and he wanted to remember everything down to the smell of the wax used to form the Papal seal.

He took a deep breath before reading.

Dearest Father Santini,

I have heard of your work enough times now in a very short period of time that I felt compelled to send you some personal correspondence. The lovely nun you sent to us for some study in the archives was very complimentary of your work amongst all of those here with whom she interacted. She says you are very creative in your methods of getting the congregation members involved in the local community, something the Church has not been as pro-active at as we should have been in recent years.

The Church is an important factor in providing an anchor of any community, at least once upon a time that was true. Perhaps as an organization, we have become lazy and are not doing enough to expand our flock in order to hold a position of importance in the daily lives of a greater number of people. Your work may show us the way, and perhaps we can use your example in other communities. Perhaps you have been chosen by God to show us that way in the modern world.

When I first heard of you it was after the incident with local police outside of an eatery that thrust you into the public eye. Now I have come to understand you have taken that moment in the spotlight and are doing television spots during violent crime reports to spread a message of peace and love. Apparently you have also used your spotlight to master the social media platforms that remain one of life's great mysteries to me.

Bravo!

Overall, what you are doing reminds me of a passage from The Book of Deuteronomy:

20:1 When thou goest out to battle against thine enemies, and seest horses, and chariots, and a people more than thou, be not afraid of them for the Lord the God is with thee, which brought thee up out of the hand of Egypt.

20:2 And it shall be, when ya are come nigh unto battle, that the priest shall approach and spark unto the people,

20:3 And shall say unto them, Hear, O Israel, ye approach this day unto battle against your enemies: let not your hearts faint, fear not, and do not tremble, neither be ye terrified because of them

20:4 For the Lord your God is he that goeth with you, to fight for you against your enemies, to save you.

I believe your work is waging a true battle against evil, and I know that God is on your side. I shall pray for your successful advancement to Bishop. Once that matter is decided, one way or the other, you must come to Vatican City so we can have lunch and discuss your future. One thing I am very interested to know is what motivated you to become a Priest. We should capture your story in our history and perhaps actively seek out others with similar histories as your impact has been extremely positive and should be used as an example for others to follow.

One thing is certain, whatever mission God has placed in front of you is being accomplished. Keep up the great work.

Yours in Christ,

The Bishop of Rome

The Pope said that his work is ordained by God. His mission must expand and expand rapidly. There must be a way for me to get others involved, or maybe that is going a step too far. Maybe that is something for God, not for a simple priest to determine.

Dear Lord, I shall not fail you. I shall remain your humble servant.

***

Richard Hartke was looking through the bits of junk mail someone had tossed on his desk when an envelope fell on the floor. As he was about to toss it all in the trash because everyone knew that anything important came in by email, he noticed something that stood out. He saw his name written in now-familiar calligraphy and froze for a moment.

He carefully placed the envelope back on his desk, put on a pair of rubber gloves, and shouted to the other side of the open work area, "Special Agent Ross, I need you, immediately. I have something here you must see."

The agent let out a sigh of disgust, got up from his desk, came over and asked, "More theories Mr. Hartke?"

"No theories, but I think we have a love letter from

our guy, and somehow, he knew enough to send it addressed directly to me. I was not comfortable opening it alone," Richard said.

"What? Why would he be sending letters to the authorities? He can't be that dumb." the agent reached the desk, his eyes widened as he looked at the envelope, "Fuck, I think you are right. This one is weird, or maybe arrogant enough to think nothing will ever lead us directly to him."

"Is that a theory, Agent Ross?" Richard asked, wishing he hadn't been sarcastic out loud and regretted it the moment it left his mouth.

"Sorry about that, I was an asshole, it is a job requirement at my level. Now, carefully open that and make sure we keep it preserved so we can get any prints or DNA from this, if possible. I doubt we will find any, but you never know," the FBI man instructed unnecessarily.

Richard carried the letter over to a clean workspace on a larger table and carefully placed it on the surface.

"Good, now carefully, don't touch it more than you have to," the Special Agent looked around the room as Richard carefully unfolded the letter.

The Special Agent pointed to one of the lab techs, "You, give me that camera. We need to get this photographed and translated then analyzed for any trace materials. How do we get it out of Latin and into English quickly?"

"I can do that," Alex Steele announced to the room,

joining them.

The two men stood out of the way of the overhead light so that the letter would be as readable as possible while Agent Ross operated the camera to capture the text from every possible angle. Later it would be examined for fingerprints or any kind of chemical traces that could tell them something about this suspect that they didn't already know.

"Ok. Now, carefully bag that. You...translate it from these pictures and put the translation on that screen as you go," the agent said as he pointed to a large flat-screen mounted high on the far wall.

The words started appearing almost immediately.

Dear Investigator Hartke,

I have been watching your efforts to identify a specific criminal. I understand your efforts in this field have been successful for many years, at least as effective as someone can be in your situation when bringing the guilty to justice so that they may pay for their crimes. The system and laws of man within which you operate are flawed, so I do not blame you for the rising crime in our nation, or the lack of true consequences for criminal behavior.

The help I have given you is with criminals, that because of the rules you work within you were unable to prosecute, or even manage to bring to trial.

While I am sure some will call me a criminal, I know that I answer to a Higher Authority. It is the Lord's justice that I enforce. For I am His sword and His shield. Our system of justice is supposed to be based upon His, and as a society we are not doing our part to ensure that continues to be true.

I have only been able to help you with three souls who have violated the laws of God so far, but there are more to come. Someday you will thank me for my assistance, even if we never meet face to face. But know this, if the justice system of man were more efficient and effective my activities would not be necessary, and I could be left to do what I was meant to do without this annoying distraction.

> *Sincerely,*
>
> *The Cleanser*

"Three? Ok folks we have an unknown. We need a list of recent unsolved cases, and we need it now," instructed Special Agent Ross rubbing his temples.

"Or there is one that hasn't been discovered yet," Richard said.

"Hartke has a good point. Let's not forget that, and someone figure out how the fuck this guy knew to address that letter by name to Richard here," the FBI man barked to everyone in the room.

"Can we now assume the Catholic theory has validity?" Richard asked.

"A little, but keep in mind that he could still be trying to confuse us."

"Look, I think this isn't just a casual Catholic connection. Look, right there where he claims to be the sword and the shield of the Lord?" Alex Steele asked.

"Yeah, so what," Agent Ross said.

"Well in several places in Scripture that is the description of the clergy. I think we are looking for someone who either is, or once upon a time tried to become a member of the priesthood," Alex explained. "He is also flawless in capitalization of anything thought to be of God."

"Fuck me," Agent Ross mumbled as he picked up his phone and rubbed the bridge of his nose.

***

Father Santini had shared the contents of the letter from the Pope with Sister Mary Anne and Officer Pierce at a bar not far from the Church and had been discussing it for twenty minutes when Officer Pierce stopped the conversation and asked a question taking the conversation in a new direction.

"This must be a real career booster for you, not that you would have asked for one, but still, I'm sure it doesn't hurt as you look towards the possibility of a Bishop. But it occurs to me in the years that I have known you I never even thought to ask you. Why did you become Priest?"

"That is sort of a very long story, I don't think I have ever really told anyone the story in its entirety. I think my parents understand it, but they watched it unfold," Frank said before taking a sip of his beer.

"If you are uncomfortable sharing, I'm sure the officer here would let it go," Sister Mary Anne said.

"Oh, I guess it is ok amongst friends, I just don't want anyone to think less of me, and a lot of this is stuff I left behind me years ago," Frank said.

"I would never do that," Officer Pierce said.

"Ok, well, you remember about thirty-five years ago there was a case that got national news about two of the children of an organized crime family being taken hostage, and a sort of short-lived war between two families taking place?" Frank asked the two.

"Yeah, I don't remember much, I was just a kid, but I think Whitey Bulger was involved in that or something?" Officer Pierce asked.

"Well, you also remember that they never recovered one of the two young men?" Frank asked.

"Yes," Sister Mary Anne added.

"I was the other one. My name was kept out of the news because I was a minor, but I was the other one. I had to sit there for a few weeks and watch as they tortured and eventually killed my brother. They did everything they could to him for a while. They chopped off fingers, toes, and mailed them to my parents. They took a sledgehammer to his kneecap. You name it they did it and really worked him over. His body was never found. My father I think, has left that life behind immediately after I was found, and I found Christ after some very intense therapy," Frank explained.

"Father Santini, I, I, I can't imagine what that was

like," Officer Pierce said.

"Frank, why didn't you ever tell me?" Sister Mary Anne asked.

"I guess. Honestly, I don't even think about it very much anymore. But you know, it was some real old-school medieval torture stuff. It made me want to live a life far away from that sort of criminal element, it made me want to try to get people back on the road to righteousness. Although, I did intensely study the Inquisition for a while and there were some parallels in some ways. But at least in that case it was in the name of absolution. It was the guilty who fell into the hands of the Inquisitors, and those who were known heretics being punished in the eyes of God.

"But that was the Church then. It is a different day and a different time. I made my peace with what happened to my brother. I hope that worldwide organized crime is also becoming a thing of the past. But those guys were brutal. I can't imagine what has to be wrong with a person for them to be able to do that to an innocent person, whose only crime was being related to someone else," Frank explained and took a deep drink, finishing his beer and motioning to the bartender for another round.

"Truly organized crime isn't as prominent as it used to be, but it does still exist. I never knew that was your dad. I knew the last name was the same as that crime family, but I just assumed it was a coincidence," Officer Pierce said.

"Yeah, he has told me over and over that he's been out of that business basically ever since that incident.

He says he is completely legitimate now, and honestly, I'm not sure how involved he really was and even if he ever really was, I wouldn't know what it was he ever did that was criminal, if anything," Father Santini said.

Sister Mary Anne remained silent. Her mind racing a million miles an hour. Not wanting to believe her friend had this tragedy in his life, and at the same time thinking that he might very well have been the one who did an Inquisition style bit of penance on a particular lawyer. But could he have been responsible for that thing down on the Cape? Surely not. Surely, he wasn't capable of such things, despite this childhood trauma. He couldn't possibly have killed those people.

Dear God, could Frank have done this? Surely not. But if he did, is it really a bad thing? Is he just removing those who are beyond absolution making way for the truly righteous to live in peace?

Chapter Twenty
Looking for Help

Father Santini had been working on a sermon when his phone rang. Seeing Amanda on the caller ID, he quickly answered, "Hello, Amanda, how are you today?"

"Father! I'm glad I got you! I am well. How are you?" she asked.

"Fantastic so far! How could I help you today?" he asked.

"I have some great news that I wanted to share," she said.

"Oh? I always like good news. Tell me what is it?" he asked.

"Those two guys from the parking lot that night, they have decided to plead guilty, so there will be no trial. I was so scared I'd have to sit in a room with them and look them in the face. I will never, ever, have to see them again!" she said excitedly.

"Well! Thank God. That is good news. I know I prayed for this. Any news on their sentencing?" he asked, hoping for another bit of good news and not just a slap on the wrist.

"Yes, they each got three years. I guess they could get parole before that, but I guess it's good enough," she said.

"Well, remember, if they repent, and truly are sorry for what they have done, it is our responsibilities as Catholics, assuming you are still converting, to forgive them their sins," he said.

"Well, of course I'm converting. And thank you for the reminder, you are always the fine upstanding Catholic reminding me of what I should have been doing all these years," she laughed.

***

Investigator Hartke and Special Agent Ross were making their way through traffic in an unmarked vehicle on their way to a meeting at the Archdiocese of Boston Pastoral Center in Braintree. It was time to start asking a few official questions of those involved in the religious organizations around town, especially those within the leadership of the Catholic Church. There seemed to be an obvious connection, and in a case like this the difference between successfully prosecuting a criminal and a case that eventually goes cold, remaining unsolved forever was all based on number of man hours spent looking into any and every possible connection, no matter how small the lead.

They pulled into the small parking lot and walked inside. The reception area had a few comfortable chairs, some Catholic themed paintings and a few well-tended potted plants. On the right-hand side was a small desk with some brochures about the Faith and various Worship Services offered by the

Church as well as an elderly woman sitting in a comfortable looking office chair who looked up from the novel she had been reading.

"Can I help you gentlemen?" she asked with an inviting smile.

"Good morning. I am Richard Hartke, a Crime Scene Investigator, and this is Special Agent Ross of the Federal Bureau of Investigation. We are here for a meeting with the Bishop," Richard said politely.

"Oh yes, His Excellency is expecting you, and waiting in his office. If you go down the hallway it is the second door on the right," the woman said pointing down the appropriate branch of the hall.

"Thanks," Special Agent Ross said.

"I should warn you gentlemen that His Excellency is about to retire, is in his eighties, hard of hearing, and if you let him, he will ramble on for hours on subjects you may not care very much about and are not at all relevant to your visit if you aren't careful," the receptionist warned, keeping her volume only slightly above a whisper.

"Thanks for the tip," Richard said with a wink.

"Hopefully we can get something useful out of this meeting and we aren't just wasting our time," Special Agent Ross said annoyed as usual, as they walked down the hall.

The office door was open, revealing an ornately decorated office with Catholic relics covering virtually every inch of space on shelves going from floor to ceiling. The man occupying the office had obviously spent a great deal of time choosing each, and lovingly placing them in some semblance of order.

The FBI man knocked on the doorframe, "Your Excellency," he said using the formal method of addressing someone in this religious post. "I am Special Agent Ross from the Federal Bureau of Investigations, and this is Richard Hartke one of the local Crime Scene Investigators, thank you for agreeing to meet with us. It is possible you could be a great deal of help clearing up some questions we have about an active case we are working."

"Good to meet both of you. I am not sure why you think I could be of use, but I am always happy to try to help those in law enforcement any way I can," the old man said warmly.

"I just want to start off by saying that we aren't here to arrest anyone, nor do we suspect anyone specific in your organization of any wrongdoing, we are really just hoping for your help trying to sort out some confusing information we uncovered while working one of our ongoing investigations," Special Agent Ross explained, speaking a little more slowly and loudly than normal out of courtesy to the Bishop's advancing age.

"I am afraid I don't understand. What help can the Church offer beyond the random musing of an old man, and the more public work of our Father Santini helping out the police up in his area and going on the news every few days to talk about how a little Faith in something greater than ourselves can aid our everyday lives. I don't know that there is a lot we can offer a criminal investigation, especially one that brings the FBI to our doorstep," the Bishop said.

"I know all about Father Santini, he seems like a great guy and from what I can tell looking online people seem to genuinely like him. What he is doing honestly doesn't apply to this case in any way, despite how important his work is. My team is focused on stopping a particular type of criminal who keeps repeating their crimes, not some random bar parking lot crime in progress. That is more of a right place right time sort of thing, our problem is someone who plans their actions way in advance, and we have a specific criminal we are chasing," Agent Ross explained.

"We are proud of him. He is one of the up and comers who is in the running for my job as a I finally retire. Although if he is chosen as Bishop my suspicion is that they would send him somewhere else then bring in an outsider to take my post. It helps keep things fresh, that way ideas and directions for a particular region of the world don't get stale," the old man said.

"How long have you been a member of the clergy?" Mr. Hartke asked as he began taking notes.

"Almost sixty years, but I have been active in the Catholic Church my entire life, which is now a very long time, much longer than I care to say out loud," the old man said.

"Well, that is a long time. I am sure you have seen a lot of changes inside the organization across all those years," Special Agent Ross said trying to be friendly, but hoping to get the discussion moving towards the investigation. But with his years of experience, he knew it was best to get people comfortable in the presence of law enforcement with some small talk, once that was achieved a more probing conversation was possible, which could yield results for an investigation.

"Some might say there are no surprises left for me, that I have seen it all at least twice, and forgotten it at least once. I love the Lord, but at this point the Diocese deserved better than a complacent old man at the helm, they deserve someone with a new vision for the future. So, I am giving up the office, and retiring," the Bishop said, with a touch of melancholy in his voice.

"Well, perhaps we can help you go into retirement with something you haven't seen before. We have a few details we are stuck trying to figure out if they are applicable to a direction we are going with respect to an open investigation. Before we go any further, we need your assurance that this conversation will go no further than this office. As I said, this is an ongoing investigation about an open case, not to mention one that is already getting a lot more press attention than I care for, and we can't have this information getting out or it would certainly slow if not completely stop our progress, such as it is," Special Agent Ross explained.

"I will keep this conversation as private as if it information conveyed in the confessional," the old man said moving forward in his chair.

"I am not a Catholic, and I have always wondered

exactly what that meant, how far does that confidentiality go," Special Agent Ross said.

"It means what you tell me will be kept in the strictest of confidence. I can't discuss it with anyone, ever, with the exception of the case when you are intending to commit a crime, which I assume neither of you are planning on doing given what you gentlemen do for a living," the Bishop said with a grin.

"Well, that is comforting. We have this problem. There is a criminal who seems to be taunting us. He keeps leaving behind notes at crime scenes, and he likes to quote Scripture, in particular the one about an eye for an eye stands out in his writing. Now we can, and have, looked up and read the entire book that passage comes from, but we are hoping you can give us some deeper understanding, and maybe interpretation of these words, and specifically what someone deeply familiar with Scripture and Catholic teaching might think these words mean. For instance, are they a call for action? Are they a guidance for what to do when they are the victim of a crime?" Special Agent Ross asked, leaving the questions intentionally ambiguous.

"Ah, the book of Exodus. Everyone's favorite passage to partially quote, but never fully think about or understand. In fact, it isn't something that appears just in Exodus. It is found, if memory serves, three times in the Old Testament and quoted by Jesus himself in the New Testament as well. So, it is obviously important to the faithful.

"The origins of this are actually very well known. It

was first brought about as a concept when the Hebrews were escaping slavery in Egypt. According to historians there were around a half million people involved, traveling together, and having a common set of rules for everyone to follow made the trip easier, especially when considering that the rule of law wasn't as universal as it is today. This was one of many laws, or rules, they had for everyone, that way there was something that could act as a guide to live by. They set up a system of governing that was different than the rules under the Pharaoh they were running away from. The concept was that the poorest of the people among them would have the same rights as the most wealthy and powerful. Some might say this was the basis for modern society, at least the laws we have on the books in modern society, before lawyers started to argue the meaning of those laws and fuzz the lines in between wrong and right. Back then, in that ancient society things were more black and white, and not as dependent on the talents of your personal lawyer, as I heard our Father Santini say on the news recently," the old man explained.

"Sounds like we have come to the right man. Were these laws literal or were they open to interpretation by someone in a position of authority?" Special Agent Ross asked.

"As far as we can tell from historical records it was never used as an exercise for extracting one for one style retribution. It is generally understood that some proportional, but typically although not always humane punishment, was used to settle issues where someone was wronged or harmed in some way," the old man explained. "What does this have to do with a criminal investigation? Don't we have laws to enforce, are you searching for a way to bring someone to trial who might be on the fuzzy line between legal and illegal we seem to be faced with that Father Santini seems to rail against these days?"

"This is not public information, but we have a repeat offender who we believe is responsible for more than one in a series of particularly brutal murders, and that he is more than likely planning more. He likes to leave behind notes, written in Latin, quoting Scripture, and claiming to be lending the police a helping hand to punish those who need to be punished. In one of these notes, he directly quotes the passage from Exodus. But these murders also have other factors that set them apart from what we typically see," the Special Agent explained.

"I am afraid I don't understand," the Bishop said.

"Well, for one, the victim in each of these cases were bad people. One of them we knew was a criminal, we just couldn't prove it, and had no actionable leads that would even rise to the level of opening an investigation, much less bringing charges. In another case we knew about the criminal activity but had no leads on the identity of the criminal until his body was discovered and undisputable explanations were left on the scene about his illegal activity," Special Agent Ross explained trying not to be too detailed.

"Is that thing that happened out on the beach one of these murders? I saw that video, I think what I saw was the unedited version, and it was particularly…messy," the Bishop said.

The two lawmen looked at once another, the FBI man nodded.

Mr. Hartke answered, "Yes, it was. We have an operating theory that this killer out doing these things is either a member of the Catholic Church or at least familiar enough with some of the teachings of the faith and leaving hints behind to make us think he is a member of the Church. We also believe that this individual is interpreting scripture for themselves and taking liberties in doing so in a way that depart with typical theological teachings."

"Whomever is doing these things has gotten, for lack of a better term, creative in their method of killing. They seem to be punishing their victims, torturing them in some shockingly painful if not demeaning ways before allowing them to die. It is almost like he keeps them alive on purpose for a period of time to extend their pain, it seems as though he is trying to make the punishment fit the crime," Special Agent Ross said.

"When you say torture, I instantly think of something medieval, surely you can't mean that, you must be overstating things," the Bishop said.

Special Agent Ross reached into his backpack for a file folder, "Unfortunately that is exactly what I mean. But before I show you these photos there is something else you should know. We believe this man to be insane, and a member of some organized religion, so the person we are looking for could be an upstanding member of society somewhere. He could very well be sitting in one of your pews every single Sunday. Insane people, sometimes, are able to blend in and be highly functional and even pleasant people. However, he has told us in one of his notes that he believes himself to be above the laws of man, and answers to a higher authority. Does that mean anything to you?"

"In the Church we do believe that the Laws of God are above those of man. Now I am starting to understand what led you to my door. I am just an old man, and I am no lawyer, but I do know people. If you really do have a criminal on the loose that does not believe the laws of the Earthly plane of existence apply to him, there is a real problem. If that individual is capable of crimes such as murder in some gruesome manner such as you have said, I can see the challenge you face," the Bishop said.

Special Agent Ross slid a photo across the desk of a body that had been picked apart by everything from crabs to birds to ants.

The Bishop did the sign of the cross and slowly picked it up to examine it more closely.

"Obviously this body has been damaged beyond the actions of the criminal. However, he certainly did put into motion a series of events that are, for lack of a better term, horrifying. But the way the body is displayed, I think I have seen before. This looks a lot like what went on in some rather well researched and documented cases with the inquisition. Is this the only example or are there more?" the old man asked.

"Unfortunately, we have one more example of what this person is capable of, but I'm afraid it only gets worse from there. However, I can say that the second case we know of perpetrated by this individual, the punishment seems to have fit the crime, whereas with the first crime we believe he was just out to cause pain and not have it be anything other than torture. So, as you suggest, something proportional, but not exactly identical," Mr. Hartke said.

"I'm not sure I want to see worse. I am afraid I can't disagree with your theory that he is likely familiar with the Church history at the very least. But I don't know who would do such a thing. How do you see the Church being of help?" the Bishop asked.

"Well, you seem to agree with our internal people that this criminal is a deeply religious person by nature, and as you say, this could be copying something from historic Church activities, although certainly not current day. Is there someone from your organization who might be able to help us in more detail? Maybe figure out what he might do next, and if there would be any specialized equipment needed for him or her to perform these tasks in the name of the Lord that we could trace? Maybe there are somethings we can put on a suspicious purchases list and chase down anyone buying them in quantity?" The FBI man asked.

"I have just the man. Let me call him right now, and I'm sure he'll jump at the chance. He has a history of working with law enforcement and is eager to have my job, this could help him and I think he would be a good fit to help you. You have probably heard of him; his name is Father Franklin Santini."

"That name just seems to have come out of nowhere

recently. Has he been one of your members for very long?" Special Agent Ross asked.

"He has been around for a while, and until recently was just doing his duty without ruffling any feathers. Then, for some reason, he decided to start getting involved helping the local police and ended up in a parking lot fight to break up a rape, and now he is one of our more popular public figures, we don't have many, so we appreciate his efforts," the Bishop explained.

"I see, any idea what caused him to change his habits?" Special Agent Ross asked.

"Oh, probably just one of those things," the old man said as he dialed his phone.

***

Father Santini sat in his modest room staring at his smartphone. God loved him, why else would the Bishop have called to recruit him to help the FBI and other law enforcement agencies in solving a series of murders.

He knew everything about them, and they needed his help in solving them. He almost laughed. God clearly loved him.

Chapter Twenty-One
Confession & Law Enforcement

"Bless me Father for I have sinned. It has been one month since my last confession," the man behind the privacy screen said.

"Tell me your Sins so that you may be forgiven," Father Santini replied, he was getting bored this evening. It has been completely routine. People coming in with everything from thoughts of cheating on their spouse, to one person who had cheated on their spouse but seemed to feel actual remorse, to someone who was cheating on their taxes, and other, far more mundane things. But nothing that rose to the level of needing to be Cleansed. Maybe the tide had turned, and his mission was nearing the end?

"I have lusted after money, and I have tried to take every shortcut possible to get rich. You see, Father, I hate hard work, and I know people who are rich, many of them, in fact that don't work very hard at all. So, who are they, and why should they get to keep it all to themselves," the faceless man behind the privacy screen said.

"Perhaps these rich people you are talking about worked hard to earn the money you are lusting after, and have finally reached a point in their lives where they can now rest and enjoy the fruits of their labor? Just desiring someone else's money isn't a sin, but sloth is. There is a large difference between normal laziness and sloth. Do you keep enough of a job to pay your own way through life?" Frank asked trying to determine the depth of the problem, or if it was just a sin of desire.

"I guess, but some people have so much, and I know that I should work hard to get it, but there are days when I just want to just find a scam of my own to get to where they are and get there fast," the man said with a snap of his fingers.

"What do you mean scam of your own?" Frank asked, his interest in this confession growing.

"I know some people got rich by hard work, but many others did it by scamming people until they got where they wanted to be. Like a buddy of mine, he has been running this web app for people to make bets on different things. He then rigs the outcome so that he's on the winning side no matter what. He's been getting away with it for a while and made something like a hundred grand last weekend alone. I could do something like that, then I would never have to do any real work again," the man explained.

"Ok, now I see what you are saying. You haven't done any of these things yourself? These are just thoughts?" Frank inquired.

"I haven't acted on them yet, but part of me wants to and for that, I must confess a Sin, at least I think it is a sin," the man confessed, sounding truly repentant.

"My Son, you have not committed a Sin of any kind, but your friend sounds as though he is worshipping money, being terribly dishonest, and several other

Sinful acts that I can think of," Father Frank said.

"Oh, he certainly has done that. The app is just the tip of the freakin iceberg with him," the man said.

"Well, for your penance, you must not emulate your friend, push these thoughts from your brain, and attempt to find the help of either a support group or a psychologist to get you on the correct road. We have several groups here at the Parrish that can help. Now, why don't you tell me more about this friend of yours, and his specific actions," Frank said.

***

Frank made his way back to his room in the rectory to change. He didn't want to run down to the FBI offices for the meeting dressed this formally. It wasn't horribly comfortable, but he preferred this when hearing confessions, or performing certain official public facing duties.

As he was buttoning his shirt he heard and email alert from his phone.

Father Santini,

My name is Craig, my partner Jack and I are the two people that operated the drone that caught the footage of the murder scene out on the beach in the north shore area that has now gone viral. We saw you on the local news a few times discussing violent crime and have seen your video on YouTube in the bar parking lot as well following a number of your public statements and social media accounts.

We have a podcast that is getting far more hits than it once did due to this viral video and our shift into local crime coverage and discussions about the impact of those crimes on our community. We would love to have you on our video podcast to discuss the wave of crimes that appear to be hitting the Bay State. I think it could really help get your message out while further growing both of our social media audiences because there is some obvious crossover appeal. We look forward to your reply!

Jack and Craig
Bay State Crime Blog

Frank thought about it for a minute, then tapped out an email agreeing to go on. God really was working in mysterious ways. Making him famous for his opinions on how violent crime was the problem in society all the while being involved in what these people were referring to as extremely violent crimes, which really were just God's justice finding a place in the modern world.

His mission was truly blessed. God seemed to be throwing more and more ways at him to spread the Word of the Lord, and faster than he would have ever imagined. Things were changing for the better.

The Bishop had been vague about what the FBI needed. He assumed it was some kind of public relations thing, but it had to be something that would help his mission. God would not permit anything to derail him now while he was doing so much good. He finished dressing and headed out the door.

***

Richard had been in the lab looking at data for hours. He wasn't sure how, or even if it was possible to break this case open based on what they had, but he was certain if what they needed was here the necessary bits of information were in the letters combined with the details of how the various people were killed. Something had to be there that led to a suspect of some kind. Things were just too specific for it not to be a very small list of people who could have done this. There had to be a way to build a short list.

It had to be someone who either wanted to be a member of the clergy at some point or someone actively involved in the Catholic Church. It could even be a member of the clergy, there was no way to rule that out at this stage. Maybe it was someone at one of the non-denominational Christian organizations that seemed to be popping up all over the place.

He leaned back in his chair and rubbing his eyes as the door opened.

"Richard Hartke," said Special Agent Ross, "I want to introduce you to Father Franklin Santini. He is here augment our Catholic specialist team. Maybe he can see something that the rest of us have overlooked."

"Father, good to meet you. I have seen you on the news, and I have been wanting to ask, are you any relation to the infamous Santini crime family? As far as I know they aren't active anymore, but I have been curious ever since you were first thrust into the public eye," Richard asked.

Richard noticed Special Agent Ross' typical poker face was not as unreadable as normal. This was new and surprising information for the agent.

"Yes, but I have been asked by the family lawyers to always say, alleged crime family. I can say that if any of my relatives were ever involved, I have been told that they left that line of work decades ago and the statutes of limitation have long since come and gone. I was a teenager when the transition happened and honestly, I never knew much about my family business at all. I was called into God's service in the middle of my teens and never have asked many questions about that kind of stuff. There are some things I would just rather not know," Father Santini explained with a well-practiced smile.

"Well, that sounds like a discussion for another day, or maybe even one for that book I keep wanting to write as soon as I find an interesting enough topic. Thanks for coming in on short notice. I want to be sure that you understand what we are about to discuss with you needs to be kept in the strictest of confidence. These are the kinds of things that just can't get out on the news or social media. I took the opportunity to look into you a little bit and you have a growing public presence. Some of what we will show you is not public information and could destroy our case if it ever got out. If you can't agree to these things right now, and by that, I mean sign our Non-Disclosure Agreement which lays out the penalties for revealing this information I'm afraid this conversation can't continue beyond some friendly introductions and maybe discussion of your colorful family history," Special Agent Ross said trying to get down to business as always, not taking his eyes of the Priest, looking at him like he was a rare zoo animal.

"Do I need a lawyer to review this?" Frank asked.

"You are certainly entitled to that if you want, but I will tell you that the Bureau has used this same form for years and isn't likely to change anything. Really, all you have to do to stay in compliance is just don't discuss any of the details of these cases you aren't already familiar with outside of this room. The easiest way to do that is to just not discuss these cases in any kind of detail with anyone that isn't actively involved in finding the person or persons responsible for these crimes and bringing them to justice. Rail against violent crime publicly all day, and you are good at that which helps us out in ways, but just don't divulge any leads, or lack thereof about this case," Special Agent Ross explained.

"I'll just treat it like are in the confessional," Frank said with a smile.

"That's exactly what your Bishop said, he also said you want his job so far from what I see publicly is looks like you are kind of ready to take that step," Richard said lightheartedly.

"It's a priest thing, and I didn't go looking for that promotion, the leadership approached me, and nothing is decided yet," Frank retorted with a smile as he signed the document.

"Ok, Richard here, who is one of the best crime scene investigators I have ever worked with, is going to walk you through what we have and see what you think about it. Maybe you will see something we haven't," Special Agent Ross said before taking position behind a nearby desk to keep an eye on the two men as they got to work.

"Ok Father, please have a seat this is going to take a while," Richard said as he prepared to walk Frank through their evidence, such as it was.

"Please, call me Frank," he offered.

Richard spent a half hour showing Frank various bits of evidence before Father Santini said much of anything besides the occasional "Who would do such a thing," or other such comment.

"And that brings me to the letters," Richard said.

"Letters?" Frank asked, knowing exactly what he meant.

"Yeah, this person seems to like to leave us letters at every crime scene and once through the mail," Richard said.

"Can I read them?" Frank asked.

Richard slid an envelope across the desk with copies

of the letter which Frank picked up and proceeded to read the letters he had written.

"Well, whomever it is, their Latin is impeccable, and you don't see that too often," Frank offered.

"Couldn't you get that off of Google Translate?" Richard asked.

"Well sure, but the nuance is very clearly from Catholic teachings. You tend to get a very academic translation through websites like that, and this isn't that. It is very specifically the way a member of the Catholic Church would phrase things, and a classically educated member at that," Frank said.

Special Agent Ross joined them after hearing this.

"What else can you tell us Frank?" the Agent asked.

"Well, I dunno, not much, I guess. Maybe he views himself as some kind of amateur detective who doesn't like rules that much?" Frank suggested finding it humorous that he was the one God had chosen to sit here and answer these questions.

"Really? To me it seems like he very much cares about rules," the FBI man argued.

"But whose rules?" Frank countered.

"He seems to like those of God more than those of man if you read these letters fully," Richard said.

"Well, God's rules did come before those of modern man. Besides, whomever this is does get many things correct, and he does seem to indicate he is of the belief that the rules of God are above those of man, and that is a Catholic belief, as well as many religions around the world," Frank said, confirming the suspicion of the law enforcement team.

"That was our thought as well. It is like he doesn't think these are crimes or something," Richard said.

"Well, in a purely theological sense it can easily be said that this person is correct if what you are saying is true. Perhaps in his point of view these aren't crimes as, perhaps, he is punishing these individuals in ways that the Lord would prefer?" Frank offered, wishing he could say more but leaving it there.

"I see," The FBI man said leaning in a bit, laser focused on Frank.

"What else can you tell us Frank? What do these crime scenes make you think these people, the victims, could have done?" Special Agent Ross asked.

"Oh, I wouldn't know. But I bet if someone felt that the things done to these victims were the punishment that fit their crime or crimes, whatever they did had to be pretty bad. This one," Frank said pointing to some pictures from the beach, "looks like something direct from the inquisition period of history. The other one, who knows, maybe it was justified based on whatever crimes the man had committed, and available to him at the time."

"The second guy had done some pretty bad stuff. But the other question we struggle with is how does this guy find the people he punishes? Law enforcement knew these guys were shady, and this guy left us information that certainly would have helped us bring them up on charges. We have no idea how he got it, or how he even is choosing who to punish, and why not just give us the data dump, and let us deal with it," Special Agent Ross said.

"I dunno, maybe this person is a criminal or has connections to other criminals somewhere and is getting paid to do this sort of thing. Like a modern day hit man, that just happens to be religious. Historically speaking that wouldn't be unheard of, in fact it is probably something that still happens today, at least in some parts of the world," Frank offered.

"Ok, that is a possibility. Anything else you can think of Father?" Special Agent Ross asked, obviously realizing the meeting was coming to a close, and that Father Frank was starting to run out of useful information he was willing to share.

"Not at the moment but give me some time maybe something will come to mind. Sorry I can't be more help," Frank said, standing up.

"Sure, give us a call. Richard, make sure he has your contact information," Special Agent Ross instructed while staring directly into Frank's eyes.

Frank locked eyes with the lawman. He hesitated for a moment. He had never seen such eyes. They looked like a predator seeking prey.

"Here you go Father," Richard said handing over a business card.

"I'll be in touch if I think of anything," Frank said as he left the room.

Frank gathered his things and left the room.

The two law enforcement personnel watched Frank as he exited security and disappeared from view.

"Well, Mr. Hartke, what do you think about our publicly notable Priest here?" Special Agent Ross asked still looking at the door Frank had exited.

"Based on how quick he got to the Latin thing, and his body language, how he chose his words, hell even his family connections, I think he knows something we need to know, and he isn't telling us," Richard said.

"I think that you and I agree on this one, and perhaps we will trust our feelings this time. Hopefully we aren't both so desperate for a lead that we are willing to see one where nothing exists," the Special Agent said.

"Could he be our guy?" Richard asked.

"What?" said the FBI agent, almost sarcastically.

"Well, look, I know you caught this. The dude didn't flinch when I showed him the detailed crime scene phots, and everyone reacts in some way, except this priest. When he spoke about it, something in the way he did it seemed like he almost admired whoever is doing this," Richard said.

"Yeah, I noticed that. That bit about the tools available about the victim down on the Cape Cod crime scene was oddly specific. We need to watch this guy. He's on a list," Special Agent Ross said.

"What about the family connection?" asked Richard.

"We need to dig into that. Is that family really out of

the business or are they just hiding it. I really want to know," said Special Agent Ross.

"Yeah, here in Massachusetts there is a long history of organized crime, and not a long history of them talking very much outside of their trusted few. It also blends into our prolific history of political corruption," offered Richard.

"Yeah, I'm not sure exactly where all this is going to go. Why is it they never call me in on the easy one," the Special Agent said shaking his head and going back to his desk.

***

Governor Baker had been answering questions at the press conference for almost thirty minutes when the one he was hoping wouldn't come up, finally did."

"Mark," Charlie said, pointing to the reporter from the Boston Globe.

"Governor Baker, given the rise in murder rates, in particular brutal murders taking place in the Bay State how do you respond to those critics who say your office isn't doing enough to bring violent criminals to justice, and that judges are growing soft on crime," the reporter asked.

Charlie wanted to sigh, but cameras were pointed at him.

"First, I'd like to remind everyone that many types of crimes are on the decline here in the Bay State. But we do have a spotlight on us due to some really specific murders. My office has recently requested some specialists from the Federal Bureau of Investigation to assist on these cases and they are hard at work with State Officials to do exactly what you say, bring more criminals to justice.

"In that series of murders that I'm sure you are specifically focused on, which have become the topic of many social media threads I find something disgusting. This killer has a growing list of what appear to be fans. Fine, maybe he took out some bad people, but that isn't how we do things in this country. This person is a killer, murderer period, end of statement.

"Finally, if anyone knows anything that can help bring this or any criminal to justice place call our tip line, and if you see a crime taking place, please dial 9-1-1 immediately.

"Thanks everyone, that's all the time I have," Governor Baker said as he walked out of the room.

As soon as he and his entourage turned the corner out of ear shot of the press, he looked at his assistant, "Get that investigator, I think Hartke was his name in my office as soon as possible, this isn't going away. We need to deflect these questions somewhere else unless they are about to solve it, then we need to take as much credit for it as we can," he said, ever the politician.

Chapter Twenty-Two
A Theory, a Cleansing, and an Interview

"Everyone, lunch is here," Special Agent Ross announced to the entire team.

Richard stopped what he was doing. The man in charge had never ordered so much as a team coffee before. Something had changed. The Special Agent was getting more involved in the day-to-day details of the work and less focused on administrative tasks the longer the investigation went on. He assumed there was pressure from above to solve this before it got worse or received more news coverage or maybe it was before the killer's public popularity surpassed some politician. There seemed to be a daily expose on national news about how Massachusetts was now ground zero for horrific murders, even with just the two, albeit two spectacularly violent ones. Unfortunately, more details than the investigative team would prefer had been released to the press either by amateurs with drones, or by local cops, which had slowed their progress a bit.

"Grab a sandwich and take a seat. I want to review some stuff and throw out an operating theory," Agent Ross instructed.

Everyone grabbed one of the sandwiches from the pile of subs.

"Ok, I prepared a PowerPoint, which you all know I

despise but this time we are going to do it," the Agent said as he turned on the largest screen in the room.

"We all see, and at this point all agree, that there is some kind of Catholic connection here. We don't know specifics yet, but it is there. We also all agree that he is taking out bad guys. His victims are clearly people that even if we deployed all the manpower in the world on it we likely wouldn't be able to make anything stick on either of these victims.

"Now, the first victim. The lawyer had no known connection to the Catholic Church other than an altercation with a Nun in a hospital emergency room after being involved in a DUI. When it comes to the DUI, he was surely guilty. He hurt some kid really bad and bought his way out of it with some huge settlement and there were no charges pressed. That was far from the only shady thing about this guy. He represented people who were certainly guilty of any number of things and for years, and always used money or intimidation to keep himself and them out of prison.

"The second victim has no religious affiliation whatsoever. None, zero. Zip. However, he is married. His wife regularly attends Catholic services down on the Cape Cod. She is a frequent traveler around the state and known to attend services, even on Wednesday nights wherever she is.

"How is someone with a catholic beef picking these guys you ask? Well, I don't know. But here is one other little tidbit," the agent changed the screen to show Father Santini.

"That famous guy, Father Santini, who we had in here the other day, he is connected to the nun. They work in the same Church. Father Santini in his bid to become a Bishop is running around the state and doing favors for everyone who might help launch him into the job, so he knows people all over. He also has connections to organized crime, which is coincidentally his own father. I really have a hard time believing in any coincidence, and this one is just too big to ignore.

"Is it at all possible that there is another Catholic cover up here? Kind of like when they covered up clergy doing things to underage kids that they shouldn't?" Agent Ross asked.

There was a pause in the room as everyone let the quick presentation sink in.

Richard spoke up, "Maybe Father Santini is the connection? Maybe he is even the bad guy? Or maybe he knows who the bad guys are and he helps point them at a target...maybe?"

"I don't know if he is the guy or not. But he certainly has the connections, he has the family ties, and he is in position to make sure things don't leak. If he's not the bad guy, then someone like him could be. His profile is just too good. But I have been doing this a long time. When we got lucky and brought him in as an 'subject matter expert' I could tell that he wasn't telling us everything he knows. There is something there, I just have no idea what, and at this point I can't prove anything. What we have is so thin that if I took this forward to discuss bringing charges or even getting a search warrant, I would be laughed at.

But I'm not wrong, someone in the Church is involved here, and Father Frank knows more than he is telling us," Agent Ross said.

Richard wondered if he should make a joke about this being based on feelings rather than facts but decided against it.

***

Frank was getting cold sitting in the Jeep watching the front door of the high-rise apartment building. Many people in Boston wanted to live in these sorts of places so they could enjoy the "lifestyle." Frank never saw the appeal. The apartments tended to be undersized and overpriced. In all his time in the Boston area he had come to realize that there were two kinds of people living in them. Those that lived in the oversized penthouses who could afford to live anywhere they chose, and those who aspired to live in the penthouse, some of whom would do whatever it took to get there.

He was passing time by reading emails on his phone. The decision for Bishop was being made and he was getting emails of support from all over the area. They were nice to read, and the level of support made him feel proud, but that was not his plan for the night, and the decision would be official soon enough. Time to turn off his phone and concentrate. He knew this target of his came out every night about this time to go out for a drink. Of course, he wouldn't go to some local watering hole for a simple beer, no that just wouldn't do.

This man always went to an upscale place and drank high end, top shelf cocktails. Frank had followed him a few times on his routine evening and knew it as well as the man himself.

He had even spoken to him at length one night. He had learned enough about the man that he hoped given the cold air he could pull off his plans. It was mostly flawless but depended on the target doing one voluntary thing, otherwise his plans would have to be abandoned until he could figure something else out.

There he was, coming out the door turning right, as usual. Frank cranked the engine and pulled down the street.

He pulled up close to the man, "Hey it is you! Dan! Want a ride? I was headed down to the Oak Room for a drink if you want to come along."

"Absolutely!" the trim man said as he climbed into the jeep. "What the fuck you doin' down here again?" Dan asked.

Thank you my Lord.

"I was thinking about what you said, and I am really thinking about jumping in and getting involved. What makes you think that we can really make that much money and not get caught?" Frank asked, trying to verify what he already knew, that the man was indeed beyond absolution, while thanking God this sinner had not recognized him.

"Because the fuckahs losing money to us are so rich they don't ever miss it. Besides, they took it from someone else so it ain't really *their* money, and they won't come looking, even if they figure it out. All we do is take the bets, we know the outcome a few seconds before them, and we only bet when we know we will win. We make thousands a day. We then launder that through crypto which no one understands anyway and the volatility of that crypto means any profit we make can just be called a rise in the price of crypto," the well-dressed man said. "It is just that simple."

"Since it is all done through an APP how do you know the people betting are criminals?" Frank asked.

"Who else would bet the minimum amounts we require?" Dan said.

"Someone desperate for a quick influx of cash, but might not be able to really afford losing it?" Frank asked.

"Well, if they are too stupid to know better, screw em', they deserve to lose their ass. In this world it is survival of the fittest man, rules of the jungle, ya know?" Dan said with a dismissive wave of his hand.

"That's all I needed to know," Frank said. It was dark out; they were in a part of town where almost no one would bother to look inside a car. He jabbed a tranquilizer into the man's leg through his high-priced pants. It took less than a second before he was out cold and leaning against the passenger window.

If anyone looked in and saw him would think he was passed out drunk, which was not an uncommon occurrence in Boston.

It was a short drive to get out of the city but took a bit longer to get Sudbury. That suburb was not nearly as densely populated as many cities in the surrounding area and offered enough isolated space for what he had planned.

Once they arrived and found the wooded area Frank had scoped out for this evening's use, he parked on the gravel shoulder on the side of the road, and heaved the smaller man over his shoulder, carrying him into the woods.

The trees would allow him to not have to deal with driving stakes into the ground that was already half frozen due to winter weather. This would be quick, and painful, once this man woke up.

Frank placed the man far from any residence. It was at least a mile to any man made structure. Plenty of space, no one would hear the screams, and if they did, they wouldn't know where they came from or what they were because they would be muffled anyway.

Twenty minutes later Frank was praying when the man woke up.

"Dude, what the fuck man," Dan said between hard blinks of his eyes trying to wake up.

"The name isn't dude. It is Father Franklin Santini, and it is time for you to confess your sins," Frank said giving the man a chance.

"What?" the man said in disbelief.

"You have committed many sins, the gravest of which is worshipping money above all else. Money, the root of all evil in this modern world and you have placed it above the Lord. You have even chosen to take it from people by being dishonest. That is another big no no in the eyes of the Lord," Frank explained.

"And I am giving you one chance, and only one chance to confess and absolve yourself of your sins, to wipe the slate clean so to speak, or I shall have to offer you some penance that you may not like," Frank advised.

"Fuck, I thought I recognized you. Through me off that you didn't have on the collar. You are that vigilante priest that beat the shit out of that guy who keeps showin up on the news. Dude, I ain't even religious. There is no God, your life is a joke. Now let me out of this and I won't turn you into the cops," the man said.

"That's me, and I do not answer to the laws of man. I answer to a higher authority. Now, if you don't see that you have done anything wrong, if you are truly not sorry for what you have done, we, well, I mean you, have a problem," Father Santini said reaching into his bag.

"Oh whatever. Now let me up and we'll forget about the whole thing. You will find out someday that money is what really matters. It is the only thing people respect. It is the only way you get laid, not that you would know," Dan said, growing angry and impatient.

"Well, if that's how you want to do this," Father Santini said, speaking very slowly.

He made his way to Dan. He shoved a rag deep into his mouth. Any shouts would now be greatly muffled.

"Let's see. How should we do this. I have a variety of tools here. The breast ripper is really designed for women. So that's kind of out.

"How about this?" Frank asked as he held up four-pronged device, with each prong twisted like a corkscrew and extending from the corners of a square device.

"See, now that you have told me to just go away, to forget about God, I deem you unworthy of this world. Very soon you will meet a Saint named Peter and he will decide where you go. I advise you to become repentant for your Sins between now and when you enter the next world. Now, normally I would make this take a while, but I have a lot to do tomorrow morning, and I need some rest. So, we will have to substitute extreme pain, for elongated suffering," Frank said.

Frank took out his knife and cut the man's pants off. With his manhood exposed Frank took the four-pronged device and jammed it into the man's testicles and twisted.

Dan's eyes went wide, and he tried to scream. The pain must have been intense, but Frank didn't care. There would be no mercy, and he had no time.

He gripped device as tightly as he could and twisted it in a complete circle, ripping apart a very sensitive area of the man's body.

The man kept trying to scream, but Frank had inserted the rag too deep for him to make much noise. He knew from his research that the man would die from these injuries, but it would speed things along if he stabbed through the artery in his leg, he didn't have time to wait, and refused to run any risk that the man would survive. Time was short, and he had other matters to attend to.

Frank shoved the device into the man's leg where the medical book had said an artery was position, and massive amounts of blood began to flow. The man's noises, and blood flow rapidly ended.

"And now, I hope you are repentant, or there is an eternity of damnation waiting for you," Frank said as he carefully placed the note he had written, administered the Last Rights, and headed back to the rectory.

***

Frank woke up to a knocking on his door. He put on his bath robe and made his way to the door, where he found Sister Mary Anne was the source of the noise.

"Sister, what can I do for you?" he asked.

"Frank, can I come in for a moment?" she asked.

"Certainly," he said, closing the door behind her.

"Frank, I know it was you. I know you punished that lawyer, and I don't care. But if I can figure it out so can someone else," she said.

"Sister, I have no idea what you are talking about. You know I don't have it in my to do that sort of thing to another person. You have the wrong Santini," Frank said remaining outwardly calm.

"Frank, I don't care. That isn't why I'm here. I just got a call. You made it; you are the new Bishop. Now, take the promotion and ask to be moved somewhere else in the world! They will do that for you to help you grow your influence, and it is a good influence. Continue to do the work you do, keep up the work, just don't do it here or someone will catch you," she said.

"Sister, I only do work commanded by God. I will do as instructed, of course. Where did you hear this news about the decision?" Father Santini asked trying to ignore her comments about anything other than the promotion.

"I have my sources. Now check your email, and I won't ask why you were out so late, or how that muck got under your fingernails that I usually only see on ER medical personnel who didn't have time to put on gloves when a bleeder comes in," Sister Mary Anne said as she left the room.

"Sister," he called as she was making her way down the hall. "I will think about what you can do to help."

She nodded, smiled, and continued down the hall.

Frank knew that God would keep him safe, and he now had an ally. One that he was certain he could trust.

Frank shook his head, trying to wake up. He looked at his laptop and checked his email. Sister Mary Anne was not wrong, he did indeed have the job once all the formalities were complete.

He thoroughly showered and shaved to prepare for his video podcast interview to discuss the violent crime wave sweeping the area, which was about to have a new announcement.

He turned on his computer, clicked the link they had sent and waited a few moments for the meeting organizer to let him in the online room.

The screen shifted and he saw Craig's smiling face.

"Father Santini, good morning thanks for joining us. We are going to start recording this and just dive right in unless you have any questions," Craig said.

"What if I say something so dumb it shouldn't go public?" Frank said with a grin.

"We'll edit out anything too bad if we have to, but normally these things just get a little promo stuck in the front and go online. It is no big deal at all. You ready?" Craig asked.

"I'm ready if you are," Frank said.

"Great!"

There was a short pause as the two men on the screen clicked some keys then sat back.

"Hello viewers, we are here with Father Franklin

Santini, a local Catholic priest, who you might remember from nightly news, or from the video of his...altercation in a parking lot with a drunken criminal. Father Santini, how are you this morning?" Jack asked.

"I am doing better than I have been in a long time, Jack," Frank said.

"Cool, any particular reason why?" Craig asked.

"Yes, I just found out I'm being appointed as a Bishop inside the Catholic Church, but I don't know where in the world I will be sent to perform my Service, just that I am being moved up a ladder rung in the Church leadership," Frank said, beaming with pride, then admonishing himself for anything other than being grateful for serving the Lord.

"That's great news, congrats, and all that hard work is paying off," Craig said.

***

A few hours later Special Agent Ross was watching the podcast. He saw the announcement and started sending emails.

Cleanser Task Force,

Our favorite Priest just became a Bishop. He is now in an even better position to mastermind a coverup, if he is even our guy or knows who is. But we could be wrong so don't fixate on this one suspect. Follow the data wherever it goes.

S.A. Ross

***

Inspector Hartke had just finished reading the email and watching the video podcast when Special Agent Ross came in the lab and announced, "We have another one, Hartke get your kit and come with me. From what I understand I hope you haven't eaten recently."

"Got it, let's go," Richard said.

A silent twenty-five-minute drive later the pair was on the scene. The ground was frozen with patches of ice here and there making walking among the hilly wooded area challenging. Richard almost fell twice, cursing each time.

"There have to be footprints, or a trail left in the ground with the snow and ice. Nothing new fell last night. Unless this body is older than that." Richard said.

"Let's hope we get lucky," Special Agent Ross said wistfully.

They could see police tape surrounding an area and Richard took a deep breath, "At least we are in such a heavily wooded area with evergreens here we don't have to worry about drones. Has the news of this one broken yet or are we going to have the scene to ourselves for a while?"

"So far, the only people that know are the local cops, the resident whose dog found it, and us. This should be as clean of a scene as we have found," the Special Agent said.

"Let's hope we find our break this time," Richard said as he went into investigative mode.

"Whose footprints are these? Anyone here?" Richard asked as he approached the body.

"No one wanted to come close to that body. We circled the area and found only one set of footprints in and one out other than the dog," a local officer said.

"Show me the ones coming in," Special Agent Ross said.

The officer pointed to the other side of the crime scene.

"You take the prints, I'll get a first look at the victim," the FBI man said to Richard.

They parted ways and quickly got to work.

Richard found the trail and noted just how good the impressions were. It was clear, one of the clearest he had ever seen. Then his heart sank.

"Special Agent Ross," Richard called. "These are the guy. You can clearly see where he came in and where he went out. He obviously carried the victim because the prints coming in are deeper than the prints going out. Thankfully the area was somewhere between damp and frozen when all this happened. However, we have a problem."

"Everything you just said sounded like a good thing. We can probably get his weight, his height, a shoe impression. How can any of that be a problem?" the FBI man asked incredulously.

"Because he wore two different shoes, the tracks are clearly different and one is at least a complete shoe size larger than the other one," Richard said.

"Well fuck, this is a smart one. I found his note, and I'm not sure I want to know what this guy did to deserve this punishment," Special Agent Ross said.

"Huh? How was he killed? I mean the other two were pretty bad how much worse..." then Richard saw the wound.

What used to be the victim's genitals looked like it had come through a meat grinder. Strings of flesh dangled down and were stuck to his inner thigh in the dried blood. Blood had sprayed around the area for nearly ten feet in all directions.

"How did he not leave here covered in blood," Richard wondered aloud.

"I bet he wore a raincoat and then dumped it someplace between here and home. We'll never find that; this one is too smart. But, one thing we can get is the approximate height from his stride and weight from the depths of the footprints leaving the area," Special Agent Ross said.

"Let me go figure that out, I can have it in like five

minutes," Richard said.

He got to work measuring the depth of the footprints leaving, the stride, then entered everything into his computer about soil type in the area and the answer quickly appeared up on the screen.

"Agent Ross! You aren't going to believe this," he said.

"Let me guess, the approximate height and weight of our priest friend," the agent answered.

"You got it. You know the only trouble with that?" Hartke asked.

"Yep, it matches about fifty thousand people who live within driving distance of here," the agent said rubbing his temples.

"What does the note say? Is it in Latin again?" Richard asked.

"Yes, it is in Latin, but this time he doesn't quote scripture. It was the top sheet on a quarter inch pile of paper that appears to be this guy's gambling racket where I think he was cheating people. But the note itself is actually very short," Special Agent Ross said.

Richard took the tablet that had been used to access google translate function and it really was shorter than ever.

Dear Authorities,

I have another one for you. He was worshipping money more than God, and that is not permitted.

Please start doing your job so that I can stop. I really do have better things to do with my time.

Yours in Christ

The Cleanser

"Well, looks like he is either tired of talking to us, or busy and really does want to quit," Richard said.

"Yeah, like busy about to become a Bishop," Special Agent Ross retorted.

"While I wish I could say I disagree with your gut feeling we have absolutely no evidence to prove anyone else is responsible. As in none," the crime scene investigator pointed out in frustration.

"I am well aware, and aware that we only have a suspicion and some very circumstantial evidence," said the lifelong FBI man.

"But I don't think you are necessarily wrong. If it isn't him, he knows something. The trouble is he is really smart, and famous. We can't go after him without it coming back on us with some kind of political repercussions at the least, not to mention his family has some great lawyers experienced in this kind of stuff. Plus, he really is taking out super bad people, but does still need to be brought to justice," Richard pointed out.

"Yes, we do still need to catch him before he changes targets. Not to mention with the level evidence we have I couldn't get a tap on his lunch order much less any other kind of surveillance through a judge with any kind of knowledge of the actual criminal code at all," Special Agent Ross said.

"I am well aware. Now, let's hope that he left something behind that can help us, although based on the other crime scenes I am going to bet that he didn't," Richard said.

Agent Ross' phone rang.

"Ross," he said into the device. He listened for a minute before hanging up without speaking another word.

The Special Agent looked at Richard, "Your local guys found an unsolved really weird but not nearly as violent murder of a parishioner in Father Santini's Church. The victim was actively engaged in a series of affairs and was killed in what looked like another night of extra-marital sex, but no note. I wonder if this could also be our guy, when he was just getting started, and again it does in some weak way point back to one guy at the center of all of this."

"Fuck, it has to be him. Now we just have to prove it," Richard replied.

***

Governor Baker had been answering questions about

his new budget when the tone changed, and the brutal murders became the focus again.

"I had a chance to speak with the Special Agent in charge of the investigation on these murders. He and I decided we should remind everyone of a few things.

"The overall crime rate around the nation is starting to decline, just a little, but it is the first decline in a long time. This isn't just here, but it does apply to us, I mean coast to coast there is a growing discussion of crime and how it negatively impacts all of our communities, and that has probably been part of what has led to this dip. Hopefully that trend will continue. Also, donations to charities are up, so perhaps that is an indicator of even more good things to come.

"Yes, we had another very brutal murder here but so did four other major metropolitan areas. The only common thread is that the killers are unknown, but they are extremely brutal, and the victims are all suspected of high crimes themselves.

"I would personally like to urge everyone to not take matters into their own hands. People could get hurt, and at some point, an innocent person is going to get killed. We have an entire justice system designed to get to the truth. Not just one person who happens to decide someone must be punished.

"Policing is best left to the professionals. If you suspect someone of a crime, do not take matters into your own hands, please report it to the proper authorities. Despite this killer's popularity, this is not someone whose behavior anyone who can hear my voice should choose to emulate.

"That's all I have, we will see each other again soon," the Governor said as he turned to walk out to a series of shouted questions.

Chapter Twenty-Three
Promotion and Confusion

Father Santini was sitting in front of his computer in full ceremonial robes with his heart racing as he waited for the virtual meeting to begin.

Becoming a Bishop was not an instantaneous thing. It involved discussion, meetings, a voting process and finally, approval of the Pope. Typically, this final step was a formality, but not today. Upon the official announcement of the decision, word had gone to The Vatican, and it quickly became known that His Holiness wanted to have a "quick chat" with the Father Santini.

Father Santini was a few minutes early and time was appearing to stand still. His heart was racing faster and faster, and suddenly he realized that the debilitating headaches that had once plagued him for years had become almost non-existent since the Cleansings began. All of this, including this promotion had to be part of God's plan, and his heart began to quiet, and he felt a calm come over him.

He had truly been touched by God as some people had claimed?

Suddenly the screen changed, and he was face to face with The Holy Father.

"Father Santini, it is a pleasure to finally meet you, at least electronically," the Pontiff said in heavily accented English.

"Your Holiness, I am honored. In my entire life I never imagined I would find myself in direct contact with someone in your position," Father Santini said, calmly, his nerves completely at bay, subdued by the knowledge that this was all part of God's master plan.

"Anyone who shows your level of devotion to the Lord deserves no less. There are so many in our ranks who would merely politic their way to the top. You, on the other hand, have done things the old-fashioned way through hard work and dedication to the way God wants us to live our lives and serve the Faith. On top of that, you seem to have cracked the code on social media with the youth and that is resulting in increased participation in your region of the United States by this very important demographic. Somehow you have done this in like three months. Simply put, you are what we need in our leadership roles, and we must work to expand the influence of people like yourself," the Pope said.

"Holy Father, you are too kind. I merely do my best to be worthy of God's Grace, and part of that must be performing whatever duties He asks of me, to the best of my ability," Father Santini said.

"I would like to talk to you about your service and perhaps we should call it mission from God. Specifically, I'd like to understand how you see your role, but I think that is not a discussion for a video conference. I'd like to see you and discuss these things in person," the Pope said.

"Holy Father, I would cherish the opportunity to meet with you in person," Father Santini said with perspiration forming on the palms of his hands and adrenaline pumping into his veins with excitement.

"Let's settle it now. You will be a Bishop. We will get someone sent to your local Parish to take your place immediately. Yours will be difficult shoes to fill, but we will find someone young and energetic. Perhaps you can act as a mentor from a distance," the Pope said.

"Holy Father, I am but a humble servant, it will be as you instruct," Father Santini said, beaming with pride, and trying not to let his excitement show.

"Fantastic. You will travel here to Vatican City as soon as you can get everything arranged. We will then get together and discuss your true Holy Mission, and how your example can influence the future of the way the Church conducts business around the world," the Pop said with a smile. "This may include putting you in charge of our global social media strategy. At the same time, I am elevating another deserving young priest from England to the rank of Bishop, and he will go there to Boston due to our retiring member."

"As you wish, Holy Father," Father Santini said.

"Excellent, once your travel itinerary is known, get word to my office and they will make all the arrangements for you on this side," the Pope said as he terminated the video call.

Frank picked up his phone to text Sister Mary Anne and Officer Pierce.

We all need to get together for a drink. I have news that I must share. I will be at the bar down the street from the Church in thirty minutes. If you are free, please come.

Then he sent a text to his parents.

Mom, Dad, I need to come by for dinner. I have some amazing news.

***

Frank got to the bar in twenty minutes and sat watching a hockey game drinking a beer until they arrived. The nun and officer walked in together.

He stood up and shook hands, motioning for them to sit and grabbed the waitress's attention.

"Before I share, we need to order some drinks," Frank said.

"What can I get for everyone?" she asked with a smile.

"I'll have a mojito," the nun replied.

"Old fashioned," Jonathan said.

"I will have another," Frank said pointing to his almost empty glass of stout.

The waitress went to go get things moving.

"When someone is elected Bishop, the Pope has to approve that promotion. Normally that is just rubber stamped, but I was asked to do a video meeting with him. He approved me and has asked me to come to Rome for a private audience to discuss my future role in the Church," Frank said smiling ear to ear.

"You spoke to the Pope…himself," Officer Pierce asked with his jaws agape.

"Frank, that is amazing. Do you know who is going to take your place here?" Sister Mary Anne asked.

"I have no idea. His Holiness did say that they would find someone young. While I am in Vatican City it sounded like we will figure out where I go next, they are bringing someone from England to fill the bishop role here," Frank said, finally coming to realize he was leaving Boston, possibly for good. "So, I am going to dinner at my parents' place tonight and give them the news."

"Seeing them is probably a good thing if you are leaving," Officer Pierce said.

"I have to admit, I was so excited I briefly considered just buying an airline ticket and leaving today," Frank admitted.

"Well, it goes without saying that we are here to help with anything you need," Sister Mary Anne said.

"I appreciate that, and I don't want to leave without saying goodbye to the congregation. I am sure I'll be here until after Sunday Services, but I was so excited I wanted to share the news with those closest to me, as soon as I had something official," Frank explained taking a drink of his beer.

"Are you still going to help the FBI task force from a distance?" Officer Pierce asked.

"I'm afraid I will have to leave that to someone else. I'd really like to help bring more people to justice, but I am afraid I can't help them in this case," Frank said vaguely.

"Well, I'm sure they will find someone who can help. A case like that is difficult under the best of circumstances," the officer said.

"So, Frank, tell us more about His Holiness, "Sister Mary Anne said, shifting the topic away police investigations.

***

Frank and his dad decided to sit in the family library drinking coffee after dinner.

"Frankie, I am proud of you. Even if you aren't here in Boston, we will come visit you, wherever you are," Leonard Santini said.

"Thanks Dad. Hey, you mentioned a book about the history of the mafia, something you said I needed to read?" Father Santini asked.

"Sure, right here," Lenny said as he reached for a leather-bound volume.

"Thanks, Dad. Listen, I need to talk. But what I am about to tell you absolutely can't leave this room,"

Frank said.

"Of course, son."

Frank proceeded to tell his father everything about his Cleansings. To the old man's credit, he barely batted an eye.

When he finished, the old man asked, "Are you under any serious suspicion?"

"I don't think so, but you can never be sure," the priest said. "Sister Mary Anne did figure it out, but all she wants to do is help. I think she understands that what is being done is right, and I know she understands that the laws of God are above those of man. So, I am concerned that if she can figure it out, someone else can as well. The FBI has a massive group of investigators working on the case."

"So, what can my organization do to help?" Leonard Santini said, all business.

"Actually, that depends. I hate to ask, but are you still active? I mean in the parts of the business that are absolutely outside the legal portions of the family enterprise." Father Santini asked.

"Mine is not a profession you 'retire' from. I have just kept it quiet. Really quiet. My guys do things much worse than you have done, but our disposal process is much better," Leonard explained.

"Ok, well then I have a plan that will divert any attention away from me. In the very least this plan should throw any suspicion that exists away from me, and render their case if they had one worthless," Frank said.

"Son, I have been doing this a long time, you let me be the judge of what will and won't throw off a police investigation," Leonard Santini said.

"You know, I hadn't actually considered that, maybe I should have," Father Santini said.

"Never count an old man down, the body may not be what it once was, but the brain is still fully intact," Leonard Santini said.

"Ok, well, part of how these things have to be done is to render in such a way that the punishment is proportional to the crime, kind of like in confession. If we don't stick to that rule, we fall outside of Scripture, so that must be front of mind," Father Santini said.

"Got it, now, what's the target, and why?" Leonard Santini said.

Chapter Twenty-Four
Rome and the Pope

Father Santini had somehow managed to finish the book he had borrowed from his father and get a great deal of sleep on the plane to Rome. The Uber driver had dropped him off directly in front of Saint Peter's square. He stood next to his two small bags taking it in. He took a photo and posted it to his main social media account with the caption:

I just arrived in Rome and will be meeting with the Pope later today for a moment! At some point the leadership here will define my new role! So excited!

As Frank stood there in front of the famous square, a Priest approached him.

"Father Santini?" the robed man asked.

"Yes, I assume you are Father Paolo Grigolini, it is good to finally meet you in person. After so many emails and texts I feel as though we are old friends," Father Santini said shaking the man's hand.

"Welcome to the Vatican, that you for letting me know you landed. We could have sent someone to collect you from the airport instead of having to muck around with Uber," Paolo said.

"Oh, I didn't want to be a bother to anyone," Father Santini replied.

"Well, no problem then. Now normally we have a driveway in the back for people such as yourself that takes you directly to the residences, but with this being your first-time visiting Vatican City I thought meeting you out here in front of Saint Peter's square you might enjoy the experience of seeing this amazing series of monuments," Father Grigolini said as he helped Frank by taking one of the two bags.

"I really appreciate that. All of the pictures I have seen over the years do not do this place justice. Until one sees it with their own eyes you just can't understand. The majesty...This is amazing. Truly worthy of our Lord," Father Santini said trying to take it all in.

"What makes me think, and honestly really astounds me, is that all of this was done in the late sixteen hundreds. It makes you really wonder what we could do today if we put our minds to it. I'm not sure what we could do better, but there must be something, with all our modern technology. Now, we just need the will to do it," Father Grigolini said.

"Yes, it certainly does," Frank replied.

"Wait until you see the inside of the Basilica itself," Father Grigolini said as they started to make their way through the tourists. "More than once the square has been host to more than three hundred thousand of the Faithful coming to celebrate the Lord at a single point in time. The square is home to one hundred and forty statues of Saints that were also completed in the late sixteen hundreds by the disciples of Bernini."

"Simply amazing," was all Frank could say.

As they approached the obelisk in the center Father Grigolini said, "The two fountains are to memorialize Bernini and Maderno while all twenty-five meters of the obelisk was carried in one piece all the way from Egypt to this very spot in the year fifteen eighty-six."

Father Santini performed the sign of the cross, becoming overwhelmed by the majesty of his surroundings.

"I will give you a proper tour of the Basilica later today, but I want to get you to your room. We have just enough time for you to get settled and ready for lunch. Today you will be eating privately with His Holiness," Father Grigolini said.

Frank stopped walking, looked at his companion and said, "What? I thought it was going to just be a quick meet and great."

Paolo smiled at him, "His Holiness has requested to be your luncheon companion today."

"Really? Just the two of us? Who else will be there?" Frank said as he started moving again, his body parts back under his control.

"Just you and His Holiness from what I was told. He has been following and impressed by your work on public outreach, including television and social media. He wanted to see you first thing to get something moving, I don't know exactly what. His Holiness is an old man, but one of action, and he thinks the Church needs to move into the modern world," Father Grigolini said.

"I can't disagree with the Holy Father," Father Santini said.

*****

Father Santini had been shown to the Papal dining room and left alone to wait for His Holiness, the Bishop of Rome.

Frank was in formal attire looking around the fairly ordinary room. He knew that former Popes had enjoyed and, in some cases, insisted on lavish surroundings for their apartments, which would include priceless religious artifacts hidden from public view and only seen by a select few clergy.

When becoming Pope each member of that select group chose a Papal name for their time in Service as the head of the Roman Catholic Faith.

This Pope had chosen the name Francis in honor of Giovanni di Pietro di Bernardone, better known as Saint Francis of Assisi. He had always been known for his humility. He chose not to move into the normal Papal apartments, choosing instead a small guest quarters on the Vatican grounds. The man was known to be an advocate for the poor and believed in God's mercy but was also known to have a very strict adherence to Scripture applied to the modern world.

Father Santini was not going to sit until the man was

in the room and seated. It would not offer the respect he deserved. He had paced the room a few times when the door opened.

"Father Santini, thank you for coming," the Pope said with a heavy accent.

"Your Holiness," Father Santini said as he knelt and kissed the symbolic Fisherman's ring.

"Do you speak Italian?" The Holy Father asked.

"A little," Father Santini answered.

"Great, so between your Italian, and my English perhaps we can figure this out, without the need for a translator," The Pontiff quipped.

"It is wonderful to meet you in person. I don't do much of anything fancy for lunch and often cook my own meals, but there will be some sandwiches here any minute. Why don't you sit and tell me what it is that brought you into the Service of the Lord, I'm always interested to know what drew people in," The Pope said as they door opened and two plates with sandwiches were delivered by a Nun.

Father Santini sat after the Pope out of respect, "Well, Holy Father, that is a bit of a long and strange story."

"Take your time, I have half of my afternoon clear for you," Pope Francis said.

Frank almost didn't believe what he had just heard. God had to have a hand in this. The Pope must be supporting his mission without clearly saying so. Some things are better left unsaid.

Frank decided to start at the very beginning. He

explained his family involvement in the mafia, his abduction, the murder of his brother, until finally taking his vows. The Pope asked a few questions along the way but was mostly captivated by the story.

"Very interesting. And that is much different than any I have heard before, but everyone's journey is unique. Is your family still involved in organized crime?" the Pope asked.

"They are, but I have never been, and I really have no insight into their doings," Father Santini said.

"Being here in Rome we see some of the families that are suspected of this way of life. We even get them in confession from time to time. In some cases, their intent is good, but their methods are a bit out of bounds for the laws of man. I'm not as certain about the laws of God, I don't know enough about how they actually conduct their business. Perhaps we can have a longer discussion about that someday," His Holiness said.

"Until recently I never really even asked about the family business," Father Santini said honestly.

"What happened in your life that caused all of these changes of late? From my staff I learned you took your vows around twenty years ago, yet until these last six months or so you seem to have remained content with the more routine aspects of the priesthood," His Holiness probed.

"Holy Father, recently the routine of it all frustrated me. Very specifically some congregants in the confessional have caused me to get more active outside the confines of the Church," Father Santini said.

"What about confessions caused such a change?" the Pope asked, moving forward in his seat and take a bite of his sandwich.

"I had been with that same congregation so long that I know the voices of many confessors and can 'see' the faces and names of many despite the privacy screens. More than a few confessors would come in for the very same sins over and over and over again. Then one day someone came in and essentially attempted the very sin they were confessing while in the confessional," Father Santini said.

"How is that even possible?" the Holy Father asked with a laugh.

"She was confessing, again, to infidelity, and violating the Covenant of Marriage. While confessing, she then attempted to get me, a priest, to engage in intercourse as part of some checklist of sexual conquests she wanted to finish before ending her extra-marital activities but felt that each time she could just confess, and it would be fine. A conversation her and I had engaged in multiple times," Father Santini said.

"What was your response?"

"I pleaded with her to stop and seek professional help, which she refused to do. She then tried to justify her actions by claiming since we are all made in the image of the Lord therefore, he must want her to do these things. This pushed me over the edge of going against the local guidance and becoming more involved in getting out into public so people can see what living a good life could lead to and clean up many of the misconceptions and misunderstandings held by many. Then, a parishioner in law enforcement offered to get me involved with them, which led to the parking lot incident with the two drunk men and the woman, that lead to social media infamy, some appearances on television, and now here," Father Santini explained.

"God must certainly have a very specific plan for you," the Pope said. "What do you think we as the leadership of the Holy Roman Catholic Church can do better?"

Father Santini recounted his story of the lowering of standards for students and how in the United States this has seeped into laws and their enforcement in society, "Holy Father, I feel we need a return to the point where there is certainly to be forgiveness granted for those that are truly repentant, but for those that are not, there must be consequences while here on the mortal plane. I feel this is especially true for those coming into the confessional who are looking for a 'free pass' for their Sinful behavior."

"I can agree with you on this. How can we do this for those who do not join us? Have you determined how to get people back into the ranks of the Faithful?" His Holiness asked.

"By being more visible. For far too long we have closed ourselves off and been content to live inside our four walls and only make these rare appearances on Sundays, weddings and funerals. We need to interact on a more personal level with the members as well as non-members of the faith. Take my little congregation just outside Boston. The moment I started getting out with the police, social media and the local news we had a much larger number of people than ever before inquiring about converting to the Catholic Faith both online and in the pews," Father Santini explained.

"I see. This clinches it. You are going to be a goodwill ambassador, officially posted here at The Vatican, but in reality, you will be sent to different parts of the world, to the most troubled areas, to spread the word and these ideals. In reality you will only spend about half of your time here," His Holiness said.

"Holy Father, I am humbled. What would you have me do while here?" Father Santini asked.

"You will be in charge of our global social media strategy and work hand in hand with me helping grow our flock. Starting today. You have given me an idea," the Pontiff said picking up his phone and speaking in his native Spanish to whomever he had dialed.

"You and I will go from here to the Sistine Chapel, which will be filled with tourists today, and you and I will meet them together. Perhaps lead a few tours. We will be seen together, photographed together, and this even can be used to launch your position. Perhaps later we can take a short walk around Rome and meet people in the streets. For that, I will need to coordinate carefully with the Swiss Guard as it can cause chaos with traffic," the Pope explained.

Father Santini was speechless and smiling from ear

to ear.

***

"Holy Father, we will be unable to guarantee your safety. We haven't fully cleared those in the Chapel. It could be anyone in there," the head of the Swiss Guard warned the Pope in an attempt to get him to change his course of action.

"I don't think anyone in there came here today prepared to harm me on the off chance I may just drop in amongst the crowd. What we are about to do has not happened in more than a hundred years to my knowledge," the Pontiff replied with a warm smile.

"Holy Father, we will do our best, but if a threat emerges, please follow us out of the area as quickly as possible," the guard said.

"Father Santini are you ready to see my favorite room in all of our places of Worship?" Pope Francis asked.

"Yes, Your Holiness," Father Santini replied trying to get used to where he suddenly found himself.

The door opened, the Swiss Guard led the way, with Father Santini and the Pope Francis walking side by side with a photographer following close behind. The tourists fell silent and turned to stare as the Pope smiled and waved.

The official Vatican photographers and

videographers captured everything from multiple angles.

"Hello everyone, bless you, thank you for coming to visit our chapel," Pope Francis said to the crowd in Italian, then Spanish, and finally English.

A noise came from the crowd as everyone tried to speak at once. The Holy Father held up his hands for silence.

"You all came here today to see the Sistine Chapel, not talk to a wrinkly old man. Let us not waste time talking, and instead focus on the beauty these artisans brought to the world as a tribute to our Lord," The Pontiff said.

"In fact, I will be a bit of a tour guide for a few moments," the Holy Father said to the cheers of the tourists.

Frank was amazed.

Thank you for this Lord. Your plan is more than I deserve. I will stay worthy.

"Now if you will look over at that wall you will see six frescos painted, I believe in the late fourteen hundreds. They depict some of the events of the life of Jesus Christ. On this wall we have six events from the life of Moses. The tapestries hanging around the room depict events from Gospel, and these were designed by none other than Raphael and date back to the early fourteen hundreds.

"Please shift your focus to our famous ceiling painted by Michaelangelo and depicts events from the Old Testament. My personal favorite thing in the entire room is our westernmost wall also by Michaelangelo. Together the works in this room are considered to be amongst the finest paintings in the world.

"The western wall over there is known as The Last Judgement and is said to be inspired by Dante's Divine Comedy. This painting shows the second coming of Christ, as well as God's final judgement on humanity," the Pope said.

Father Santini focused on this painting and ignored the rest.

Lord, I see what you are trying to tell me. It's Your final judgement that matters, and through me you have been judging the worst among us.

"Who would like a picture with me and my friend here, Father Santini?" the Pope asked the crowd to the chagrin of the Swiss Guard.

***

Frank was back in his room; his head was spinning as he flipped through the pictures the photographers had emailed to him.

There he was, standing in the Sistine Chapel, right

next to the Pope and posing like they were old friends.

He picked out a few and emailed them to his parents before turning to his social media accounts.

He picked his favorite one and posted it with the caption:

I was humbled to meet Pope Francis today and discuss a new role I will be performing within the Church. More information to come in the next few days!

***

Craig received an alert about a new post of interest. He opened his phone to see Father Santini standing with the Pope and some tourists.

He quickly tapped out a text to Jack.

Dude, the priest we had on is in Rome and getting his picture taken with the Pope. We have to do whatever it takes to get him back on!!!

Chapter Twenty-Five
The Dog Fight

Leonard Santini had thought long and hard about the conversation with his son. Upon find out that Frankie was taking out some very bad people the police just couldn't get anything on, he had been proud, possibly more than he had been in a long time. It was like his son, the priest, was fulfilling the intent of the mafia of long ago and following in his old man's footsteps, but from a much different angle, but overall, the reasoning was the same. The same son was now having his photograph taken with the Pope. What father wouldn't be proud of a boy like that.

Frankie had requested a favor. He needed to ensure no suspicion was falling on him, which was smart. The kid had real instincts. It was how his crew would handle the situation, find a way to throw suspicion somewhere else. But they were much better at disposal these days. People just seemed to disappear, never to be heard from again. But Frankie had wanted to make examples of some particularly bad people, which had value if you were trying to change attitudes of a larger group of individuals.

Normally Lenny would send someone for this sort of thing, but this was for his son. He would handle this personally. He did briefly wonder how Frank had found out about a series of illegal gambling events he wasn't aware of already, especially a monthly underground dog fighting event with what sounded like a group of high rolling regulars. On top of that it apparently wasn't this guy's only nefarious activity. Lenny had insisted his work have some legitimate slant to it, but sometimes you had to do what you had to do. This didn't sound at all legit, or even make an attempt at anything that wasn't just out of bounds. Not like taking bets on the Patriots, or Red Sox for a cut of the action.

The location was a bit of a drive from Boston, but if you had something like this you would definitely need privacy, which meant distance from downtown. As Lenny made his way up the two-lane state highway, he was feeling good about being back in action instead of just issuing orders. He wondered what his son had written in the note sitting on the passenger seat and wondered even more how he had come up with the punishment, but those details didn't matter. The stack of papers describing what this man had been doing was thick. How Frankie had gotten all of that must be interesting. He had a source someplace as none of those activities had ever been attributed to a name. According to Frankie, this person was supposed to die, and it needed to hurt, it needed to hurt a great deal, and if half of what was on those pages was accurate, there was certainly a valid reason for that.

Lenny found the turn, started up the winding gravel driveway and was waved down by a large man sitting on the three-foot-high stone wall that lined the left side of the drive.

He lowered his window and said, "I'm here for the fights."

"I don't know who you are, and this is private property," the muscle-bound young man said.

"How about now?" Mr. Santini said as he handed the kid five hundred dollars in cash.

"Do me a favor, park down by the road and walk up so no one realizes I let you through. I don't wanna get in trouble."

"No problem," Lenny said as he turned around, found a place to put the Jeep that wouldn't be easily seen in the dark, and walked up the hill towards the smell of barbeque.

He sat on a large rock out of sight in the woods and watched for a bit.

There was a large barn that could have easily dated back to the late eighteen hundreds in this area given its appearance. It had obviously been well maintained, but all the antique buildings around here had that same look. Live in the area long enough and you can easily pick them out.

There was a crowd coming in and out of the structure and the action was clearly inside.

He decided there was no risk in checking it out. With the lighting, his cold weather scarf and jacket, no one would be able to give an accurate description of him, if asked.

As he made his way around the corner of the barn, he found a huge barbeque setup with a cook who had obviously been at the bar more than he should have been.

"Want part of last month's losers? It's really good shit man," he slurred.

"No thanks," Leonard replied, not sure if it was really dog meat, and besides, he wasn't here for a snack. He rarely thought about the animals he ate but he probably couldn't brin himself to knowingly eat a dog.

He entered the barn and found what had to be a hundred people watching some announcer.

"Ok, betting is closed on this round. Here we are at round three! So far tonight we have two dogs who are repeat winners, real bloodthirsty beasts. For our third round we have a special event. We have two dogs that have been in the pits many times before, and have barely gotten so much as a scratch, two huge winners who have a real taste for blood. This is going to get nasty!" the man said to the cheers of those watching.

Now that he knew who was in charge Lenny went back outside and ducked into the woods. He discovered that even the drunk at the barbeque had abandoned his post and other than the guy on the driveway, no other security seemed to be around anywhere other than the one guy inside holding all the cash at the betting table, who didn't appear to even be armed. He found a comfortable spot to wait and watch the door. He waited, then waited some more. What sounded like four more rounds of dog fights took place across about ninety minutes.

Finally, he heard the announcer say there was only one round left. Lenny had observed enough of the place by this point to realize this guy had a decent setup but was a real amateur, this was clearly his actual home.

No one who had any experience in setting up illegal gambling events would ever use dogs as someone who would normally make a great mark and gets pissed about the animal cruelty might turn you in to some animal rights group, and those fuckers would investigate harder than the cops. This sort of thing had to be someplace you could have some measure of plausible deniability.

When the final fight ended the crowd came pouring out. Once the idiot running the place was the only one left, Lenny casually walked up and knocked on the barn door and let himself in.

"It's over dude, time to get out. Come back next month," the man said.

"My name isn't dude, it's Leonard Santini, you know who I am?" Mr. Santini asked.

"I know you by reputation, but this shit is mine man. I ain't gonna share," he said.

"That is no way to have a friendly discussion. This is not my sort of thing anyway, but let's keep this friendly. What's your name and what other little enterprises do you have we might partner on," Leonard asked.

"It's Brian, and what do you mean 'partner'?" he asked suspiciously.

"Well, I have connections, you are obviously entrepreneurial, maybe we can work together to grow one of your smaller but promising enterprises," Lenny explained.

The man looked him up and down carefully, "You really the organized crime boss, I thought you retired. Or are you just working with the cops now and trying to get something real on me?"

"I am no fucking cop. But I do have my hand in a lot of stuff in the Boston area, and men like me never retire. Now what else do you have that I can help with and make bigger? Then we can both win." he said.

"Ok. Well, there is one thing I never had time to grow, maybe you can help. Once a year I manage to get over to Asia. I always bring back one of those really young bitches for people to come out here and fuck in weird ways for a month or so before sending her ass back. I make so much money in those few weeks I always wanted to do more of that," Brian explained.

"How much do you pay the woman?" Lenny asked.

"I don't fucking pay them. Fuck that. And they aren't women, these bitches are young. All I do is tell them if they do it they will get to stay in the country, then when they start to ask questions, back they go," Brian said.

"How young?" Mr. Santini asked, better understanding why Frank had this guy on his list.

"I dunno, fifteen, who the fuck cares, it's easy

money," spittle flew from the man's mouth as he spoke.

"I see, well maybe, anything else?" Lenny asked.

"Look, it's late. I got a ton of shit to do," he said as he got up, and turned his back on Mr. Santini to get back to work closing the place up.

Lenny pulled out his pistol and based the guy in the head twice, knocking him unconscious.

He zip tied the man's arms and legs, then went to the tool chest on the other side of the barn. He found a fully charged battery, slammed it into the drill that he found in a cabinet, put a large bore drill bit in, and tightened it in place.

It was just a matter of time now.

Lenny looked around the barn and found a pit that had to be ten feet deep and twenty feet on each side. There was a covered ramp on each side that would allow dogs to be loaded from cages directly into the pit with some well thought out flexible pathways that could be moved between the cages quickly.

There were a few dog carcasses with horrific injuries in the back of the place and a number of pissed off looking large dogs in cages that could be connected to the pit from their modified horse stalls.

Lenny had an idea. It was a little more than Frankie asked him to do, but it seemed fitting.

Mr. Santini left the barn and checked out the surrounding area, including the interior of the house. No one was anywhere to be found. An amateur like this, who wasn't even armed did not deserve to survive. The fact that he hadn't gotten caught and put in jail was a miracle. There was some real arrogance in this sort of behavior.

He went back to the barn and grabbed the man's wallet out of his back pocket, and saw his ID. He was a State Representative. Dirty politician. Well, that explained the arrogance and how he got away with it.

Twenty minutes later the asshat started to stir.

"You finally awake?" the Leonard Santini of old asked.

"What the fuck. Turn me loose. Do you know what kind of shit storm I could cause you?" he yelled, wincing at the pain in his head.

"Yeah, that is just not going to happen. What happened next is going to hurt. More than a little," Lenny said with a smirk.

The mafia boss tightened his gloves, picked up the drill, pulled the trigger a few times to make sure things were good to go. Satisfied he knelt down across the man's calves and drilled large holes in each of his ankles, rendering them completely useless.

The screams were loud and long. They would occasionally stop as he screamed "You fucker!"

With both ankles out of commission he reset his weight higher up on the man's legs and took out both kneecaps, this his elbows and wrists.

The sound of a drill going through flesh and bone was like a strange combination of cutting a steak and visiting the dentist. Both wet and not at the same time. Lenny had forgotten about that, but it didn't slow him down, this wasn't his first time.

"Now, we have you immobile, so you won't be going in search of a phone, or whatever. I didn't hit any arteries, so clearly, I haven't lost my touch and with the help of a doctor you could survive. But I have another idea," Mr. Santini said as the man's eyes went wide with fear.

"What the fuck are you doing? Please? Stop!" he begged through tears.

He dragged the man to the edge of the pit and shoved him over the edge. Lenny then casually made his way around to the dogs ignoring the man's sobs and pleas for mercy.

Lenny found the largest, angriest looking dog he could, connected the pathway to let him into the pit and released the hound.

The animal went directly into the tunnel, down into the pit and went to work. It grabbed the man by the neck, bit hard, and shook him like a toy. The screams from the pit continued for less than a minute. He looked over the edge and realized that the man was clearly dead.

Lenny went back to his Jeep, grabbed the stack of papers and the note, positioned them in the barn in an obvious place, listened to the dog growl from the pit for a minute, realized the smell in the place meant that dog had probably penetrated deep into the abdomen by now, and left on his way home.

He briefly wondered how long it would be before the body was discovered, but that was irrelevant. He was tired and needed to get some sleep, and burn these clothes.

***

"I am starting the recording in 3…2…1," Jack said.

"Your Excellency, congratulations, and great to have our on our little video show again," Craig said using Bishop Santini's traditional honorific.

"Thank you, and it is great to talk to you again as well," Bishop Santini said into his laptop.

"Thanks for taking the time for us, and I know your time is very limited today, why don't you tell us how things are changing for you," Craig said, leading Frank where he wanted to go.

Frank explained what his new position would be, what it was like to be in Vatican City, some new directions the Pope was planning on taking, and even took the time to explain how much he was going to miss Boston.

"Well, that is a lot. Certainly different from what you were doing here in the Bay State," Craig said.

"Not really, I am spreading the Word of God, and helping people see that it can apply to their everyday lives. I just get to do it to a much larger group of people than I did before," Frank explained.

"I see, well is there something you would like to say to kick that off, something you can tell us that you haven't told anyone else, perhaps an exclusive!" Craig said getting excited.

"There is one thing actually, it isn't really new, but it is how I would like people to think about their daily lives.

"Has being a huge conflict person ever helped you get where you want? Have you been involved in a large number of arguments, fights, domestic disputes? Do you always seem to be the one at the center of some disagreement?

"Try thinking with your heart instead. Think, would God want me to do this? Can I use words instead of physical force?

"If we all love one another unconditionally it will make our lives so much better. God has shown us how to do this, we need to take those lessons outside the Church walls and live our lives in peace with one another. Not everyone will return that love, but that doesn't mean we should respond in kind. We should always respond with love," Frank said.

"Thanks for that, Your Excellency. I think that's all the time we have today," Craig said as the recording stopped.

"Your Excellency, thanks for being on again, any chance we can make this a regular thing?" Jack asked.

"Maybe, but I have a few conditions," Frank said.

"Ok, what are those?" Craig asked, visibly excited.

"First, I can only come on once a month with my new schedule. But I am willing to do thirty-minute slots once a month. However, only if you agree to do a once-a-week spot on how religious organizations can and do help people who are not even parts of their own parish. I want you to find a local person involved, hopefully a different person each time, to come on and discuss how being part of organized religion has changed their life," Frank explained.

"What kind of guest, someone who is a leader in the church, just a member, from any particular religion?" Jack asked trying to wrap his head around this.

"It can be anyone from a member that attends services, to a priest, to a rabbi, as long as the message is that religion doesn't bite. We aren't here to do anything but help those who need help. We protect the innocent from evil. But you must do your best to not be evil. If you do fall, and do something you shouldn't, just get better. Be better every single day. If you will just keep that theme the same and I don't care what organization they come out of, just keep the tempo," Frank explained.

"I think we can do that," Craig said.

"Ok, then we have a deal," Frank said with a smile.

Chapter Twenty-Six
The Pile of Flesh

Susan Cahill turned off the road and onto her father's driveway to run by and check on him. She always got annoyed at being forced to leave East Boston, but he hadn't so much as answered a text message in a few days. She hoped he wasn't passed out drunk again. He had worked to kick the habit, but since the divorce (his third) he had backslid more than once. It annoyed her that a twenty-four-year-old woman had to spending time taking care of a parent like this, but such was life. You do what you must for those you love.

She parked in front of the house, got out of the car and heard some dogs barking and howling from the barn. Something was weird. Her father didn't have dogs, he despised them. She let herself in the front door, noticing it wasn't locked and thought that was odd.

"Dad! It's me!" she called, getting nervous.

No answer.

Making her way into the kitchen she found nothing out of place and no coffee in the coffee maker, which for this time of morning with him was also bizarre. Maybe he went out of town and didn't tell her. She was always fussing with him to be more considerate, but then why was the front door unlocked? What the hell were dogs doing in the barn. Something was wrong.

She went through the rest of the house and found no signs of life, but nothing surprising, and nothing obvious was out of place.

Making her way outside, cell phone in hand she went to check on the barn. As she approached the smell was horrific. Worse than the time the septic system leaked.

What the hell was that smell?

She opened the barn door and realized something had to have died inside. Something was very very wrong. Flies were everywhere. She had not set foot in that barn for a long time, and the dog tunnel mechanisms caused her to instantly dial 9-1-1 and she couldn't bring herself to set foot inside.

Something stopped her.

"Nine one one, what's your emergency," the operator said.

"Yes, hello, my name is Susan Cahill, I came out to check on my father, I haven't heard from him for a couple of days, and I think, I think there is something illegal and probably something dead in his barn," Susan said.

"Are you in danger?" the operator asked.

"I don't think so, I dunno, maybe?" she stammered, starting to think that it was possible that she might be.

"What's your location?" the operator asked.

She relayed the address and told them to be careful coming up the drive as there is a sharp right turn.

"Can you wait someplace safe?" the operator asked.

"I don't think I'm in danger, but the smell, something has to be dead in the barn. It could be an animal I guess, but last I knew my dad didn't have any out here," she said.

"Ok, can you get to someplace visible, and wait for the local police to arrive? I have a car on the way already," the operator said.

"I guess I can wait by my car," she offered.

"Great, I'll stay on the line with you while we wait for the car to arrive. It should only be about five minutes before they get to your location. Do you require an ambulance?"

"No, I don't need an ambulance. I'm fine," Susan said.

"Is there anyone else on the premises?"

"Not that I can find, and I looked through the entire house. The barn on the other hand, I couldn't bring myself to enter, that's where something is clearly wrong, and smells like something died. I have never seen so many flies," she explained.

"What do you think it is?" the operator asked.

"I saw a bunch of dogs in cages, and it looked like some kind of weird tunnel system to allow the dogs to move around, but it disappeared into the ground, and there is a smell like something large died in there," she said.

"Oh my God! What if it is my father in there? Should I go in? Maybe he's in there and he can't yell, and he needs help!" she asked the operator starting to panic.

"We have a car just a few minutes away. I will get a second on the way as well," the operator said.

***

Craig pulled out his cell and called Jack. He didn't wait for him to respond when he picked up.

"Dude, get the drone, we gotta go, I have a feeling something big is going on just outside of town. I heard on one of the websites that let you listen to police radio that they just sent a bunch of squad cars to a State Reps house. We need to get the drone out there," Craig said, speaking quickly.

"You think it is another one of these killings?" Jack asked.

"I dunno, but something big. It can't hurt us to get a drone over the top of it and be first with something going down at some politician's private residence."

"Let's go. I will be there in like five minutes, get the shit and packed and let's get our asses out there," Jack said.

***

Susan was leaning against her car when the squad

car pulled up, "They are here," she told the operator.

"Ok, I will leave you in their hands, thank you for staying with me," the nameless operator replied.

"Ma'am, are you Susan Cahill?" the officer asked.

"Yes, I am the one who called, this is my father's house," she said.

"I am officer James Fisher. You don't live here?" he asked.

"No, I moved out about a year ago and I'm over in East Boston now, but he wasn't answering calls, and hasn't for a few days, so I came out here to check up on him," she explained.

"Do you have some identification on you?" the officer asked.

She retrieved it from her purse in the car and gave it to the officer.

"Thank you, is there anyone else here that you are aware of?" he asked.

"No, I went through the whole house and didn't see anyone, but then I opened the barn, and something is wrong in there," she pointed to the open barn door.

"The door is open; you didn't go inside?" he asked.

"No, the smell, and something is clearly just not right in there. It smells like something died. I couldn't bring myself to go in there," she said, a tear coming down her face.

"Ok," he reached for the radio microphone on his shoulder, "Dispatch, Officer Fisher, I'm going to examine the barn, I am the only one on scene. No immediate danger, but I will need backup."

"Affirmative Officer Fisher," came the radio voice.

"Ok, you just wait here ma'am. I'm sure we can clear this up quickly and have you on your way. Probably just some animal that somehow got in there and died, happens more often than you'd think, especially this far out of town," he said trying to calm her nerves.

"Still wouldn't explain where my dad is, but that would be good I guess," she said, wiping her face.

"Let me go take a look, I'll be right back," he said as he made his way over to the barn.

He slowly entered, calling out, "Anyone in the barn? This is Officer Fisher, Police! You are in no trouble, just please make your presence known!"

There was no response and he slowly walked in, covering his face with one hand because of the smell.

He quickly emerged.

Susan could hear him talking into the radio, "Dispatch, this is Officer Fisher, I need everything. I need CSI, ambulance, coroner, and whatever detective is available. You better call the chief and get him out here also. We have a mess out here. I have never seen anything like this."

"James, are you sure? Is there any danger?" came the radio voice, sounding concerned.

"No, no danger that I can see, but we will also need animal control. Just get them here fast, and get someone out here to do traffic control, news media is going to show up fast," he said.

"Ma'am. I don't know exactly what happened in there, but you were right to call us," he said as he approached Susan.

"Did you see my father?" she asked, starting to cry.

"I honestly don't know exactly what I saw," he said trying to remain composed.

***

An hour later the small yard was full of emergency vehicles. The local chief of police was now in charge of the scene. There were two officers at the entrance to the property turning anyone away that wasn't part of the first responder team.

Animal control was the last to arrive. According to the chief they had taken their sweet assed time.

"You guys should go in the back entrance. The front is a real mess. Plug your nose, that place stinks," Chief Brown shouted.

"Did anyone get in touch with that FBI team yet?" he asked the group.

"Yes, Chief. They said they will be here shortly, and not touch anything before they arrive," Officer Fisher said.

"Well, we can get the damn dogs under control before they get here at least," the Chief said, clearly annoyed with the FBI demands.

"Ma'am you really should go inside and wait, we have fully cleared the house, it is safe, and this is going to take a while," the Chief said to Susan.

"Why do we need the FBI? Has anyone managed to locate my father, even by telephone?" she said, the stress of the situation exhausting her.

"Ma'am we have not reached him, but we found his phone in the barn, so I don't know where he is. You should really not be here for this," the Chief said without an ounce of empathy.

"Miss Cahill let's go in and have coffee," Officer Fisher said.

"Ok, I guess," she said and went inside with the officer.

"Let's hope that isn't her state rep father at the bottom of that pit," the Chief said to the group standing with him.

A drone flew overhead.

"Is that one of ours?" he pointed.

"Probably FBI," someone offered, and the drone was ignored.

"Where the hell are they? Didn't someone tell them to hurry the fuck up?" the Chief asked.

"They said they will gather their equipment and get here from Boston as soon as possible," his deputy said.

They all stood laughing at the animal control team

debate how to best get things under control for fifteen minutes when two men walked up carring arm loads of equipment.

"Are you the Chief here?" one of them asked.

"Yes, I am Chief of police Brown. Who are you?" he asked, reluctantly shaking hands with the man.

"I am Special Agent Ross, FBI, and this is Crime Scene Investigator Richard Hartke. Has anyone entered the barn?" agent Ross asked, all business.

"Just me, one of my officers, and animal control who went in the back, all the real stuff you need to see is in the front," the Chief answered dismissively.

"Ok, this is now my scene. EVERYONE. I need everyone out of the barn right now," Special Agent Ross shouted.

"Your scene, thank God," one of the animal control team said.

"Is that drone yours?" Special Agent Ross asked.

"No, we assumed it was you," The Chief said.

"How about you guys do something useful, find out who is flying that thing and get any video they have already captured," Agent Ross instructed.

Agent Ross and Investigator Hartke put on latex gloves and approached the main barn door.

"What do you think?" Richard asked the Agent.

"I hope these guys didn't fuck up the scene, and I hope this isn't another one from our guy," Special Agent Ross said.

As they entered the barn Richard pointed to the note and stack of papers clearly displayed to be easily located on a hay bale, "I think we can rule out it not being out guy."

"Fuck, yeah, well at least we get a somewhat intact scene this time," he said picking up his phone.

"Shit, this is a mess," Richard said as he looked over the edge of the pit.

The Agent looked over the edge, then dialed and said into the phone, "Send the whole team, and don't eat lunch on the way, you'll understand when you get here."

The pit had one of the largest dogs he had ever seen, his fur matted in blood. It was happily sitting in a corner and surrounded by piles of flesh, bone, and body parts strewn about all over the pit.

"The odds he just fell in?" Richard asked.

"About the same as me winning the lottery without buying a ticket," Special Agent Ross said.

"Well, without the package of information our guy loves to leave it would be down to DNA to identify this one, so at least we know who it is. But now, why is the only question," Richard said.

Outside of a butcher shop he had never seen anything like this. It had to be a few days of work for the dog to do all of that.

"How the hell are we going to get the dog out?" Richard asked.

They made their way back outside.

"Chief!" Agent Ross called.

"What?" came the terse reply.

"This is now a murder scene. I need you to close this area off. Then, get that damn drone out of the sky. Animal control!" Agent Ross shouted.

"Yes, sir!" someone responded.

"We have a number of dogs that need to be gotten out of there without disturbing things wherever possible. Including one that is in a pit with some human remains. I need whomever on your team has the strongest stomach," the Agent said.

"I'm going to go inside and read the love note," Richard informed the Agent.

"Yeah, probably as good a place as any to start," the Agent shrugged.

Richard went back into the barn, tried to ignore the smell and opened the letter. It took him a few minutes with Google Translate to figure out what it said.

Dear Authorities,

This man abused his power, abused children, and used his influence to prevent people from even looking into his bad behavior. I don't know how many people he blackmailed, or paid off, but he was a very bad man.

He did not deserve to walk the Earth with God's creations.

He is no longer a problem for you, he will answer to Saint Peter.

I hope I won't have to do this much longer, and you'll start doing your job.

Yours in Christ,

The Cleanser

He walked up to Agent Ross and showed him the translation.

"Well, when we catch this guy, he won't have to ever do it again," the Agent said with a sigh.

"That is the most messed up body I have ever seen, I have no clue what this guy did yet, but it seems like our guy took out another bad one. The folder with what he did was at least a half inch thick this time," Richard said.

"Yeah, and what happens when he decides we are evil for trying to enforce the laws of man, and he believes that to continue enforcing the laws of God he has to come after us?" Agent Ross asked.

"I never thought about that," Richard said with a shiver.

***

Chief of Police O'Malley had never wanted to make a phone call less in his life. This one was going to hurt.

The phone rang, and part of him hoped it would go to voicemail. No such luck.

"Hey Chief, what can I do for you?" Governor Baker asked.

"Nothing Sir, but I had to give you some information before it hit the news," he said.

"Did that guy hit again?" Governor Baker said, tired of getting questions from news reporters about this serial killer that was starting to have more popular support than he was enjoying.

"Yes, sir he did," Chief O'Malley said.

"Where? Will I get asked about it quickly or is at least out of the Boston area again this time?" the Governor hoped.

"No, Sir. This one is still in close by and this time he took out State Representative Cahill," The Chief said rubbing the bridge of his nose.

"Fuck. I knew the guy was dirty, but I thought that was just politically. Well, let's get a briefing before I am seen in public again," the Governor said.

"This one is apparently really messy sir. You really aren't going to like this either. I just talked to the FBI and you know that Priest that is making all the news up North of Boston lately?" the Chief said.

"Yeah, Santini or something I think," The Governor said.

"Yeah, that's the guy. He's the only suspect at the

moment."

"When was this guy killed?" The Governor asked.

"Looks like two days ago, body was just found today by his daughter," the Chief said.

"Couldn't have been him. Tell the FBI to pull their head out of their ass," Governor Baker replied angrily.

"How can you be so certain? In law enforcement we have to be sure," the Chief said.

"Because every day for the last week or maybe a little more he has been in Rome posting pictures of himself and the Pope all over Instagram. I think his alibi is solid," the Governor said.

"Fuck."

***

Special Agent Ross slammed the phone against the wall of the barn.

"Bad news?" Richard asked.

"Yeah. Our prime suspect, our only suspect, can't have done this," Special Agent Ross said to the team growing team picking through every corner of the barn.

"How can you be sure?"

"He's been in Rome with the Pope for the last week and posted pictures of himself there every three to four hours during the daytime over there since arriving, including one just a few hours ago," the Agent announced.

"How the fuck did we miss that?" Richard said. Not entirely upset this guy was still working to help them. The stack of charges against this guy, if they all proved out included everything from human trafficking of underaged girls, to embezzlement of state funds, to drugs. It would not be a big loss on society. "I need to show you something that might be interesting."

"What?"

"In every other case the victims were drugged, then we suspect he waited for them to wake up to do whatever it was he did because it gave him a chance to secure them. Look at the back of this guy's head, you can clearly see he was bashed in the head with a pistol a few times, likely hard enough to render him unconscious for a bit. So, this MO is different. Maybe he just ran out of drugs, but given what he was using is easy to get, I kind of doubt that," Richard explained.

"Maybe there is a cover up going on and this is a second person, and they missed that detail," the Special Agent suggested.

"Maybe, but it is clear our suspect is the wrong guy," Richard said, annoyed.

"Yeah, but maybe he trusted his dad, and asked for help while he was out of town to fuck with us," Agent Ross suggested.

"Can we prove any of them were involved, or even get a warrant of some kind based on what we have? There isn't some method the FBI has to get these things done we don't enjoy at the local level?" Richard asked.

"None at all. I can't do shit to either of them, and it is now worse with our guy gone," Agent Ross said remorsefully.

"So, basically we have piles of data, and no one we the raises to more than circumstantial evidence," Richard summarized.

"Fuck, yep, that's about it."

Chapter Twenty-Seven
A Press Conference and a Trip

Governor Baker stepped to the podium. He briefly wondered if the moron who said no press is bad press were still alive today so he could punch that person in the face.

This press conference was the one he wanted to do the least in his career.

"Everyone, before you ask questions, I do have some prepared statements. So please, let me get through this.

"We do indeed have a serial killer at large here in the Bay State. You may think we are unique in this and in ways we are, but at any given time the United States has between twenty-five and fifty of these individuals at large. The one have does indeed have a little more flare than most.

"The most recent victim is indeed State Representative Cahill.

There was a collective gasp from the reporters in the room.

"Let me inform you of a few things you may not realize. This serial killer has four victims we can identify for certain and a fifth suspected. All of the victims do have a common thread. They are all people of highly questionable legal or moral practices.

"The first was a lawyer with known ties to criminals both white collar and blue collar. He himself had been guilty of multiple DUIs and always bribed his way out of trouble.

"His second was guilty of chartering boats for some illegal sexual practices out on the water off the coast of Cape Cod.

"The third ran an illegal gambling ring and was taking money from people in a scheme that wasn't just gambling it was fixing the betting and taking the life savings from people they had scammed.

"The fourth was Representative Cahill. He was guilty of running a dog fighting ring, human trafficking, drug dealing, embezzlement, and a few other things we are still looking into…allegedly.

"The common thread here is these so-called victims are themselves criminals we would have never had enough evidence to bring to trial in a million-man hours of investigation. They were too good at hiding what they were doing, and our investigators are too ham-strung by a growing number of regulations that make their job increasingly difficult.

"That brings me to two announcements.

"First, to whomever is doing these things. You seem to be uncovering information we do not have. If you, or anyone else, has information that could lead to a conviction or anything that you think could help prevent crimes, please send it to the tip line, or go to my office's website and click the link to submit it anonymously online.

"Second, to anyone heralding this individual as a hero. He or she is not. They are themselves a violent criminal. We should not be taking the law into our own hands.

"Now, as to our killer. Yes, he has been particularly violent. I will not be commenting further and will in fact be leaving you in the fine hands of Special Agent Ross of the Federal Bureau of Investigations. Thank you," Governor Baker concluded as he left the podium that was immediately occupied by Special Agent Ross and met by a room full of reporters shouting questions.

***

Father Santini stood at the airport terminal waiting for his parents. He had insisted they come and visit so he could show them around the Vatican and tell them what was going on with all of his new duties in the Service to the Lord.

They were flying first class, so he expected them to come out quickly. He was dressed in black, except for his collar, which in Rome was not that unusual. In the United States it was rare, here it was not.

They came out through the gate, "Son! Great to see you!" his father said.

"Frankie," his mother said giving him a hug.

"Mom, Dad, thanks for coming. How was your

flight?" he asked.

"Long, but uneventful," his father said.

"How far are we from the Vatican?" his mother asked, clearly excited to make this trip and visit this most Holy of locations in the Catholic Faith.

"Oh, not far at all, and don't worry I'm going to give you an amazing tour," he said with a wink.

Twenty minutes of small talk later they had the bags and were in the taxi. A brief ride across town and they quickly checked into the hotel which was walking distance to Saint Peters square.

Frank walked them through the square, showing off his favorite statues of different Saints along the way. Then they got to the Basilica.

"Mom, Dad, the Basilica here is one of the most amazing things I have ever seen. It really is worthy of The Lord. Construction first began in the early sixteen hundreds under Pope Paul the Fifth. In here the Pope will preside over a number of liturgies throughout the year. But mostly it is left open for pilgrims from all over the world to come visit and experience the glory these artisans brough to our world.

"Bernini ensured that there are niches for four of the most important of Holy Relics. There is the Veil of Veronica, a piece of the True Cross, a piece of the Holy Lance, and the skull of Saint Andrew the Apostle.

"Below the Basilica are the bodies or relics of around ninety former Popes, including the very first, Saint

Peter the Apostle. The number of paintings here is incredible and are considered to be some of the most famous masterpieces of the Renaissance.

"Frankie, this is amazing. But tell us about what you will be doing from now on," his mother said.

He spent a few minutes explaining that he will be traveling the world into areas that required help getting out of the Church walls and into the public to make the world aware that the Roman Catholic Faith is still here, and not leaving anytime soon. It was certainly flourishing in some areas but needed a boost in other parts of the world. And that he would be here about half the time focusing on their social media and regular media outreach, especially to younger people around the world.

Frank's phone caught his attention.

"Mom, Dad, come with me. I have a treat for you," he said as he motioned for them to go through a specific exit.

"Frankie, you don't have to go to any real trouble for us," his mother said.

"Oh, this wasn't me, someone else insisted," Father Santini replied.

They took a five-minute walk across the Vatican to his humble quarters. The Swiss Guard was outside.

"Mom, Dad, the Pope wanted to meet you," he said as they approached the small house.

"You are kidding," Leonard Santini said.

"Not at all, and dad, he has some questions about the

family business and is on our side," Frank said to his dad with a wink. "And thanks for taking care of that thing for me. His Holy Father is fully informed on everything I have done and knows our family history. He really appreciated your help in keeping the spotlight off of me. He also has some questions on what we might do better to enforce the Laws of God."

"It would be my honor to answer any questions he has," Leonard Santini said.

***

Special Agent Ross walked into the main team area.

"Everyone, it's been four months. No word from our guy, no more bodies. While I can't say he has finished, I think we can safely say he has gone dormant," the Agent said.

"Or moved to Rome, and his dad knows we are paying attention to the family," Richard said under his breath.

"Or moved to Rome," Special Agent Ross said for the group. "Either way, there isn't anything else for us to do. I am being told this team is standing down. I want everything boxed up, and inventoried. This guy could pop back up someday, and I want to be ready.

***

Father Santini walked into the Pope's office, knelt down and kissed the Fisherman's ring.

"Holy Father, how may I be of service to you?" Bishop Santini asked.

"Your Excellency, I have a first assignment for you," Pope Francis said.

"Where would you like me to go?" he asked.

"We have an assignment for you to go to Slovenia for a few months," Pope Francis said.

Frank knew that God was calling on him to enforce judgement once again.

Holy Father, I will not let you down.